DOUBLEDAY New York London Toronto Sydney Auckland

THE ANCIENT CHILD

a novel

N. SCOTT MOMADAY

PUBLISHED BY DOUBLEDAY
a division of Bantam Doubleday Dell Publishing Group, Inc.,
666 Fifth Avenue, New York, New York 10103

DOUBLEDAY and the portrayal of an anchor with a dolphin
are trademarks of Doubleday,
a division of Bantam Doubleday Dell Publishing Group, Inc.

Library of Congress Cataloging-in-Publication Data
Momaday, N. Scott, 1934–
The ancient child : a novel / by N. Scott Momaday. —1st ed.
p.   cm.
1. Billy, the Kid—Fiction.   I. Title.
PS3563.O47A78   1989
813'.54—dc20   89-31304
CIP

ISBN 0-385-27972-8
Printed in the United States of America

October 1989

4   6   8   9   7   5   3
BG
Book Design by Guenet Abraham

FOR REINA

This is a work of fiction. Henry McCarty, alias Billy the Kid, is a figure out of history, as are those who immediately surround him, notably Pat Garrett, Bob Olinger, J. W. Bell, and Sister Blandina Segale. So are Set-angya and Maman-ti figures out of history. To one extent or another, all are put to fictitious use. The other characters are products of the author's imagination. Any resemblance to actual persons, living or dead, is purely coincidental.

The author acknowledges with thanks the generous assistance of the Helene Wurlitzer Foundation of Taos, New Mexico. And he acknowledges with special thanks the advice and encouragement given him by Bernard Pomerance and Bobby Jack Nelson.

**For myth is at the beginning of literature,
and also at its end.**

Borges

Characters

LOCKE SETMAN, called Set, an artist
GREY, a young medicine woman, a dreamer
HENRY McCARTY, Billy the Kid, a notorious outlaw
KOPE'MAH, an old medicine woman
BENT SANDRIDGE, Set's adoptive father, a retired man, humane and wise
LOLA BOURNE, a beautiful, ambitious woman
SET-ANGYA, an old Kiowa man, Chief of the Kaitsenko Society, a Lear-like man, a man who carries about the bones of his favorite son
THE BEAR, himself, the mythic embodiment of wilderness
OTHERS, as they appear

Prologue

Eight children were there at play, seven sisters and their brother. Suddenly the boy was struck dumb; he trembled and began to run upon his hands and feet. His fingers became claws, and his body was covered with fur. Directly there was a bear where the boy had been. The sisters were terrified; they ran, and the bear after them. They came to the stump of a great tree, and the tree spoke to them. It bade them climb upon it, and as they did so it began to rise into the air. The bear came to kill them, but they were beyond its reach. It reared against the trunk and scored the bark all around with its claws. The seven sisters were borne into the sky, and they became the stars of the Big Dipper.

❖❖❖❖❖❖❖

Kiowa story of Tsoai

Astrological pursuits, which require the secret and solitude of
night, are opprobriously classified with witchcraft. . . .
shăsh (sô'), the bear; *shăsh bichí,* his snout; *bijá,* his ear; *bokhó,*
his fire; *beetsós,* his feather. . . .
dzĭłkiji zá'nĭł, the equipment of the mountain chant, may be
identified by the bear-claw attached to it, and should contain:
tgěł bitgádĭdĭn, cat-tail pollen; *shăshdá,* bear food; *łichěě,* red
bush; *azē łichi,* red medicine; *mâ'idá,* wild cherry; and others.

An Ethnographic Dictionary
of the Navajo Language

Paulita Maxwell does not weep

"¿Quién es?"

Well, where do you come from?
And where do you go?
Well, where do you come from,
My Cotton Eye Joe?

"¿Quién es?" he said again. And in that moment the first shot was fired and then the second. The first bullet entered his body at an upward angle, passing beneath the bone and into the heart, and he was already a dead man. The second shot was wild; it struck the adobe wall, then rebounded against the headboard of a wooden bedstead, so that there seemed to have been three shots in all. But in fact there were only two, both fired from the same gun. He fell upon the floor of the dark room. John Poe, standing just outside,

heard everything—the words, the shots, and, as he stated afterward, "a groan and one or two gasps from where I stood in the doorway, as of someone dying in the room." Pete Maxwell, whose house it was, brought a candle and set it burning on a windowsill. In the bare light the dead man lay yellow on his back, stretched out, a butcher knife near his left hand. His body was almost obscenely pale, the color of clotted cream, nearly hairless, blue veins at the wrists and temples. His mouth was slightly open, his teeth protruding. His eyes were closed. He was dressed only in pants and stockings. And he was positively identified. Very soon after the shooting people began to gather there, some of them crying. The women pleaded to take charge of the body, and they were granted permission at once. They carried the body to a carpenter's shop on the grounds and laid it out on a workbench and placed candles all around it. And the next day they laid it in a grave in the old military burial ground nearby, and there was composed a report of the coroner's jury in the hand of one Alejandro Segura. It began:

Salud:

Este día 15 de Julio, A.D. 1881, reciví yó, el abajo firmado, Jues de Paz del Precinto arriba escrito, información que habia una muerte en Fuerte Sumner.

In the distance there were the voices of children. The air was very still. Paulita Maxwell, Pete's eighteen-year-old sister, did not weep, could not, though her heart was breaking. She kept to the darkness, her eyes open wide, as if to see something there take shape, the invisible become visible. She felt her skin tighten and become as hard and brittle as pottery. She believed that if someone should touch her she would shatter. She did not dare to open her mouth. Any sound that came from her now would be horrible—gagging, or a strange rodentlike whimper. She gnashed her teeth, and her mouth and throat were so dry that her breaths were like burns. Neither could she pray, even silently. She could express nothing but that her grief was inexpressible. Her hands were folded, her fingers laced and locked. A fly had lighted on the nail of her right thumb; she was oblivious to it.

> Well, I come for to see you,
> And I come for to sing.
> Well, I come for to show you
> My diamond ring.

"*¿Quién es?*"

Somewhere a raven calls

The boy.

The boy ran.

The boy ran after his sisters. There was a bursting of the boy's heart. He stumbled and gasped and stood still. The cries of his sisters pierced his brain like a madness. He caught his breath—or not his own breath, really, but the breath of something other and irresistible and wild. The ground was almost cold. Dust floated in the long, slanting rays of the sun. Somewhere a raven called. And when the boy looked up his sisters too were standing still, off among the trees, and their faces were pale and contorted with fright. In their eyes was certain disbelief—and certainly love and wonder. And they began to run again, and again he took up the chase.

The next moment is forever to come

Never had Grey to quest after visions. She lay on her back, stretched out on the prairie grass, looking up at the great, drifting clouds and grinding her hips. "Aw, damn it to hell, anyway, Billy," she whined. "Jeez, you had the drop on the son-ofabitch. Why didn' you blast him—*zap!*—blow the fucker away, huh?" She thought of bursting into tears, which she could do at will—she raised the back of her hand to her forehead and feigned anguish—but suddenly she thought better of it, preferring to laugh instead, and so she sputtered with glee, bringing the fin-gertips of the same hand to her pursed lips in a parody of decorum. "Hey, Billy, remember that time?—that really boss time we had at Lincoln, remember? You was up there in the courthouse with ol' Bob an' ol' Bell, an' I come to see you, remember?—said how much I'd admire to shake hands with a honest-to-God outlaw an' all. *Hooooeee!* An' ol' Bell, he said, well, he reckoned it'd be all right. An' ol' Bob, he fussed and fumed so an' liked to have a fuckin' fit. And I shook your hand, Billy Bonney, remember? And you rattled your handcuffs for me like castanets, just flashin' that shit-eatin' grin of yours, that cool, shit-eatin', buck-toothed grin, an' I slipped you that note—*hooo ha!*—that ol' unsurpassed-in-glory, never-to-be-forgotten, cigarette-paper, outhouse note, re-member? *Ho, hooooo ha!* And later, when you an' ol' Bell was talkin', an' you told him you had to take a pee—*hooo haw!*—the ol' hogleg was there, huh, Billy? Oh, Billy, I'd put it there on the floor, in the corner under them newspapers, sure enough, wrapped in the *New Mexican,* oh my! *Hooo heeee ha!*—the ol', stinkin' single-action outhouse special! An' you, Billy, you just fitted it to your hand like a glove, huh? An' you flat hauled off an' done the deed, Billy. You done it. Oh, glory, glory, hallelujah, you *done* it. You done *it!* An' you rode away from Lincoln town on Mr. Burt's horse, just as sassy as you please, to the cheering of the crowd. Oh, the cheers, Billy, the *cheers!* I can hear the cheers, Billy, I can hear them now. Can you, Billy? Billy, can you? Can you hear the cheers?"

She sighed and wiggled the toes of her bare brown feet and marveled at the bright, ephemeral horseman in the sky, moving into a massive, rolling thunderhead, wonderfully backlighted. The pale centaur moved evenly through a crystal canyon shimmering above the world's rim. And just before it dissolved into the swirls and facets and fissures of light and shadow, a long streak of the sun struck fire to the clean, curved wingspan of an eagle that soared in the blue aura of the handsome, black-hatted head.

Never had Grey to quest after visions. They happened upon her irresistibly and all the time. A chill wave on the wind rolled over her and lifted a hank of hair across her throat. She returned her mind's eye to the Maxwell house and braced herself. But the death scene which had been so vivid and immediate a few moments before was not revealed to her again. Rather, it approached and was anticipated, then simply and cleanly let go, as if it were something shameful relegated to a far confinement, some oblivion at the farthest reach of the mind. And yet the review, as far as it went, *was* immediate, profoundly present: It remains that moment, not yet midnight, on the fourteenth of July, 1881, at Fort Sumner, New Mexico Territory. The hollow air touches the leaves of peach trees. The moon is small and flat and far away, and yet its light is strangely pervasive. Pat Garrett is sitting like a wax figure on the side of Pete Maxwell's bed. John Poe and T. L. McKinney are outside in the boundless night. Then the pale form, moving not quite hurriedly, glides within arm's reach of Poe and into the black room, and there is then the urgent voice and the question, *"¿Quién es?"* And that is all. The next moment is forever to come.

The tipis are tall and luminous

Ah-keah-de: *They were camping. That summer the light was hard and brilliant, and the meadows were high with grass, and the grass was thick with wildflowers, blue columbine and lupine and paintbrush. The sky was very deep, and the mountains seemed to sound its depth. The days were warm and the mornings and evenings cool. Two of the people died, but it was understood that they were old and tired and that they had lived their whole lives well. A boy child was born. There was no sickness to speak of, and nearly everyone got on well together, without anger or envy or deceit. The rivers and streams were swift and cold, and the hunting was good. Children invented games. The women talked incessantly, and their voices were excited and high-pitched, and their words ran into laughter again and again. The men talked too, mostly of hunting, but sometimes they teased the women and boasted of how handsome they all were, both men and women. We are indeed a handsome people, they said, and they laughed. The men greased their hair* *and dressed themselves in fine skins and beautiful feathers and all the trade goods they could lay their hands on—quillwork, bits of bone and shell, talons and teeth. The dogs slept and grew fat. Now and then a man or a woman—or even a child, if it was old enough to be careful— would walk away from the camp and turn around in the distance just to look back, full of pride and admiration. The camp was big and alive, set out like a scattering of great white stones in the green, rolling plain. It shone and shimmered against the dark, timbered hills. The tipis were tall and luminous. Long vines of smoke crept up from the cooking fires; sometimes the smoke was blue, sometimes gray or violet. There was always the smell of meat roasting. And the camp was full of sound. There was much dancing, and the voices of the singers and the beating of the drums carried far and wide.*

Then one day there was a quickening of the blood and a falling off of the laughter and the singing and the drums—and in that lapse and hush the people let the summer go, mindful that the earth was going on from season to season, bearing them to a destiny.

Grey considers her appearance

Grey considered her appearance in a small metal mirror that she had drawn from her shirt pocket and now held between the tips of her right thumb and middle finger, both stained with grass and the juice of wild plums. She concluded in an instant that she was beautiful. These grave considerations were innumerable, and the conclusive revelation was always the same. Once she had seen a Kiowa doll in a museum. It was very old, and it startled her, for it seemed to comprehend her in some personal, immediate, and mysterious way. And it was beautiful and fragile in its age. It was dressed in buckskin; it had long black braids of real hair, and it wore tiny beaded moccasins. Again, she had seen a Navajo doll at Hubbell's trading post. Its hair was done up in a queue, and it was dressed in a velveteen blouse, dark blue, and a long, pleated, cream-colored skirt, and it wore rich red moccasins and exquisite silver and turquoise jewelry. She had looked hard at these dolls, trying to see to their centers. She believed that they were somehow involved in her own being, that they were masks that stood for her in some profound, fated way, and for no one else. And she began to love masks. Her father was Kiowa and her mother Navajo, and the two cultures came together in her easily, more or less. English was the language of her childhood home at Lukachukai, but she hoarded bits of the Kiowa and Navajo languages as she could. She learned early to read, and she read voraciously. Through the extraordinary kindness of a third-grade teacher and bibliophile at Chinle, Miss Penelope Sweetser, who taught for thirty years, was married for five days, and retired to a little house in Flagstaff with window boxes filled with petrified wood and hothouse cacti, and every room a library, there were books at Grey's fingertips, and she read them during her most impressionable years. She read Homer and Shakespeare and the Bible. She read Will James and Walter Noble Burns. She read Robert Service and Emily Dickinson. *Laughing Boy* affected her so deeply that she had to remain in bed for three days. When she read *The Saga of Billy the Kid,* she swooned and ran a temperature of 103 degrees. And in her delirium she dreamed of Billy, who, as nearly as she could recall his words, recommended that she read *Meadows of Audhen,* by M. A. (Motto Asam) Candy, which he admired for its lyrical intensity, but she was unable to find it.

Here on the Oklahoma plain with Dog, she described herself in these terms: Dog, Dog, Dog, is it any wonder that I inspire the praises of Master Bonney? No indeed, for I *am* a bonny lass. I have enjoyed eighteen wondrous summers, all of them in the vastnesses of the wilderness, which is my incomparable element. I am tall and limber and well formed. My mind is clear. I am as trim and graceful as a doe, and I am free of the strictures of "civilization," so-called. I have dark, lustrous hair, gathered becomingly behind my shell-like ears, sparkling green eyes, an aquiline nose, a small, shapely, delicate mouth like a Cupid's bow, and a whole, symmetrical, and lovely face. My profile is comely and well defined, classical. My skin is olive and translucent, and my bearing is graceful and dignified. My unpretentious attire is altogether appropriate. It consists of a chamois sheath, with leggings beautifully made by hand, and a tunic, woven of wolf's hair, similar to garments worn by kings and queens of yore. My small alabaster feet are encased in tiny moccasins, elaborately decorated with bright beads, and a string of iridescent shells encircles my long, slender, curved, unblemished throat.

In fact Grey was nineteen. She stood not more than five feet five inches in height, but some quality of her posture made her seem taller. She was slender and supple, but her body was compact and strong. Her hair was long and thick and black, so black that it bore a purple sheen. Her eyes were striking; their color ranged from gray to green to violet. They were eyes out of an ancient myth, epic and holy; they might have been Callisto's eyes. Her brows were heavy and black, and one was habitually raised, so that there was an asymmetrical aspect to her countenance—an expression of mischief and wonder and sagacity. Her cheekbones were high and pronounced. Her nose was not aquiline, but rather short and tilted. Her jaw was square and precise, and her mouth was full and shapely and lascivious. Her lower front teeth were slightly crooked, and there was a mole under the left corner of her mouth. Her throat was indeed long and curved, with a down upon it that seemed in certain lights a coppery aura. Her shoulders were round and rather narrow. Her arms were long and expressive and downy too, and her hands were small and shapely. Her breasts were full and jutting, high on her body, her waist narrow, her legs full at the thighs and calves like a dancer's legs, her ankles small, and her feet firm and arched, with long, articulate toes. Her skin was dark and smooth and taut. Her movements, especially in the presence of men and horses, were athletic and animalistic. At the nape of her neck and under her arms, at the lower curve of her belly, and along her inner thighs, there emanated a scent like musk and mace and the rinds of limes. Except on special occasions, when she dressed in the fashion of one or the other doll, she wore rolled jeans and a shirt knotted under her breasts—and sometimes a floppy hat with an eagle feather in the band—and nothing else. On the whole, she was beautiful beyond the telling.

The strange, disinterested figure
approaches so close as to be intimate

The grandmother, Kope'mah, turned on her side and fixed her sightless eyes on a memory. What she saw was the K'ado, or Sun Dance, of 1887, held near the mouth of Oak Creek, a small southern tributary of the Washita River above Rainy Mountain Creek. There was a great round lodge, bright with boughs and pennants. An expression of wonder came upon Kope'mah's ancient face, the same expression she had worn there on Oak Creek as a child ninety years before. It was early summer again; a heavy heat rose from the river, and scissortails and magpies darted above the lattice of limbs and vines. There were many people, and they were all milling about, brightly dressed, talking, singing, laughing. She was a young girl again, and she was highly excited and glad, simply and wholly *glad*. She approached the lodge, her heart beating hard and fast, then entered into the cool darkness of that deep, intricate space. And Tai-me was exposed there, Tai-me, the sacred

Sun Dance doll and most powerful medicine in the tribe, more powerful even than the *tal-yi-da-i,* the ten bundles containing the "boy medicine," one of which was kept by her uncle T'ene-taide. She dared to look upon it; the stiff, polished figure gleamed in a splinter of light, and the downy feathers of his headdress trembled on the warm, sluggish breeze. She placed a patch of blue wool among the other, richer offerings. The presence of Tai-me was palpable; it was as if she had walked into a warm, slow-moving stream; the presence lay against her like water.

Long afterward, when she had thought about it a thousand times, she told her eldest son that it was then, that day on Oak Creek, that she had become powerful, in that distant, bright commotion, once and for all, when she was still a girl and could not have dreamed of such a gift. From that time on she was greatly respected among the Kiowas—and feared, too, so that there was in her the profound loneliness of medicine people. The power she simply accepted and never questioned, and she was always careful to use it rightly. And now, as an old woman at the end of her life, she summoned her great-granddaughter Grey every day, at least once and sometimes twice or three times, and whispered to her. Her little quivering hands described an urgency, for now death was closely involved in her power, and all save her death itself, that strange, disinterested figure approaching so close as to be intimate, yet always vague and tentative, became clear to her. Death was a rightful riddle, she understood. It was appropriate that there should remain a riddle at the center. It was her due; in the turning of a hundred years she had earned a riddle.

Butterflies spring from the grass

The horse Dog bolted, and butterflies sprang from the grass. They rose to spangle the sky, to become the prisms and confetti of the sun, to make a wide, revolving glitter, an illumination on the air like a magnified swarm. He beat his hooves into the rosy earth, throwing up clods like hail. He raced along with his head and tail high, making a streak like smoke on the skyline. Then, dispassionately, he returned to the girl on the knoll and began to graze again.

They are too far away

From the opening of her tipi, from the highest point in the camp, the old woman Koi-ehm-toya saw the children moving across the wrinkles of a meadow toward the trees. Zeid-le-bei! she thought; a bad business, dangerous. It was well past noon, and the light had begun to deepen. There were golden glints in the air and a faint haze on the woods. Koi-ehm-toya squinted and blinked her eyes, trying to see who the children were, but they were too far away, moving off, their backs to the camp. She counted them—five, six, seven—then counted them again. No, there were eight. Where did they think they were going? Were they being sent out to forage? That was not likely, after all. All the racks were hung with meat; no one was hungry. The children bobbed and skipped and tumbled away in the distance. Oh, they were only at play, she decided, running around and wasting their time, as children will do, giving not a thought to their safety. She clicked her tongue and set a mask upon her face, a perfect scowl. And in the very way of an old woman she wondered *aloud what was to become of the people, they had grown so careless. She scolded the children under her breath, but she could no longer see them. They had already entered into the trees, into the darkness that seemed to Koi-ehm-toya absolute. Zeid-le-bei! Well, after all, someone had to worry. She sighed. If no one should worry, what then? The very notion made her shudder. A hawk sailed past the sun, its shadow slithering in the grass.*

She fixes him in an evil-eye stare

—————————————

The horse Dog cut grass meticulously, methodically. He was a handsome, deep-chested, four-year-old sorrel stallion with black ears, black mane and tail. He was well muscled and short in the spine, and he was fast. On this range, three or four generations before, he would have been well known as a hunting horse, and he would have been greatly prized. He would have inspired deep feelings in those old Plainsmen who beheld him in his grace and beauty, in his hunter's attitude, anomalously quiet and alert, and full of latent, violent motion—especially in those who touched their hands to his hide or to the heat of his breath. He and the man who touched him, so long as it was done in the proper way, would have made a good and true story, a sacred equation.

"Dog!" Grey's voice exploded. The horse had nuzzled her bare toes, had wrested her all at once from her nap, and her reflexes were sharp; her whole body snapped, contracted into a fetal fold. Dog threw his head wildly, tensed, and shivered. He regarded her warily, his nostrils flaring, showing the whites of his eyes. She, then he, relaxed.

"Dog, Dog, Dog, Dog, Dog, Dog," she said, inflecting each "Dog" differently. She fixed him in an evil-eye stare. "You do that again," she said sweetly, "and I'll hog-tie your ass and play spoons on your balls."

Grey stood, yawned and stretched, then swung herself easily upon the horse, walked it from Bote, Oklahoma, across the creek and through the trees, then set it loping southeastward, in the direction of the gray house on the red plain where the old woman Kope'mah lay dying.

Grey had learned of horses as a child at Lukachukai and as an adolescent at Dulce. Her mother's eldest brother, Ashkii Tolichee, whose favorite niece she was, owned a string of mustangs and a herd of sheep, and these he turned into money, and with the money he bought mustangs and sheep. He was of "the Chinle crowd," his wife said, a longhair and an entrepreneur. And Grey's first lover, a Jicarilla man with a white scar across his left ear and jaw, whose name was Perfecto Atole and who had no use for money but who owned notwithstanding a piebald roper and a black cutting mare—and four pairs of handmade boots—infected her with a passion for rodeo. Grey became a performer of star quality. Early on she performed, once and for all flawlessly, the Pony Express mount and lost her virginity, in that order, on the same day. She had once, in a dozen days, won twenty-eight barrel races, roped and tied thirteen calves in a total time of three minutes and four seconds, and sat for more than eight seconds a famous bucking horse named Jackhammer, alias Havoc, alias Kidneypuncher.

And so, one day when she was talking to Worcester Meat's leaseman, Dwight Dicks, it happened that Dwight's son, Murphy, led the horse then known as Murphy's Law close by, within fifty feet of where she was standing. It was suddenly there on the periphery of her vision, discreet and gratuitous, and she turned her head ever so slightly and turned it back, spilling not a syllable of her discourse—she was speaking of manure. But in that glimpse she had taken the measure of the horse. The horse stood some sixteen hands high. Its head was somewhat small in proportion to its body, and well shaped, with large wide-set eyes and small pricked ears, their tips pointed inward. The head was held high, so that the long neck was arched, and the profile straight, the nostrils flared, and the expression at once benign and alert, signifying sound intelligence and instinct. It was short and straight in the back, deep and wide through the brisket. Its hind quarters were muscular, the muscles well articulated. Its legs were long and straight and clean, set under the body well. The hooves were small and shapely. The veins in the neck and forequarters were prominent. The coat was deep in its color and glossy. The mane was long and the tail long and flagged. Even led at a walk, its energy and strength were near the surface, so that it seemed about to prance or wheel or rear up. And in the same moment she determined to have it, not to own it in the ordinary sense but to have it at the disposition of her will, to the extent that the creature would allow it, to have it in her hands and between her legs, to count it among the things that defined her. And already she knew it by the name Dog. It was about this time, too, that she proclaimed herself the Mayor of Bote, Oklahoma.

The bear is coming

One night, when the crickets and frogs made a strange synchronism on the creek and the green moon seemed to bob and float on the clouds, the grandmother Kope'mah whispered to her great-granddaughter Grey—it was unrelated to anything she had said before—"The bear is coming." That night Grey dreamed of sleeping with a bear. There were spots and streaks of blue and yellow pollen at the great, soft eyes and above the long, shining lips. The bear drew her into its massive arms and licked her body and her hair. It hunched over her, curving its spine like a cat, until its huge body seemed to have absorbed her own. Its breath, which bore a deep, guttural rhythm like language, touched her skin with low, persistent heat. The bear's tongue kneaded her—her feet, her belly and her breasts, her throat. Her own breathing became exaggerated, and there were long, orgasmic surges within her; she felt that her body was flooding with blood. The dream was full of wonder.

That is all

"**H**ell, it was worth the horse," Murphy said. He wasn't looking at her directly. It wasn't what he wanted to say; it was his father talking. He was ashamed.

"I know," Grey said.

"He's a whole lot of horse," Murphy said.

"The best," Grey said.

And that was all.

They sit so, like mother and child

That evening, ladling beef and onion broth into a bowl for the grandmother, Grey, dreaming, caught sight again of the fleeting figure on the porch. Then there was a narrow interval in which time came to a stop—there was a perfect stasis—and began again. Deluvina Maxwell, an old servant and a Navajo woman like herself, burst from the house and hurled curses down on Pat Garrett's head. She had to be restrained.

Some days before, in the blackness which enclosed her, the grandmother Kope'mah entered into a boundless state of mind, a personal and immediate consciousness, strangely lucent and euphoric. It was a state in which she became for the last time her own being, as wholly contained in her nature and innocence as on the day she was born, a hundred years ago, a state utterly without distraction, in which time had no function. She spoke a language that was current when she was a girl, and she spoke it to people who had been dead for sixty and seventy and eighty years. She saw things that had withered and worn away in time, but she saw them now new and undiminished and beautiful. She smelled the fresh, airy fragrance of a wild rose that she had pressed in the pages of a hymnal in 1913. She felt the heat of fires that had burned on the plain when she was a marriageable young woman, and the mothers and grandmothers watched her, waiting to prepare her— to perform a ceremony of preparation—for her and her man. She heard wolves howling in the moonlit reaches of the Llano Estacado. Holding her father's hand, she saw at a distance of a mile on the peneplain of the Washita a herd of ninety buffalo, keeping in the shadow of a great gray cloud. They seemed to her very noble and meticulous and, indeed, sacred, as they moved in slowest motion through a mist of colored rain. They were familiar and wild at once. At a glance she could pick out the calves, even the yearlings. She and her father sat cross-legged, high on a mustard slope, and watched the herd mow the prairie, the undulant grassland with its pools of color—rose mallow and bluebonnets and buttercups. A bolt of lightning struck down in the herd—Man-ka-ih—and there was a sudden brief commotion, an upheaval so concentrated and transient that it left no mark on the scene. The herd seemed a great, black, bushy vegetation on the earth, moving like sediment in water, slow as the shadow of the summer cloud. But that night her father told her, to her astonishment, that the herd was already a day's ride to the west.

She appeared to be asleep. Someone had brought in a kerosene lamp and set it in a corner of the room. Kope'mah could see nothing, not even in the deep, pervasive yellow light, but she could smell the oil and the smoke. She knew the flicker of light upon the walls of her room, on the bedcover she had quilted in 1929, on a blue enameled pitcher and basin in the far corner, on the tumbler of carnival glass near her hand. For she had seen these things once upon a time; there was almost nothing in the room that was not there when she still could see, twenty years ago, only the scented salves and smooth stones and velvet ribbons that Grey brought to her. She held all the colors and shapes and textures of an earlier time in her memory. But she no longer knew what her memory was.

She thought she had spoken to the bearer of the lamp, but she was not sure. There had been no reply in any case, and she did not care. It had been Worcester; she could smell him. It had been her son Worcester, to whom she had little to say. He was her second son and fourth child. He was nothing like her eldest son, Kauliteh, who was a prophet, nor like her last and favorite son, Walker, who was Grey's grandfather. These were proud, headstrong men. But Worcester was careless and dispassionate. He was affable, old-fashioned, imperturbable. He had never opposed anything, as far as she knew, and that rankled her. Maybe, she thought at times, he was simply right in his bland attitudes, practical, after all, worldly-wise, sensible enough to live at peace in a dangerous world. But she had little respect for such wisdom, if wisdom it was. She preferred a sagacity like Set-angya's, which was spiritual, an otherworldly intuition, a kind of holy madness, as she thought of it, a wild and native intelligence. Set-angya had been a warrior and a chief. Worcester Meat was merely a benign original; and he was seventy years old. And to benign originals she preferred legends. Set-angya had been killed, shot down by soldiers at Fort Sill before she was born, and he had been contemptuous of death, and in the face of it he had sung the song of the Kaitsenko. Bravery was a madness in him; he was one of whom to hear in a story; all her people loved the mad warriors, the storied ones, the legends.

Again the door opened, and Grey came into the room, bringing the bowl of broth. Kope'mah knew at once who it was, and she uttered the little exclamation that was peculiar to the old women of the tribe, "Eh neh neh neh neh!" It was made with a pronounced frown, which endowed it with dignity and veneration. It would always be for Grey a charm in which were gathered the essences of surprise and delight; "glad weeping," she called it.

Kope'mah drank only a little of the broth, and when it had cooled at last, Grey took the bowl and set it aside. She sat next to the grandmother and took the little spidery fingers of the grandmother's hands in her own. Kope'mah seemed a child, drawn into Grey's embrace, her little bones angled into the young woman's supple bust. They sat so, like mother and child, for a long time in silence. Now and then Kope'mah seemed to fall asleep, and her breathing became so faint it could scarcely be heard; then it became irregular, rasping, and Grey knew she was awake. There was lightning far away. A warm, erratic wind bore the scent of rain to the south window and into the room, and there was a constant clamor of insects on the night.

Past midnight the voice of the grandmother grew up in the room, tentative at first, barely audible. Grey had not to struggle with the words, for she was not listening at the level of language but beneath it, in the deep recesses of the imagination. And then they were two women, the storyteller and her listener, telling and told the ancient emergence of light. Light appeared as a crumpled surface of dark water on the grasses, then it deepened to sand, then to copper—the wings of a ground dove—and then to squash, to dry gourds. Leaves shivered in the clear, cold light. The night wind lay low in the shifting grain. Grasshoppers bounded and struck and rebounded, glancing and popping on the earth. The two women caught their breath. A timeless rejoicing entered into their veins, into the current of their common blood.

Then the stallion, the hunting horse Dog, whinnied nearby above the singing birds and the cocks crowing. Its head was raised high; its eyes, like coals, in each of which the low orange arc of the sun shone like the spark within a crystal, gazed into the long, insisting wind; its ears were pitched forward; and its mane and tail were ruffled and floating on the air. Poised on the skyline it seemed an abstraction, the symbol of pure energy, massive, black, and singular. It was an image tinged with orange light. And when it wheeled and ran, it was an explosive and anomalous cohesion and disintegration of form and motion and color at once. It was kaleidoscopic. It was Man-ka-ih, the storm spirit. The rising sun splintered upon its rolling, rippling shoulders and flanks, the night kept at the hollows and folds of its bolting body—the bunching, the extension and glide, the terrible concentration of its hooves on the stony ground, the pounding so rapid as to constitute an entity.

Subsidence. The grandmother Kope'mah had begun to speak names: Set-pago, Set-tainte, Set-angya, Set-mante.

Setman.

Set.

He expounds: God's boredom is infinite

By the time he was thirty, Locke Setman, called Set by all who knew him, had found the truest expression of his spirit in painting. At thirty-five he had made a considerable reputation, having received several important awards and attracted the attention of critics and collectors throughout the country. It was fashionable—and expensive—to own one of his paintings. At forty he was in the first rank of American artists, and he was in danger of losing his soul. Innumerable demands were made upon him; he came to understand that success, in terms of fame and fortune, was costly in other terms. More and more often he was asked to compromise his art or himself in one way or another, and more often than not he did so, for he was inclined to be passive and naïve; it was difficult for him to say no. Those who exhibited his work, who praised and purchased it, and who demanded its proliferation began to determine it. Set went along. He enjoyed celebrity, after all. It was wonderful to be recognized, to be sought after, to be admired and envied and imitated. Men of means invited him to their clubs, prevailed upon him to speak at their luncheons, gave parties in his honor. Women took notice of him, approached him, laid claim to him, and he went along.

There were times when the disillusionment was so great that he wept. It was such a fine thing to paint, to see something—a human face or an orchard or the moon rolling—and to render it, to make a picture of it, according to his vision, which was unique, which was uniquely valid. Oh, that excited him. To see and to paint with excitement, with a child's excitement, that is what brought him to life. The child says, "Here, see. This bird I have painted, it is what I have seen in my soul. Is it not a wonderful thing? Is this not a good way of seeing?" Set strove to see and to image what he saw as truly as he could so that others could see as he did, so that they could see in a way they had not seen before. But it seemed no one cared about that, no one among his associates. He wanted a child. He wanted a child to come to his studio, to look at the splatter of paint on the walls, the floor, his easel, to see the drawings on the walls, to touch his or her hands to the thickly painted linen planes, to say to the child, Just look at this yellow, how it vibrates! Look at the blues, how they make a mystery! Could you have imagined a blue like this? And for a moment the child's eyes would have been wide with wonder. But the dealers and critics were narrow-eyed and glib, and there were calculations in all their faces.

Notwithstanding, there was conviction in him, and a commitment to be his own man. And therefore he struggled. Now, at forty-four, he found himself in a difficult position. He had compromised more than he knew. He had squandered much of his time and talent; he had become sick and tired. He remembered a time in which he had painted for the sake of painting, out of some wild exuberance of the spirit. He had been full of excitement, the excitement of learning, of experimenting, of feeling his ability and his accomplishment come close together. But he had committed his time and his work, virtually all of it, to his public. At every breath, it seemed, another painting or promise came due. Moreover, he had ceased to grow in his work. He wanted to paint a tree, but he was obliged to paint a house; he wanted to paint small, but he was obliged to paint large; he wanted to do something he had never done, but he was obliged to do the same thing again and again, without end. Yes, he had become sick and tired. And he did the only thing he could think to do under the circumstances; he withdrew—not completely, not all at once, but deliberately. He would fulfill his obligations, to be sure; indeed, he would give the best that was in him; but he would first and last be true to himself. He would endeavor to save his soul.

About the same time he painted a self-portrait, a full-length study in acrylic on paper. It was a good likeness, though Set was not a portraitist, and the likeness, though close, was stylized, essentially abstract. Blues and greens and an ivory predominate upon a background of brown and black. The figure faces us in a relaxed attitude, standing with feet well apart, the hands on the hips. Work clothes, splotched with paint, hang as on a mannequin. The body appears to be that of a tall man—the torso is long— though the shoulders and thighs are well rounded, like the shoulders and thighs of a swimmer. The hands and feet are slim, the arms and neck disproportionately long but somehow in keeping with the general character of the portrait. The head is inclined slightly to one side. The hair is blue and gray and unkempt, of a length that nearly covers the ears. The face is strong, with a high, broad forehead, a straight nose, a sturdy jaw, and a chin cleanly set. The expression is inscrutable, but we take it to be benign. The mouth, which is full, might describe the faintest of smiles. The eyes are slightly narrow, as if the subject is looking into the sun. The gaze is level and penetrating. The portrait is that of a thoughtful and well-meaning man, a man of intelligence and some experience, a man of sorrow, a man of deep feelings.

Set imagined it was to please, but it was to astonish God that he painted. His presumption and arrogance were pronounced and dangerous, for they would certainly lead to the Sin of Despair, thence to death and nothingness. Bent said so, half in jest, only half. Rather, as Set himself said on occasion, he painted in vain, in order to relieve the terrible boredom of God. He expounded: God's boredom is infinite. Surely we humans, even with our etiquette and our institutions and our mothers-in-law, ceased to amuse Him many ages ago. What sustains Him is the satisfaction, far deeper than we can know, of having created a few incomparables—landscapes, waters, birds and beasts. He takes particular pride in the stars, and it pleases Him to breathe havoc upon the oceans. He sighs to the music of the desert at dawn. The eagle and the whale give Him still to ponder and admire. And so must He grieve for the mastodon and the archaeopteryx. And the bear—ah! He used both hands when he made the bear. Imagine a bear proceeding from the hands of God!

It has the form of a wheel
of burning-glass

Set remembered:

The boy Locke Setman, called Loki, thirteen, sat in a green leather chair in the living room of the Sandridge house on Scott Street. He peered hard into the book in his hands, even when the blue Great Dane, Luke, called Luki, heaved and stretched, one massive forepaw nearly upsetting the fireplace screen, and yawned awesomely, emitting a whine that set the walls vibrating. The book was an illustrated astronomy, a text for common and public schools, published in New York in 1849. It was in bad repair, and Loki appreciated the need to handle it with care. It was fragile and all the more dear to him for that. He had brought it down from Bent's study after breakfast, and for more than an hour he had pored over it. After school he took it up again. He paid special attention to the illustrations, which were beautiful and exotic indeed, especially one. He traced carefully with a forefinger the signs of the zodiac. His signs were Taurus and Scorpio; Bent had told him so one Sunday afternoon when the two of them had taken the ferry to Tiburon and Loki had broken a bagel into pieces and tossed the pieces up to wheeling seagulls. In the illustration the bull leapt lightly in the earth's orbit, strictly enclosed in its constellation under the legend, "OCTOBER: The Earth enters Taurus 23d October and at the same time the sun enters Scorpio." The book appeared to be a mine of irrefutable information, and Loki was fascinated with it. He imagined that he was again in the Peter and Paul Home, before his adoption, standing easily at his classroom desk, holding the tall, sloe-eyed Sister Stella Francesca in his benign regard, her incredulity and the perturbation of his peers hanging lightly like leaves of laurel about his head.

Q: What is the largest telescope in the world?

A: Lord Rosse's telescope, at Birr Castle, Ireland, 56 feet in length.

Q: What idea had the Ancients respecting the shape of the earth?

A: They believed it was an extensive plain, rendered uneven by hills and mountains.

Q: What is the distance of the sun from the earth?

A: It is about 95,000,000 miles.

Q: How much greater is the equatorial than the polar diameter?

A: About 27 miles.

Q: What do the milky way and the single stars that are visible to the naked eye, including our sun, constitute?

A: They constitute an immense cluster, or firmament, entirely distinct from the other clusters or nebulae of the heavens.

Q: What is the shape of this great cluster or firmament?

A: It has the form of a wheel of burning-glass.

This image, holy, variable, and iridescent, brought tears to Loki's eyes. He saw in his imagination a great, glittering ring, or a succession of rings, spiraling through convolutions without number to a point on the far side of time. It was his first real notion of the infinite; it struck and staggered him, and then, by the grace of God, it escaped his attention entirely. The information he relished most was this:

> URSA MAJOR, the GREAT BEAR.—The first seven stars in this constellation form what is called the Great Dipper. It is situated about 15 degrees north of the zenith, and a little to the east of north. . . . There are four stars which form the dipper, and three in the Tail of the Bear, which form the handle. These stars cannot fail to be recognized at a glance. Six of these stars are of the second and one of the third magnitude. The first two, α, β, are called pointers, as a line drawn through them towards the horizon would pass very near the North Star, which is about 30 degrees from them towards the horizon.

And Set remembered:

The sun struck through the Scott Street windows, through an intricate floral pattern of stained glass. The light lay in four colors on Loki's hair and face. Even in sleep he was somehow sensible of colored light; pale washes ran, one upon another, in back of his eyes. He dreamed of someone approaching, a frail young woman, her mouth, like Sister Stella Francesca's, set never to smile, her eyes holding on to something beyond his dream. And the dream was—is—always immediate. There is a rude, round rhythm to her walk. Her hair, dark and reddish, ripples as she comes. Her breasts are taut, and yet they bob and bounce perceptibly, their motion slow and nearly pronounced. Her thighs are full, and they articulate the ivory-colored skirt of thin raw silk, the ride and sway thereof, the warm round flesh within, far beyond his understanding; and yet he could not be more receptive, more agitated or involved. She looks at him directly, neither with nor without recognition. Then she tosses her head, the thick hair swings across her bright mouth; it is for his benefit alone, this small, fastidious performance, and he winces with embarrassment and excitement. She is more than beautiful. She is extraordinarily graceful and sensual and alive. There is nothing about her that is not definitively feminine, and even on his precarious, adolescent terms she is wholly desirable in her flesh. At last she stands directly before him, over him, her feet set wide apart, and, shy and unaccountably ashamed, he hangs his head. Nevertheless he beholds with a terrible perturbation her shapely, sandaled feet, her long, painted toes.

And he dreams of his mother's touch, of her embrace, of all the particulars of her physical presence—her smell, her breathing, her sweat, the glistening surfaces of her back and hips and shoulders, the spring of her breasts and buttocks under his fingertips, the sour taste of her skin upon his tongue. The sound of her voice envelops him like music, solemn and serene. Her words, unintelligible, create and confirm his whole being. The dream becomes a story, a myth. Ritual has a place, so have good and evil, and there is an ineffable intimacy. Nothing is unnatural, and there is no question of right and wrong. There is merely a moment in the rite of passage, the irresistible accumulation of

experience. Moreover, the story is understood and accepted—
neither is there any question of condonation—by the audience,
which is gathered with hard, interested attention about the cen-
terpiece, the altar, of the story. And the story becomes a dream.
Among the attendants he recognizes only his father, who smiles
and proffers silent yet unmistakable encouragement. "Here,
Loki," his father says; there is something like urgency in his
voice. "Here, darling, see here," his mother says. Only later,
with his first woman, does the dream proceed beyond the blind
of his innocence, beyond the frustration that is like paralysis.
More fascinated than afraid, he looks into the dark recess, so
sharply described below the white mound of the woman's belly,
and sees therein the ragged ridge of pink and magenta flesh protruding like a gentian from the crisp, silky hair.

He awoke with alarm, a bitter taste in his mouth, as if he had
bitten into a seed. Luke, Luki, lumbered to his feet, to the call
of nature, and yawned mightily. Loki opened his eyes. Bent Au-
gustus Sandridge was standing on the third step of the stair,
looking down at him. Bent's gray hair was thick and forever
tousled, and he squinted through little round wire-rimmed spectacles. He wore, as usual, the oversized, shapeless black cardigan
with its many years of snags and stains. He affected a stern stance,
and the squint shaped a certain mask of irritability on his round
red face. But he was a gentle man.

"His blue, dull-witted, and farting eminence would seem to
require a romp on the Green," said Bent. "Want to come along?"

Loki rubbed his eyes and nodded yes.

"Oh, and Señora Archuleta says would you like the salmon
chowder for supper?"

"Uh, flapjacks, I think." It was a standing joke; there was no choice.

Already Loki had got in his nostrils the scent of sizzling onions and salt pork, and he nodded his approval, though he wanted to refute the charge concerning Luke's intelligence. He was still rising from sleep. But Luki's intelligence could remain in question. He was hungry. He loved Señora Archuleta's salmon chowder above all other dishes, save one—Señora Archuleta's Christmas *posole*.

Loki laughed to watch Bent work Luke on the leash. There was a boundless exuberance in the great blue animal, and an insatiable appetite for mischief. It seemed at times that he meant to do Bent in, did Luki, giving him the line to hang himself, as it were, bounding abruptly into traffic, spinning him on the edges of curbs, stairs, piers, and platforms as he, Luki, lunged after cats and kids. But later, on the way back from the Green, where Luke had struck terror in the hearts of man and beast, when he had run himself into the ground, he was placid as a mule. And Loki held the leash with both hands, grateful to be assisted on the long, steep grade to the top of Pacific Heights.

In Loki there was a certain empty space, a longing for something beyond memory. He thought often of his mother, dead almost the whole of his life. He knew that she was not the pale, lewd ghost of his dreams; she was the touchstone of his belief in the past. Without knowing her, he knew of her having been; she had given him life, even as he had taken hers; her blood pulsed upon his very heart. Her reality was that of everything on the bygone side of his existence. She was his immediate and most personal antecedent, the matter of which he was made, the spirit which drove his blood. He could imagine her, Catherine Locke Setman, in a way no one else could.

When he opened the door on Scott Street there was a tumultuous outpouring of the Overture to *Carmen*, Señora Archuleta's favorite music. The walls quaked, as with one of Luki's yawns. Bent, puffing, mumbled something from the walk below.

15

He looks remarkably like the famous photograph

Grey placed her hand on the grandmother's forehead, her dark fingers in sharp relief upon the pallid, wrinkled skin and the thin white hair. It had become difficult for the grandmother to draw breath. Now and then she coughed weakly. Grey kept the salty broth by the bed, but the grandmother had taken only tea for three days. Jessie, who was Kope'mah's granddaughter, wanted to attend the dying woman, wanted to be at last indispensable to her, but she did not know how. She was not a resentful woman, but sometimes, watching Grey come and go, she felt a faint blush come upon her, and she was ashamed. She had taken care of the grandmother for years. She had cooked the meals and done the laundry; she had seen to the chamber pots and treated the bedsores; she had greeted the guests and paid the bills and swatted the flies. But she had never come wholly into the grandmother's confidence. It was to Grey that the ancient woman spoke her mind and heart.

At the edge of sleep the grandmother had spoken of Catlin Setman, or Catlin's son, Locke. What she said had not made sense to Grey, but it had seemed serious in the saying: more than serious—urgent. Grey dozed in the wicker chair, listening to the wheezing of the old, dying woman, counting the intervals in her breathing. Though Grey was settled and relaxed, the waiting had begun to tell on her. She began to suffocate in the little room. She fell into a fitful sleep, and her eyelids fluttered, and she made little reflexive motions with her hands. She dreamed. And at some time in the middle of the night she started, was suddenly wide awake, staring into a corner of the room. There stood Henry McCarty, slouching, looking at her evenly, his eyes almost colorless above the trace of a smile. He looked remarkably like the famous photograph. He was wearing a crumpled black hat with a leather band. His face was somewhat crooked, with outstanding ears and long curly hair. His expression was passive, almost empty, his mouth slightly open, exposing his yellow, protruding front teeth. He wore a neckerchief. On his shirt were necklaces, delicate chains to which were affixed curious horseshoe-shaped emblems, arranged obliquely across the left breast, just below the shirt collar. He wore a buff-colored vest, open, with five or six buttons and little round lapels. Over this was a sweater, a dark cardigan with white fluting, the sleeves too long. His pants were of a coarse material, thick and stiff and baggy, tucked into high V-topped boots with high, underslung heels and mule ears, well worn. At his hips was a cartridge belt and a pistol in a large leather holster. In his left hand he held the barrel of a lever-action rifle, stock to the floor; the right hand, the arm slightly bowed and relaxed, cupped at his side.

"Billy, you sonofabitch, where have you been?" she asked, her voice full of surprise and consternation; she wanted to squeal her delight, but he seemed so solemn.

"Howdy," Billy said.

She imagined she was wearing a white dress. Suddenly she was self-conscious; she smoothed her hair with her hand.

"Are you . . . are you hungry?"

"No," he said. "I wanted to see you. I don't have much time."

"You need a haircut," Grey said. "I'll cut it for you."

"Another time, if you don't mind. Some boys are outside, some friends of mine. We've been riding hard. We need to move on."

"Where to?" Grey asked. She tried to keep her voice low, but she was excited. "Where, Billy? Can I come?"

"No, not this time. We're headed for Colorado—Trinidad. We're going to visit a man there, a sick friend." After a pause he added gravely, "We're going to kill the physicians."

"What?"

"The physicians of Trinidad. There are four. We're going to kill them."

She thought of asking why, but she didn't. He would tell her if and when it pleased him to do so. She curled her toes; they were barely visible under the hem of her stiff white dress. He had not taken his eyes off her. She averted hers, being bashful with him, with him only. And damn him, he was going to be solemn. He was going to leave without laughter, without even touching her.

"Well, you see," she said softly, "my grandmother, she's very, very old, and she's become very weak, and I think she's going to die soon, and I . . . ." She nodded toward the little, still form of the grandmother, Kope'mah, shriveled and curled under a blanket in the dark bed, nearly beyond the dim light.

"I know," Billy said.

She knew that he would leave at any moment. His speech was gentle and considerate, but she knew that he was bent upon some hard intention and that he could not be distracted. She thought to say goodbye, but before she could say it he was gone.

"Goodbye," she said anyway.

16

It shines like a vague, powdered mask, like a skull

Locke Setman—Set—studied the telegram that had been slipped under the door of the studio. It read:

GRANDMOTHER KOPEMAH NEAR DEATH.
PLEASE COME AT ONCE.
NOTIFY CATE.

He was completely at a loss. He knew of no Grandmother Kopemah. Obviously this was word from his father's people, but he did not know them. They had nothing to do with him. They were related to him, he supposed, but that was only an accident; they were his relatives, but they were not his family. His father had died when he was seven, and his mother, even more remote in his mind, had died giving him birth. All that he had of his forebears was a sediment in his memory, the memory of words his father had spoken long ago—the stories his father had told him. The longer he looked at the telegram, the more deeply it disturbed him. It was in Set's nature to wonder, until the wonder became pain, who he was. He had an incomplete idea of himself. The ten words were compelling, after all. Cate was Catlin, Catlin Setmaunt on the tribal rolls, who as a young man began to sign himself Cate Setman. The telegram was sent by Milo Mottledmare of Saddle Mountain, Oklahoma. Set studied it for a long time, moving his eyes from the address to the text and back again: LOCKE SETMAUNT, 1690 BEACH STREET, SAN FRANCISCO: KOPEMAH . . . DEATH . . . COME . . . CATE. The longer he looked at it the more extraordinary it became, a document which contained his name and his father's name, a thing of impenetrable meaning, an enigma, perhaps an omen. *It bore his father's name,* therefore his spirit. Here was an exigent message from one Milo Mottledmare, perhaps his father's friend or kinsman, who on the face of it seemed not to know that Cate Setman had died more than thirty years ago. But for his father's name, Set would have supposed there had been a mistake, that the telegram was meant for someone else.

The rest of the day he brooded, pacing about the studio, working sporadically at the easel. He tried to reach Milo Mottledmare on the telephone, but there was no listing. The brooding became a restlessness. In the evening he went out walking. It was clear, and there was a good breeze off the Bay. He stopped by the Edwardian for a sandwich and a beer, and he spoke briefly to a man he knew only as Gaetano, another painter and resident of the Marina. Set had never seen his work. Gaetano introduced his companion, a large, red-haired girl with a pretty face and a British accent. Her name was Briony. When they parted, she shook Set's hand and said, "Super. Look after yourself."

He had meant to go on up the hill to Scott Street and spend an hour with Bent, but he changed his mind and returned to the studio. He phoned first Bent, then Lola, and told them he was going out of town for a day or two.

There were reports of a storm moving in, and advancing winds had begun to churn the ocean, which was the color of chrysoprase. Set looked down with wonder upon the thousands of rolling white crescents, endlessly appearing and reappearing. In one or two days' time heavy gales would whip the coast and the great density of the rain would blacken the bend of the continent from the mouth of the Klamath to Big Sur. But just now visibility was nearly unlimited. The airplane banked in a wide counterclockwise turn off the Golden Gate, and its shadow touched the mainland just north of Pescadero. He could see Monterrey Bay.

On Thanksgiving Day, four years before, he had taken Lola Bourne on a picnic at Point Lobos. They had climbed out on one of the great rocks there, and the wind was so high it made their eyes tear, and Lola laughed and laughed just to feel it in her hair. The rock shuddered with the force of the sea, and Set sketched a portrait of Lola Bourne, laughing too, trying hard to hold the sketch pad steady in the wind. Lola sat away and a little above him in gray slacks, a shearling coat, and a white scarf, and her hair was fluffed and flying, full of the high wind, and she laughed. Under the circumstances he liked the sketch well enough, but Lola said that it certainly was not she, that rather it was the perfect likeness of a peasant girl named Vivienne, who lived in twelfth-century France, whose father worked for seventeen years on the south tower of Chartres cathedral, and who was said to understand the language of chickens, ducks, and geese.

And Set remembered:

Sister Stella Francesca kept him after class and scolded him. "You have a loose, uncontrollable tongue, Loki," she said. "Come, I will show you what we do with boys whose tongues are loose like yours." She sat on the edge of the desk, the dark, polished wooden desk at which she liked to loom, batlike, upon her elbows, and effect a perfect, lifeless silence in the room. The desk was glazed with the light of the autumn afternoon sun, as with honey. He heard the voices of his schoolmates on the lawn outside, the sounds of play, and he was overwhelmed with the sense of banishment. He closed his eyes, his face uplifted. "Come!" said Sister Stella Francesca again, sharply. He opened his eyes and beheld the sinister, hooded figure before him, and he felt his knees shaking and wanted to urinate. He approached with a terrible dread to the insistent beckoning of her long, trembling forefinger and placed his head in the folds of her habit; the folds gathered and receded before his brow. Sister Stella Francesca's breath became audible and urgent, and Loki vomited in her thighs. She shrieked and beat him about the head and shoulders with her fists. Loki saw, just before he threw himself backward and down upon the floor, a yellow and purple bruise inside and above one of her knees. It resembled an ancient scarab he had once seen in a glass box.

And Set remembered:

One of his instructors at the art academy, Cole Blessing, he thought it was, said to him, "You begin with the fifth line, remember that. You have to be always aware of the boundaries of the plane, and you have to make use of them; they define your limits, and they enable you to determine scale, proportion, juxtaposition, depth, design, symmetry correctly. You see, you can make something, a line, a form, an image. But you have to proceed from what is already there—defined space, a plane. You can make something out of something, but you cannot make something out of nothing. That is God's trick. But with a lot of learning and a little talent, not to say luck, you can make something out of something. You say you want your drawing to exceed its subject, to improve upon the object it renders. That is out of the question. Look at this model. She is beautiful. Her figure is exactly what it should be, must be. Her body is whole, vital; every bone and muscle and tendon is in place. Her body is soft and yet firm, resilient, round, smooth, delicate, endlessly expressive; and it functions, it serves its purpose. You cannot create such a thing. Can you improve upon it? Emphatically, no. You can remove this mole; you can straighten this nose; you can set this hank of hair. But that is not to draw. I'll tell you what you can do, what you had better do to the very best of your ability. You can *affirm* what is there. Art is affirmation. You can look at this model, and you can look again, and you can keep on looking until you have seen her more clearly and completely than you have ever seen anything before, and then you can—maybe—conform your hand to your eye in such a way as to affirm her being on the picture plane. You can—maybe—describe a shadow that is worthy of the substance."

Set drew in charcoal a piece of driftwood twelve times. It was like a fetish, in the shape of a dolphin leaping, with a little chamois pouch tied to its back. Of the twelfth drawing Cole said, "You have begun to understand. . . ." Set listened for the object of the verb. There wasn't one, and he went on to something else.

He dozed. But even with his eyes closed he could see the coastline reaching away into the horizon's haze. Somewhere he had read that thinking is language spoken to oneself. A dream, like thought, took shape in his mind's eye, and he returned to a day a dozen years in the past and conjured it with words: Once in the early morning I walked along the beach. The tide was out, and there were pools in the sand. Then I saw something in one of the pools, under a large piece of driftwood. It was an octopus, small, motionless, only partly submerged, and it seemed to be dead. It filled me with curiosity, for I had never seen such an unlikely creature before. I stood over it and studied it for a long time, and it did not move. It was supple and stark in the water, the color of bone, and I was afraid to touch it. Then I picked up a stick and probed at it. Suddenly it blushed pink and blue and violet and began to writhe about. This stiff reaction, total and grotesque, alarmed me, for everything about it seemed to describe some profound agony. It took hold of the stick and clung to it. I carried it away to the surf and laid it down. I supposed, I think, that it would go off at once into the depths, but no, it settled again and lay still. I wanted to think that it might have been dealing with me, that in its alien ocean mind it might have been struggling to take my presence into account, that I had touched its deep, essential life, and it should never lose the impression I had made upon it. It was still there when I came away, and it had not moved, except that it rocked very gently to and fro in the water.

And I wonder, What does it mean that after these years I should dream of the octopus? It may be that I saved its life. But I know very little about the life of an octopus, and I shall not presume to say what salvation is worth to either of us. Only just now, as a strange loneliness, it occurs to me that this creature has, for some years, been of some consequence in the life of my mind. And I wonder if, in the dark night of the sea, the octopus dreams of me.

Again, he had read somewhere that a man, very near this place of the octopus—a man named Viscaino, three hundred years ago—had seen grizzly bears feeding upon the carcass of a whale. Cate Setman knew about such things. Unlikely as it seemed, Cate Setman knew of octopuses, whales, and bears. From his early childhood, Set knew that Cate Setman knew.

Coming down out of the clouds toward Oklahoma City, Set thought of puzzles. He gazed upon the immensity of red and green and yellow geometry—rectangles, triangles, squares, jigsawn shapes. The geometry rolled out forever to the skyline. Oh, but there, he thought, look; there is exception and redemption, a redeeming disorder, the opposing aesthetic of the wilderness—the green belts slashing through the boxes like limbs of lightning, like sawteeth and scythes. It was a country of rivers and creeks, prairies and plains. In school Set was taught that art was resistance. In one way or another all his teachers said so, even Cole Blessing, whose drawings were alive. But Cate Setman knew better. Cate must have spoken the truth to Set, and Set must have known too, even when he was not looking, listening intently, and he would somehow keep the knowledge. Look, he said to himself, the wild, crooked courses, reaching in every direction. Water follows the line of least resistance, and it is itself irresistible. It has shaped some of the most impressive forms on the face of the earth.

Cate had long ago told him something about his name. What? What was it? It lay on the farthest edge of his memory. He had not yet begun to believe in names.

At Will Rogers Airport, with some trepidation, he rented a car. Lola Bourne made him keep current a driver's license, but although he traveled widely in connection with his exhibits, he almost never drove, and he had never owned an automobile. He said he wanted air conditioning. The freckled-faced girl behind the Hertz counter giggled and touched his hand. When he stepped outside the terminal the heat stunned him, and when he got into the car he had to open the windows in order to breathe. The girl had given him a map. He opened it and laid it out on the seat beside him, but he didn't think he would need it right away. He drove west. There was country music on the radio. The highway had been cut straight through the waves of grassland, and all along there were slashes of bright embankment on both sides—quick, bold strokes, as Jason Fine would say. Jason was Set's agent, and he was knowledgeable and shrewd, but he spoke of painting in clichés. This landscape of Indian red, Mars yellow, and burnt umber would be in Jason's terms brooding, vast, uncompromising, preeminently honest, and commensurate with man's capacity for wonder.

At a crossroads near Saddle Mountain he drank root beer from a can. It did not slake his thirst, but it tasted better than the water he had drawn from a great blue inverted bottle into a tiny paper cone; the water was warm, and there was a tincture of oil in it.

"Oh, yeah," said the small arthritic man at the cash register. "Miz Kopemah lives out yonder with the Mollymares—Reverent Mollymare an' his missus, you know—out a ways on Cradle Crick, I b'leeve it's called. Yuh cain't hardly miss it. Jist take the first left an' folley the road, oh, seben, eight mile, I reckon's all. Fine folk, them Mollymares, the Reverent an' his missus, fine Christian folk." Then a cloud seemed to pass over his face. There was a moment in which his concentration seemed prodigious. "But, say, I declare I b'leeve ol' Miz Kopemah passed on. Yessir, jist day before yestiddy. They was a burial out to the cemetery, I declare."

There was a house in a grove of trees, a creek beyond. It was an old house, in bad repair. He was glad to be done with the dirt road. All the way from the blacktop he had veered in and out of ruts and plunged into deep, soft dirt, granular like sand, barely keeping ahead of his own dust. He brought the car to a stop and turned off the ignition. The engine died hard, coughing and sputtering for a time.

At close range the house seemed even older and more dilapidated than it had from the moving car. He had never seen such a house; it seemed as old as the land. The ground was grown up with weeds and wild grass, and there were patches of bare red earth here and there, dusted with ash and stained with dishwater and cooking broths and other kinds of waste. There was an anthill at his feet. A rangy, tawny cur, her teats large, dark, and distended, ambled wearily in the shadow of the house, followed by three round, dusty pups; they paid him no attention. He wanted a drink of cold water.

No one was at home, he thought; the house gave no sign of life. It was past five o'clock. There was a peculiar stillness on the earth; it seemed strangely appropriate to that place. Beyond the house and the grove, a long, rolling plain lay before the creek, extending east and west. It seemed almost white, like the moon.

Then, as he wiped the perspiration from his forehead, he saw the boy. The boy stood—seemed suspended—in the black interior of a lean-to, a brush arbor, perhaps thirty or forty yards away. He peered out of the depth as out of a cave, across the bright foreground, without expression. Set thought at first that the boy must be deranged, so strange and unsettling was his sudden and wild appearance. But his gaze was a good deal more incisive than an idiot's. It was indeed so insistent and penetrating that it made Set squirm.

"Hallo!" Set called loudly, surprised to hear the consternation in his voice. "Say, I'm looking for someone, an old woman. I'm afraid I—"

"Oh, you're too late, Mr. Setmaunt. Gran'ma . . . Kope'mah . . . well, Gran'ma died already."

Set was so intent upon the boy's face, as much of it as he could see, that the voice, nearer by, startled him, and he turned sharply around. It was a woman on the porch of the house who had spoken, a handsome, matronly woman, perhaps fifty years old, of medium height, rather stout, with thick black hair in which there were streaks of gray. He looked at her for a moment, trying to swallow, but his mouth was too dry. He felt suddenly very tired and depressed. He had come all the way to this remote and godforsaken place for reasons he could not fathom and, now it seemed, to no purpose whatsoever. The grandmother, Kope'mah, was dead. He was weary and off balance; he felt that he was about to collapse. For the first time in his life, it seemed, he could not bring the world into perspective. Why had he come here? What in God's name had compelled him, and what was he doing? He did not know. He wondered if he were losing his mind. He shot a glance toward the boy, but the boy was not there.

"I'm sorry," Set managed at last. "When? When did she . . . die?"

"Friday. Early Friday morning. She was buried on Saturday."

"Friday," he repeated and said again, "I'm sorry."

"You know, Mr. Setmaunt, we tried to call you, several times, from the church—we don't have no phone here—but there was no answer."

It was now Monday. He had received the telegram on Saturday. It had to have been sent on Saturday. It made no sense. Nor could he imagine how anyone here could have telephoned him. His number was unpublished, and it was known to very few people, none of whom knew anything about his father's family, not even Bent. A kind of nausea was coming upon him. He felt an ant crawling on his leg.

"Yes, I'm Set, Locke Setman. Please, may I have a glass of water?"

He turned his head again toward the arbor. There was only the black, empty space within.

Inside the house Set could barely see at first. The windows in the front room were small, and they admitted too little light. The screens were old and rusted, and there was no longer any tension in them, so they billowed in and out. An L-shaped tear in one had been crudely mended with a coarser, darker wire. It looked like a great black centipede, broken nearly in two. Flies were thick at the windows. Set blinked away the face of the boy, which had remained in his mind's eye. He had never been in such a room as this. The walls were wooden, of a teal color. The furniture consisted of a small drab sofa, three chairs of assorted shapes and sizes, a table, and a Franklin stove. There was a kerosene lamp on the table and several photographs on the walls, and there was one painting. The photographs were old and tinted by hand, of men and women who belonged to another age, with one exception— that of a young round-faced man in military uniform. The men and women, peering passively from oval frames, bore a certain family resemblance. They were in native Kiowa dress. From the time he had entered the room, Set was conscious of an odor, neither pleasant nor unpleasant, which he could not identify. It was both subtle and pervasive. He had known it before. It put him in mind of damp, rotted wood or of deep earth. And yet there was also something human about it. Had he been asked to name it, he might have said it was the smell of age.

"Anyway, we're sure glad you could come," said Jessie Mottledmare. "We sure been wantin' to meet you—you know, to meet Catlin's son. You must stay here tonight. You're probably tired and hungry. Milo, he's my husband, will be here soon; he'll bring some meat for supper. And in the morning you must visit the cemetery. The graves, our graves, are not very far apart."

"Our graves?" Set said lowly. It sounded not like a question. A suspicion, as cold and fragile as a snowflake, touched upon his brain.

Jessie burst into laughter. "Gran'ma's and Cate's, I mean," she said.

Set closed his eyes and held his breath. In the confusion and anxiety of being a child and an orphan, he had never come to know where his father was buried, only the abstraction: *out there, where he came from.* Catlin Setmaunt, as the name must appear on the headstone, was buried *here.* After a long moment Set simply accepted that he had been drawn unaccountably into some design of fate in which he belonged. He could not yet even begin to see the design, but perhaps he would see it clearly in time. The last words of the telegram returned to him: NOTIFY CATE. He felt that he was the butt of a bad, even insensitive joke, and he had been manipulated. He had played the part of a fool. In his naïveté he had indeed tried to summon the ghost of his father, but the ghost had summoned him instead, as it were. His life had begun to turn on ironies. In this close, quaint, ancient-smelling room, Cate was close, closer than Set knew.

After a while he wanted to stretch his legs, and he excused himself and went outside. He followed a path in the grass. It was sundown and the heat had fallen off. There was a breeze, very light, and warm rather than cool, but it felt good on his skin and it smelled of trees and grass. Again he looked for the boy, but he no longer expected to see him. The final light had withdrawn to the west, and there was a copper tint upon everything, even the shadows. The bare ground of the path was saturated with softest sanguine light. He could not remember having seen earth of that color; it was red: earlier a flat brick red, now deeper, like that particular conte crayon that is red and brown, like old blood, at the same time—or catlinite, the color of his father's name. He walked from the path along the creek. The growth there was dense, and the water was red like the earth, and the current was slow, so slow as to be nearly imperceptible. The orange bitch had followed him. He spoke to her now and then, but she paid him no mind; she ambled along in her own unhurried maternal perception of the universe, he supposed. He had the sense that she did not accompany, she merely happened to be traveling the same road.

He had a strange feeling there, as if some ancestral intelligence had been awakened in him for the first time. There in the wild growth and the soft glowing of the earth, in the muddy water at his feet, was something profoundly original. He could not put his finger on it, but it was there. It was itself genesis, he thought, not genesis in the public domain, not an Old Testament tale, but *his* genesis. He wanted to see his father there in the shadows of the still creek, the child he once was, himself in the child and in the man. But he could not. There was only something like a photograph, old and faded, a shadow within a shadow.

Then something moved. The motion was sudden and without sound. He had caught only a glimpse of it out of the corner of his eye. And then he was looking hard across the creek, into a small brake. Dusk had settled there; the dim light was like smoke, the foliage thick and black beyond. A time passed in which he held his breath, listening, searching. And he released his breath. "Well, whatever it was, it's gone now," he said to the bitch. She had set her head and was staring intently into the same recess. The hair on her nape was raised.

When he returned to the house, lamplight glowed from within, and Milo—the Reverend Milo Mottledmare—was there. Milo was extremely ill at ease. He offered Set a limp hand and undertook to make him welcome, as best he could; the dirt road was very rough, wasn't it? The light was very dim, wasn't it? But the old lady, the grandmother, you know, wanted to live in the old way. She didn't believe in plumbing and electricity. She had never talked on a telephone. Milo was sorry that Set had not been at the funeral ("Beautiful, just beautiful! A bronze casket, satin-lined; Gran'ma in a blue dress with white lace and ribbons, pretty new shoes; and she was smiling so sweetly); he was glad that Set had come in any case; he had spent the whole day at Lawton on church business— his regrets, but the Lord's work had to be done; gracious, the land needed rain, the crops were burning up. Set tried to respond reasonably, but he could not think what to say. Yes, he was sorry that he was not there; beautiful, yes, it must have been a beautiful ceremony; surely the old woman would have been pleased. The more the two men talked the less was said, and the air grew stale between them. They were both greatly relieved when Jessie called them to dinner.

Set was hungry, and Jessie had prepared a generous meal. There was boiled beef, and there were fried potatoes and onions and roasted corn. Simple as it was, it seemed to him exotic, for it was not familiar to him now. And yet it was a kind of cooking that he once knew, that lay somewhere in his memory. His father had liked to boil beef in salted water. The broth was to Cate a delicacy, as it was now to Set, and he savored it. He poured heaping tea-spoons of sugar into his iced tea, after the example of his hosts. Cate had done so too. Lola Bourne should see him now, among the dark walls and the photographs of Indians, at table with the Mottledmares, lamplight flickering on the oilcloth, he thought. She would have been intrigued, and she would not have approved of the sugar and salt. Not only would she have disapproved—he smiled to himself—she would have nagged and held a grudge. He missed her.

The food revived him somewhat, and he felt decidedly better than he had when he arrived. Set liked Jessie from the first. She was warm and genuine, easygoing and full of good humor. There was nothing pretentious about her, and she was not in the least self-conscious. In this respect she and her man Milo could not have been less alike. He was painfully, comically shy. He appeared to mean well, but he was awkward and obsequious and inarticulate, and he could not look Set in the eye. Set could not be alone with such a man and be comfortable, he thought. But Jessie, in her candor and goodwill, enabled him to relax, and he conversed easily with her. Homeless again, he began almost to feel at home. In a certain way Jessie reminded him of Señora Archuleta.

After a time he brought himself to ask about the boy, whose face had become a caricature, a curious mask in his mind. Was the boy perhaps a member of the family? he asked. Both Jessie and Milo looked at him for a moment, then at each other, without comprehension. Then Jessie broke into laughter, and she said, "Oh, you mean—why, you mean Grey! Oh, she's a tomboy, all right. She's around here all the time, sure enough; but she lives with Worcester, my Uncle Worcester, across the creek. They have a little place across the creek."

"Bote," Milo said without expression. "Bote, Oklahoma."

Set was taken aback and embarrassed and was also entirely incredulous. He wanted to say, No, we're not talking about the same person. I saw a boy in the lean-to, a thin, wild-eyed boy who stared at me rudely and intensely, whose eyes expressed nothing—no, something, something like—well, foreboding, something ominous and . . . unimaginable. Don't you see? There could be no mistaking it, that it was . . . *ominous*. No! The boy looked at me, looked inside me, through me, even. It was a look I cannot forget. But he said instead, "Do you mean . . . she . . . she is your cousin? She is your cousin, then. And you said her name . . . Grey?"

Why was he being so inquisitive? he wondered. He felt himself stumbling, intruding, on the verge of revealing his own secrets, but his curiosity had got the better of him. He felt a strange excitement growing within him, and he did not know why.

"We think they're married, Indi'n way," Milo said with a lascivious wink and a strange laugh like a grunt; then, seriously, "She's the Mayor of Bote, Oklahoma."

Jessie looked at him directly, and he returned to his plate.

"No," said Jessie, "she's my niece. My brother Walker was her father; he died a few years ago. But her mother is Navajo, and Grey grew up in Arizona. My brother lived there before he died."

"Shoot, we don't know too much about her," Milo offered.

There was a pause.

"How long has she been with you . . . with your uncle?" Set asked. He could not guess where his questions were leading. He had finished his food, and he wanted a drink of whiskey. He was not likely to find one here, he thought, but there was an unopened bottle of Scotch in the car.

"Oh, maybe two years now," Milo said.

"Yes, two years," Jessie said. "She just turned up one day—I still remember it, you know? We were sitting down to supper in the arbor, Milo and Gran'ma and me, and Grey, she just appeared, came from nowhere, it seemed. She sat down with us and helped herself to everything, like she had lived here all her life. Oh, we didn't know what to think at first. She didn't tell us who she was. But she was so nice and friendly, you know? We couldn't help but like her. And a funny thing, Gran'ma liked her most of all, and she didn't seem at all surprised to see her. It's funny, you know?—like she was expecting her."

"Yeah," Milo agreed. "It was like Gran'ma was expecting her all along, an' all." He wagged his head in wonder. "Her and Gran'ma, they sure did get along good together; gracious, they got along good. And that there Grey, shoot, she talks Kiowa better'n we do. You just don't find them young'uns talkin' Kiowa like that no more."

"Nobody's going to miss Gran'ma more than Grey, I guess, unless it's Worcester," Jessie said. "He's getting old too."

"Grey and your uncle . . . she's a young woman, isn't she? I thought I saw a young . . . person."

"Oh, I bet she's eighteen or nineteen," said Jessie, "though sometimes she seems a lot older. She's been around, to hear her talk. She doesn't really *confide* in us. But she knows what's going on, you know?"

"She don't really *confide* in us," Milo put in. "She's kind of wild." Set glanced at him; for the first time they were in agreement.

"And, uh, she's a mayor . . . ?"

"She's the Mayor of Bote, Oklahoma," said Milo Mottledmare as a matter of fact.

"Oh, that's what she says." Jessie laughed. "It's a joke, I guess. She and Worcester live across the creek. There are a couple of old sod houses over there. People, white people, used to live in them back in the Depression, maybe before that. They're just crumbling away. Nobody lives in them now, not for years and years. Anyway, Grey calls the place Bote, Oklahoma, and she's declared herself the mayor."

"She's the Mayor of Bote, Oklahoma," Milo said again.

"They get along all right, Grey and Worcester, despite the difference in their ages, do they?"

"Oh, my, yes," Jessie answered. "You see, Grey likes the old ones, and they know it, and they like her too. Sometimes when you listen to her talk, you'd think she's old herself. She can talk like an old, old woman. Worcester, he's seventy, probably. We tease him about Grey, you know. Well, they live together."

"And Grey is the daughter of your brother?—you said his name was Walker?"

"Yes, Walker. Walker the Younger, we say in the Kiowa way. Our father's name was Walker too."

"We think she went to boarding school," Milo said.

Set remained curious about Grey—Grey had taken hold of his imagination—but the conversation took a turn, and he had to put his thoughts of her aside for the time being. Jessie and Milo Mottledmare wanted him to talk about himself, and so he did. He told them briefly and rather self-consciously of having lived in an orphanage, of having been adopted, of having gone to art school and become a painter. He answered their questions as best he could and did not mind that Jessie's were now and then personal. He had not married; he was a successful artist; he lived alone. She tried to seem satisfied, but he could see that she wanted to know more. She amused him, and he did not resent her curiosity; she did not resent his, after all. And he too found out something. His grandmother, Cate's mother, and Kope'mah had been very close throughout their lives, until Agabai died in 1932. Although Kope'mah was older than Agabai and outlived her by forty years, they were like sisters, or like mother and daughter. And Cate had been to Kope'mah like her own child. When he died she placed a buffalo robe over his coffin. It was a magnificent heirloom, and the gesture was worthy of a great man. Set was deeply moved to hear this; not for many years had his father's memory borne so closely upon him. Cate Setman had married Catherine Locke at Santa Barbara in the year Agabai died. Catherine died in childbirth in 1934, and Cate died in a car crash in Wyoming in 1941, when Set was seven years old. A maternal uncle intervened, and Set was not told of his father's death until an orphanage had been secured. Of course Jessie and Milo knew of Cate's death soon after the fact, and long before Set knew. They attended the funeral, and Milo's mentor, the Reverend Leland Smoke, spoke over Catlin Setman's grave. NOTIFY CATE had been the instruction of the old woman, Kope'mah. She had spoken of Set in her last days, Jessie said. And again Set was incredulous. The old woman could have known next to nothing about him, he thought, and in spite of her devotion she could not have known much about Catlin. She had to have known Cate as a child, inasmuch as he went out into the world when he was still a boy, and he died away from home as a young man. But the grandmother, in her final days, had spoken urgently of him and *to* him, Jessie said. Set wished now with all his heart that he might have been in time to hear Cate's name on the grandmother's lips. Cate was very dear to her, and in her ultimate awareness of the past he must have been intensely alive to her. NOTIFY CATE. The telegram was Grey's doing; or rather it was the grandmother's, through Grey. So narrowly had Set missed an opportunity to know something about himself, something of who he was.

They sat for a long time at the table, and at last Set became very tired; he and Milo began to yawn in concert. There was a large summer moon, and he asked if he might sleep in the arbor. The next day there was to be a meeting of one of the Kiowa dance societies near Anadarko. It was decided that Milo would leave early in the morning and set up the camp. Later Set would drive Jessie, and perhaps Worcester and Grey, there on his way to the airport. And they would allow enough time to visit the cemetery and watch a part of the dance.

The moon was high when he went out of the house. He was used to city lights, and for him this moon was brighter than any he had ever seen. In all the night it was the principal thing; every object on earth seemed to stand out in a blue and silver wash, and he could see with great clarity even the shadows of trees in the middle distance. The arbor was black inside, except the moonbeams splintered on the roof of boughs. The wide bench, on which he was to sleep, was stitched with pale blue gunmetal light. The night in its Plains vastness overwhelmed him, and just then a cool, fresh wind lifted from the Washita, and he wanted to give himself up to the deepest sleep. He wanted there to be nothing; he wanted to enter wholly into the deep element of the Plains night in which he imagined nothing was.

The hours passed, and he dreamed. He heard himself say something, and he awoke. He opened his eyes and was startled to see the girl standing over him. She made no sound, but looked down at him with great composure. He could not see her face, only her form. The moon shone behind her, set a wonderful radiance upon her. She was so perfectly still. His impulse was to shout at her, to berate her. It was such a stupid and careless and dangerous thing for her to do, to steal up on him while he slept. He might have struck out at her, or he might have been frightened to death! This went through his mind in an instant—and then all at once his shock and anger were gone. Something in her attitude, in the very way she stood in the darkness seeming not even to breathe, expressed an irresistible calm, one that infected him.

"Grey?" he managed, after a moment.

She might have nodded. She seemed tentative, ephemeral, as if she might vanish in a moment. Her hair was edged with light like mercury, a thin, concentrated brilliance.

"What? What is it? What do you want?" He was stammering.

"It is what the grandmother wants," she said. She spoke deliberately, distinctly. Her voice was soft and measured.

There was a silence. He nearly laughed in his perplexity. He was confounded. Nothing he could say or do seemed appropriate. "The old woman is dead," he said in a whisper, simply, to no one. It did not matter, he supposed. It did not matter that the grandmother was dead, or that he said so, or that the girl standing before him spoke in riddles in the night, in a darkness in the light of the moon, in a darkness that comprehended the galaxies.

"The grandmother, Kope'mah, wants me to give you back your medicine. It belongs to you. You must not go without it."

When at last she moved, it was a decisive act. She turned and walked away rapidly. She appeared and reappeared among the shadows in the undulant plain, moving with long, silent strides toward the pitch-black band of trees on the creek. He looked after her until she was out of sight, and then he heard the hoofbeats of a horse, muffled, dying away. And he went to sleep again, but his sleep was uneasy and shallow.

He dreamed of the boy. The boy seemed not to stand on the ground but was suspended in the waterlike element of darkness, hanging in the way a turtle hangs in the still margin of a stream. The body was indistinct; only the face was shaped and barely delineated. It shone like a vague, powdered mask, like a skull. But he was certain it was the face of a boy, drawn, emaciated. He could not move, but the boy approached him. There was no separation of motion in the approach; the boy simply drew up on him in that strange suspension. And the face was slowly transformed. At closer range it terrified Set. The face was that of an ancient woman, her great eyes hollow and opaque, yet glittering like faceted shale, the ropes and pouches of flesh at her cheeks and jowls seeming almost to slip from the bone, her little twisted mouth quivering as with some desperate concern to speak or cry out. Then there were strange, gurgling, rasping sounds in her throat, an awful, suffocated speech. The words were muffled and animal-like, groans and growls. And Set understood in another moment that the terrible sounds were in his own throat. It was he who wanted so desperately to speak and could not. To speak seemed the most important and necessary thing in his life, to rise from some profound and primitive helplessness to the level of speech; but he was prevented by some monstrous resistance in himself, it seemed. And the most terrible thing was, he did not even know what he wanted to say, *had* to say, if only he could say it.

And Set remembered:

There was a playing field behind the Peter and Paul Home, and beyond the field a small wood with a footpath and benches set out along the path. One day, just after the evening meal, Loki ventured out across the field and upon the path. This was against the rules of the Home, but he couldn't see the harm. He walked, talking to himself, in the late light, and then he sat down on one of the benches. The wood was dark and enchanting; he was alive to the dusk, the air, the sounds of insects like a stifled roar. As he sat down he placed his hands on the edge of the seat, and a bee, hidden underneath, stung him on the thumb. It hurt terribly, but Loki knew what it was at once, and he bore the pain manfully, though the sting resulted in an extraordinary swelling, and Loki had to go that night to the infirmary and submit to the wearing of a rubber glove filled with some milky medicine. It looked like a Mickey Mouse hand, one of his fellows said, and made of him a laughingstock. The next morning Sister Stella Francesca lectured him on the grave sin of breaking the "Castle Rules," as she liked to call the home's two-page list of regulations. And then she placed in his mind forever the notion of "bee-wolves," which she said was an old, old name for bears. Bee-wolves were rumored to exist in the little park beneath the west window of the tower. Sag's Wood, with its serpentine paths, its green benches and patches of daisies and buttercups, was in Loki's mind then a hotbed of bears. Some months later he had occasion to say to Sister Francesca, "Sister, I don't think that I am any longer afraid of bee-wolves, actually." It was a considered statement. He expected her at first to study this pronouncement—she was so often studious in her attitude—then perhaps to accept it with meticulous approval. But to his astonishment she smiled broadly at once, took him up in a great hug, and said with enthusiasm, "There's a good boy, Loki! There's a *very* good boy!"

Remote as the stars are his sentiments just now

There was a music in Grey's mind, a music made upon banjos. Never had she to quest after visions.

Her hands were trembling. The note was printed in minute letters on a bit of cigarette paper, folded several times. She held it concealed between the index and middle fingers of her right hand. She had pressed her fingers so tightly together that she could no longer feel the note. Was it there?

Grey smiled brightly at J. W. Bell, who obviously appreciated her appearance. And well he might. She had brushed her hair until it shone like obsidian. She had lain naked in the sun the day before, so that her skin was burnished and retained the merest glowing heat. She wore the long white dress with third button, just above her breasts, missing, and no undergarments, so that the full shape of her body should be visible and her movements perfectly un-impeded in the flowing folds. She had crumpled and kneaded the dress in order to take the stiffness out of it. It had become not yellow with age, nor yet was it white, but the color of tea and cream, and this certain softening of the once hard and unadulterated whiteness gave to her complexion an accent like the touch of reflected firelight. She had shaped her nails, brushed her teeth with baking soda, and gargled Lilac Vegetal, diluted with water from the well. She had looked all morning at—rather into—a thirty-carat turquoise stone, a Lander's stone, that its reflection might hold in her eyes and shimmer there like mountain rain. She had brushed her beaded moccasins with sprigs of cedar and sage, and she had patted her breasts with crushed juniper berries and rose hips and the pollen of sunflowers. She stood graceful and tall and comely.

"Oh, Mr. Bell," she intoned, "I *do* thank you for your kindness to me. It's my brother, you see. Adam owns a newspaper in Philadelphia, and he would *so* like to hear that I had met Mr. William Bonney on my sojourn in the glorious West."

She fluttered her eyelashes, and Bell blushed. Over his shoulder she caught sight of the other guard, Bob Olinger. His was a face, she told Billy afterward, that she would never forget. Hate was a living thing in his eyes; she would always, from that moment on, think of hatred as a dull opalescence in the eyes of *this* man. Olinger smiled and spat. It would remain in her mind as one of the strangest smiles she had ever seen. Afterward, too, she would try to imagine Olinger as a child, as his mother's child, but innocence and a mother's love she could not lay at his place. He had never been a child, she thought; he had not been born of woman. He was a mutation, an awful accident of nature, an incomprehensible act of God, like a pestilence. He stood in the presence of death and evil.

Yes, there was the scent of death in his hair, on his skin, at his mouth. But in this moment when she beheld him for the first and last time, she could not know that it was his own death that defined him precisely, ominous, impending, imminent. It was too far down in her intuition to grasp, but it made for a terrible fascination nevertheless. She could not know that he would die violently on this very day, in less than an hour. A subtle sweet-and-sour scent of death permeated the room, a faint putrescence.

She was distracted, and her fingers had begun to ache. Bell made an awkward gesture of presentation, and she turned to Billy. Oh, he had become so thin and pale! His cheeks were hollow, and his mouth was drawn. But he regarded her evenly, with a stiff, formal respect.

"Howdy, ma'am," he said.

Howdy, ma'am? She bit her tongue to keep from laughing and extended her hand. He took it lightly in his own, bowing slightly. The shackles seemed excessively large and cumbersome on his flat, slender wrists.

"I want to thank you for coming here today," he said. "I won't forget, no, ma'am."

She released the note into his hand. The thing was accomplished. She could not bring herself to say anything to him directly. Her heart was pounding, and her talent for seduction and intrigue evaporated in the heat of the moment. Bell's blush was gone; she dared not look at Olinger.

"Gracious me," she said sweetly, and she nodded curiously, turned, and took her leave. Her moccasins scarcely sounded on the stairs. Billy shuffled to the window, his leg irons ringing, and watched her cross the street below. The air outside smelled of lilacs and wood smoke.

When he turned, Olinger was looking at him, the strange smile still on his face, a double-barreled shotgun in his left hand, balanced delicately as on the tips of his fingers, the muzzles bobbing and weaving slowly, almost imperceptibly, never trained, but never wide of Billy's body. The shotgun was Olinger's signature.

For twelve days now Billy had listened to Olinger's taunts. They had begun on the ride from Mesilla, when Billy had been chained to the back seat of the ambulance, Olinger facing him. Two other guards were inside, three on horseback outside. They were all heavily armed, and they were a deadly dangerous lot of men. Any one of them, but most especially Olinger, would have been glad to dispatch the soul of Billy the Kid to hell. That ride, which lasted seven days, had shaken Billy. He was not afraid—it wasn't fear—but sickened by the circumstances. He wanted to be free, but he was shackled hand and foot. He wanted to be among his friends, but everyone in his immediate reach was a deadly enemy. He wanted to be left alone, but he was subjected to relentless observation, suspicion, and public humiliation. Above all, he was the victim of Olinger's sadism.

Never had Grey to quest after visions. She sat on a chair in front of Wortley's Hotel, across the street from the Lincoln County Courthouse. It was a bright April day, verging on noon. The sky was blue; there were clouds in the distance like feathers floating. The music of commerce in Lincoln had come to a stop: siesta. The bustle of the morning—and her mission—had been excitement and restoration; rarely had she felt herself so much alive. But, too, she was grateful for this lull. A delicious breeze touched her forehead. The good scents of food cooking—beans and chili and tortillas—made for a pleasant hunger in her, not a hunger to be satisfied at once but one to be borne for a time, savored like the food to come. The broad, dusty main street of the town of Lincoln, New Mexico Territory, reached away into summer. She thought of something she had once read:

> Great Streets of silence led away
> To Neighborhoods of Pause—

Sitting, the white dress drew up tightly at the breasts and arms. She unbuttoned the throat, the first two buttons. She closed her eyes. When she opened them again, a good many people had gathered in the street. There was no longer siesta. A sudden gust set a whirlwind careening in the street. There had been a shot.

She had not to quest after visions.

"Why don't you leave him alone, Bob?" Bell said. "Hell, he ain't doin' you no harm. He cain't, hardly."

Olinger spat on the floor at Bell's feet without taking his eyes off Billy the Kid. The smile was still there, crooked, without mirth. He bent his knees slightly and hunched his shoulders, making a bow of his body, and raised the shotgun and aimed it between Billy's eyes. He exerted ever so little pressure on the front trigger; his excitement was coming to an intensity almost unbearable. Spittle formed at the corners of his smile; his hands began to shake. Billy stood so still that he seemed in a trance. He did not blink, and he held his eyes, in which there was no expression, upon Olinger's. The tension was too much for Bell.

"Goddammit, Bob, stop it!"

"*Pow!*" Olinger's breath exploded. Bell flinched, but Billy did not. "Hey, lookit there! Lookit there, Bell! The Kid ain't got no head! Good God to Hallelujah! Would you lookit that!" He was animated now, warming to the performance, dancing in place, emitting hysterical laughter. "Lookit that, would yuh? Lookit, Bell! Lookit that there bloody stump between his shoulders there. Looks like a chicken's neck, don't it, what's head has been wrung off. Would you just lookit, Bell? The Kid's bloody, hairy brains is splashed all over the wall yonder, all around the window there. Hey, a goodly gob must have splashed down in the street for the dogs and chickens."

"Stop it, Bob," Bell said, but there was no authority in it; he knew that Olinger would go on.

"Hey, ol' Godfrey Gauss's dog, it must be around. Shit, that there dog *loves* brains. An' Bell, you know Widow Mora's chickens, them rangy things what's always peckin' in the road? Why, them dumb critters'll eat anything. Hey, one day I seen them chickens peck the eyes right out of a sheep's head!"

"Aw, for God's sake," Bell said with disgust.

"Kid, I'd sure like to spill your brains out there in the street an' watch the chickens peck your eyes into jelly; it would pleasure me for certain, it would." He spoke directly to Billy, who had not moved, who appeared not even to breathe.

"I had you figured for a man who liked to watch chickens, Bob," Billy said. His voice was low and perfectly even.

"Sooner watch you floppin' headless on the floor, Kid. Like to see you gropin' for your face, find it gone, find nothin' but the bloody stump. Like to see you flop and wiggle around for a spell."

"Well, if you don't blow my head off, Bob, I guess you'll just have to come to the hangin'."

"Lookin' forward to it, Kid."

"To tell you the truth, Bob, I can take it or leave it. It don't seem half as exciting as the little scene you've just laid out."

"I ain't so sure, Kid. Once down to El Paso I seen a man hanged, a man named Ficker, or Flicker, not much bigger'n you. When he hit the end of that rope, his head was just ripped right off— damnedest thing you ever seen! But I guess it happens. I 'spect we'll leave them irons on you, so's you'll have some honest weight. You got a kinda scrawny girl's neck, anyway. Shit, I 'spect there'll be one helluva pop at the end of that rope. I'll just bet you snap right in two. An', Kid, they ain't gonna be in no hurry to bury you, I'll wager. I reckon they'll cart the big part of you off first and leave your head lyin' there, an' shit, I'll bet anything them chickens'll come along and peck your eyes out. Them dumb critters love eye jelly."

"It don't sound like much of a card game, Bob," Billy said and smiled.

"May, Friday the thirteenth," Olinger said. "Fifteen days."

"It ain't a bad day to die."

"I want to see the big half with the stump flop around on the ground like a chicken with its head wrung off."

"I had you figured," Billy said.

It was time for Olinger to go to lunch. He said something to Bell, placed his shotgun in a room that served as an armory, a closet on the landing halfway down the stairs, and went out. Billy turned to the window again. He counted Olinger's steps as he crossed the street diagonally northeastward to the Wortley

Hotel—105 steps. On a chair in front of the hotel Grey sat in her white dress. She was the picture of repose. She was a girl in a painting. She was his mother on that day in early spring, 1873, in Santa Fe, when he and his brother Joe witnessed her marriage to William H. Antrim. She was, in his heroic and chivalrous intelligence, a woman to admire, to serve, to stand for, to protect, to cherish, and to die for. Such women are very delicate, very beautiful, he thought to himself—really, women of taste and breeding and refinement, so far beyond him that he could only stand in awe of them. Suddenly he thought of a nun, Sister Blandina, whom he had met at Trinidad and who had prevailed upon him to spare the physicians. *There* was a woman of mercy and charity and grace and goodness, a woman of perfect virtue. That saintly Italian woman, that woman of God, he could not have imagined her beneath her habit. He could not have imagined that she moved her bowels or broke wind or that her breath or her feet ever stank.

In front of the Wortley Hotel, Grey belched.

There had been a shot.

The scents of lilac and wood smoke had faded, and again there was a little stench of death in the room. Billy, facing the window, unfolded the note. It read: OUTHOUSE.

There had been a shot.

Billy turned. All of his instincts came to bear upon his next step. In a moment he became the creature he was best at being, an organism of inexorable purpose; his concentration was so great as to be irresistible. It was as if he already had the gun in his hand. Remote as the stars were his sentiments just now—Grey, Paulita, his mother in her wedding dress—remote beyond reckoning. He would have put bullets in the eyes of Sister Blandina, had she stood in his way.

"Hell, I'm sorry, Bell, I gotta take a pee."

J. W. Bell led Billy the Kid, straining against his chains, down the stairs and into the yard. He watched him enter the privy.

"Don't take too long," he said, and then was sorry he had said it; there was no need. He stood close by, cleaning his nails with a pocketknife. All was well. Everything was proceeding according to the established order. Except for the girl, this was a day like yesterday and the day before, and the day before that. He was not one to be bored by the ordinary. He liked everything in its place.

Bell, like so many others, had developed a liking for Billy the Kid. Billy was always ready to laugh, to joke, to pass the time in an agreeable way. He was, in fact, an attractive man. He gave a good account of himself. He was unassuming. Although famous —or infamous—he did not "put on airs," as Bell said. He seemed always to expect the best in people. He was well spoken. He liked, or was prepared to like, everyone, especially women, in whom he seemed to awaken the maternal instinct. He played a fair hand of poker, and he was known never to forget a kindness. Bell had nothing against the Kid personally. Billy was a man, scarcely more than a boy, with whom Bell could be comfortable—more than comfortable: giving, loyal, compassionate. Bell neither condoned nor understood Olinger's vicious behavior toward Billy. It was a vague and fatal notion in Bell's mind that Billy the Kid was less dangerous than he was said to be.

There had been a shot.

The gun was a Colt .44, single-action. Billy, urinating loudly for Bell's sake, checked to see that it was fully loaded. It felt like a heavy bird in his hands, then lighter, a goose that was mounting on the wind, streaking off into a distance that reached beyond the rim of the world. With his small white hands he handled it as a bear might handle a fish, with some sense of ancient respect, playfully and skillfully. Then he placed it inside his belt, under his shirt.

With difficulty he mounted the stairs to the level of the armory, Bell just behind him. There Billy drew the gun, turned, and leveled it at Bell's face.

Billy waited for a long moment, letting Bell take stock of the situation. Then he said, "I've got the upper hand, Bell. The whole show is mine now. I want you to do *exactly* as I say. The Lord knows I don't want to kill you." His voice was again low, even, almost a whisper, and he spoke slowly, enunciated carefully.

"Oh, God!" Bell said. He tried desperately to restore order to his mind. He could not, and he was then beside himself. His impulse was to run. He struggled with his fear and humiliation. In the foreground of his awareness was the realization that he had made a grave mistake, unspeakably grave: he had allowed Billy the Kid to turn the tables on him. For a fraction of a moment he heard his own hysterical laughter, like Olinger's, in his ear. No one in the history of the world had done what he had just done; no one had ever forfeited his mortal advantage so foolishly, so decisively. Beyond the mask of his station and age, he began to cry. His own gun was of no use. There was no one else on the stair, in the building, as far as he knew. He was absolutely alone with this man, this dangerous and desperate man, this cold-blooded killer, this most-wanted outlaw. He wanted to vomit. None of this was real to him; it was like a dream, a nightmare.

In this very moment he had grown old. His surprise and confusion and shame were overwhelming. He spun and bolted. His boots struck the stair, four steps below; his next step would strike the landing. There was a blind corner; the lower flight descended at a 90 degree angle. If only he could turn the corner, he would be safe. The Kid could not negotiate the stairs easily in his chains. He could not possibly pursue, Bell must have thought. But if indeed these considerations did happen upon Bell's stricken consciousness in the last moment of his life, they were idle.

As Bell lurched, Billy the Kid said to himself, "Don't do it, Bell, please." And in the same instant he pulled the trigger. The gun bucked, and Bell's body slammed against the wall, slumped on the landing, then tumbled out of sight. He was, somewhere in that infinite series of motions, dead.

Billy hobbled to the body, took the keys, and made his way awkwardly to the armory, opened it, and withdrew Olinger's shotgun. There was no hurry; he set the next few events to his own clock. He was on time; all the motion of the town of Lincoln, at midday, on April 28, 1881, was on time. He made his way to the window overlooking the main street, the only street of the town.

There had been a shot.

Olinger looked up. There had been a shot. He brought his sleeve quickly to his mouth and moved his chair backward, standing up. Others in the dining room had heard it too. They cocked their heads. For a moment there was a stasis, a silence thick and unwieldy, strange. Then each one returned to his meal, except Olinger. In that silence he was confounded. There had been a shot. He shook his shoulders and went out into the street. A girl in a white dress sat in a chair in front of the Wortley Hotel. He took notice of her and nodded, but she was looking away. She was in repose, a seated woman in a white dress. She was like no one and nothing else in Lincoln. She was like a painting by Renoir, a soft and lovely composition against a hard landscape, with its dry earth colors. It was strange to Olinger that he, a brittle man, more nearly an animal than a man, without the least advantage or sensitivity where the beautiful was concerned, should somehow be moved by the girl in the white dress. But he hadn't time to ponder. He hurried across the street, 89 steps. The voice in the window above stopped him in his tracks. "Hello, Bob." It was familiar and reassuring; everything was as it ought to be. Olinger looked up into the twin muzzles of his own shotgun. In that moment Olinger saw Billy the Kid in extraordinary detail, saw into the blue, expressionless eyes, saw the dark brows and the long curly hair with definition, saw the mouth barely open and the teeth protruding, saw the fine, articulate hands on the gun, perfectly still, saw the little bony wrists, raw with the rub of the handcuffs. And the black eyes of the shotgun, peering into his soul. There was no depth to them, or there was depth unending; they were the blackness of the void beyond the stars. In them Olinger could see eternity. Had the girl seen him walking to his death? He could not be sure, nor did it matter, really. He had seen her. Even at this most extreme moment of his life, he was acutely aware of having seen her. She was something to see. And now, looking up at the man who was going to take his life, he held on, meagerly, to the vision of the girl. He felt nothing for her, nothing to which he could give a name. It was only that she in her remote loveliness, unattainable, untouchable, stood for some cipher in the sum of his existence. He had never imagined what his last vision of the world might be; his life had been a paltry thing. He wondered that in his mind's eye, at the ultimate hour, there should be a girl in a white dress.

Billy pulled the first trigger. The load struck Olinger in the middle, dividing him nearly in two. His body was blown into the street, face down, bent at a hideous angle. Billy pulled the second trigger, and the other load exploded into Olinger's back. The body jerked violently.

Talk, a hectic murmur, was coming up from the street now. Billy made his way down to the yard behind the courthouse. There was Godfrey Gauss, the caretaker. Billy instructed the old man to bring him a horse. For a long time the old German man labored to catch a horse in the adjacent pasture. At last he succeeded. The horse was a skittish mare that belonged to Billy Burt. "Tell Mr. Burt I'll return the horse," Billy said. Gauss saddled the mare and tied it to a fencepost. Billy had been trying to remove the leg irons, but he could not. At gunpoint, old man Gauss chopped the chain in two with an ax. Billy tied the loose ends of the chain to his belt.

At last, in the bright spring afternoon, Billy the Kid led the mare out into the wide street, where the residents of Lincoln had been gathered since midday. Billy had taken his time. He had armed himself; he had secured a horse and broken his shackles; he had left two men dead. All in all, it was one of the most intense and exhilarating days of his young life. He had never been higher. The good citizens of Lincoln, New Mexico Territory, respectfully awaited the appearance of El Chivato. Bets were laid and liquor was drunk, but quietly, discretely; there was a solemnity in the town, an air of grave celebration, as on a Day of the Dead. Billy had been wounded and could not ride; he had been killed; he was searching the courthouse for a hidden treasure; he was praying for the souls of Bob Olinger and J. W. Bell; he was composing a letter to Lew Wallace, Governor of the Territory, begging pardon. Shortly after Olinger had been shot down in the street, there was a brief commotion. In front of the Wortley Hotel a girl in a white dress leaped upon a large sorrel stallion and raced away, her long hair flying and her immaculate dress whipping up like meringue high on her dark thighs. Collectively, the townspeople caught their breath.

Billy the Kid appeared at last. He bade a small boy step forward and hold his horse. Then he walked up one side of the street and down the other, shaking hands. *"¡Gracias, gracias!"* he said again and again. *"Adios."* And there was bestowed upon him the best wishes of the people. *"¡Hasta luego, Billee! Vaya con Dios. ¡Bravo, bravo! ¡Bien hecho, Billee!"*

With difficulty because of the heavy chains, which, though broken, were still affixed to his ankles, Billy mounted the horse and urged it to a gallop at once. *"¡Salud!"* he shouted. *"¡Salud y amistad! ¡Adios, mi amigos, amigos de mi corazón, adios!"*

18

There is a menace among the words

***

Dwight Dicks was sullen. He and his son, Murphy, were cleaning out the stalls in the barn. Dwight was a large, rawboned man, standing well over six feet, with a huge, balding head and huge hands. His face was weather-beaten; he seemed always, day or night, to be looking into the sun, squinting, his great mouth forever open in a grimace that was almost like a smile; there were prominent gaps among his yellow teeth, and his large lips were parched and purple. His thick legs were spread apart, and he wheezed as he worked. Murphy was eighteen, almost as tall as his father, with a thick shock of reddish-blond hair and a bland, agreeable face. He was lanky, and his body was hard and corded with muscle. Although there were resemblances between them, it would have been hard to imagine that the boy might one day look like his father.

Dwight was working with a small pitchfork, a forty-two-inch fork with curved tines and a cross handle. Because of his height he had to bend considerably to his work. He pitched the old, trampled straw out of the stall with a chain-gang rhythm, efficient and backbreaking at once. He paused now and then to catch his breath and to straighten his spine. The pain of unbending his back was a thing he had known for more than forty years; it was a pain indistinguishable from relief. This was not the kind of work he liked best. He preferred to be outside. Here in the dark barn, he raised a lot of dust, and it was hard to breathe. Every time he lifted the straw, a cloud of dust, laden with chaff and splinters and fragmented leaf, rose into the air, thickening it like a smoke palpable with cinders. It got in his eyes and nostrils, inside his collar and gloves and shoes. It was dirty work, to be sure, but by no means the worst, and he had been doing it as long as he could remember. He pitched fresh straw into the stall and dragged in a bale of hay. The fork he laid beside the bale. From the hip pocket of his overalls he removed a seven-and-a-half-inch cutting pliers, snipped the wires on the bale, and left the pliers on top of the green, compacted hay. He reached into a corner of the stall for the bottle of whiskey that he kept there, opened it, and raised it to his mouth, bending backward, wincing, taking in four long swallows of the brown, burning liquid. When the sensation of heat reached dead center, he heaved a mighty sigh and shuddered. He replaced the bottle, three quarters full, and covered it with straw.

"Murph!" he called. There was something on his mind, and he had to get it off.

"Haw!" Murphy's voice came along the stalls like an echo. Shafts of sunlight, kaleidoscopic with the swirling sediment, shone like fiery pillars before Dwight's eyes. He could not see his son.

"Murphy's Law. You give that there horse away, son?" There was a menace among the words. Murphy Dicks stopped his work. There was a silence.

"Well, Pa, not exactly."

"Not exactly," Dwight repeated. "Well, what then? You sold him?"

There was another, shorter pause, then: "Yeah, Pa. That's more like it."

Dwight considered this, a small euphoria coming upon his brain. His mood began to change.

"How much? How much did you get?"

"I got a lot, Pa. I got a whole lot."

"Well, would you go so far as to say you got a fair price, son?"

There was a jocular lilt to his voice now, one that Murphy could recognize and appreciate. Murphy relaxed. The joke was growing up between them.

"Pa, I'd say it was more than fair. I'd say it was downright generous."

Dwight Dicks's whole great face became a leer.

"You know, son, most folks would say you flat got taken. Murphy's Law is a crackerjack horse. I hope to kiss a pig he is."

"I got me a crackerjack price, Pa. And more to come too, I reckon."

Dwight Dicks slapped his thigh with a vigor that made a dusty storm on the air.

"I sure do admire the looks of that Injun gal," he drawled. "I *surely* do. And she surely can ride, can't she, son?" In a voice farther away he added, "I could surely do with some crackerjack myself. I hope to kiss a pig I could."

"She surely can ride," Murphy said.

She must serve her purpose

   Grey rode hard into the foothills of the Capitan Mountains, to the ranch of José Cordova. She told Cordova that Billy had escaped from the Lincoln County Courthouse and would soon be riding in, tired and hungry. José Cordova set about cooking the evening meal. He was very excited.

  Later, after Billy had with José Cordova's help removed the leg irons, there was a leisurely supper of the country—tortillas, a green chili stew with mutton and chicos, small tart apples, and *café con leche.* And then, under the brilliant stars, in a kind of thanksgiving with *aguardiente,* Billy, with a hard, cracking slap, released Billy Burt's mare. It went galloping home in the night.

  A single candle guttered on the table beside the bed. The bed was narrow and crude, a sack of straw on a wooden frame. Billy was too soon naked. Grey wore a pale blue flannel nightgown. They sat for a time together on the edge of the bed, almost formally, watching the light of the candle flicker on the bare adobe walls, on the *vigas* and *latillas* overhead, saying little, wondering what more to say. Billy seemed almost frail in his white skin. Grey was more than fetching in her nightgown, not directly seductive, as she could be, but simply and serenely beautiful and feminine. As if at a signal, they lay back together in the shadows. The whir of the day's excitement still sounded, but faintly now, in Grey's ears. She was overcome by the closer silence of this rustic room. In it she was safe and sound, wholly contained in the soft, bare, and shimmering walls as in a womb, lying deep in the straw mattress, warm and enclosed in her lover's arms. It seemed the most intimate moment she had ever known. Not quite against her will—it was delicious to resist, as a matter of propriety—desire came over her body, cell by cell. And Billy was quiet, patient, loving, considerate, gentle, preeminently kind to her. No man had ever been all of these things to her at once, in such measure, not even old Worcester Meat, who was the gentlest of men. She liked immensely the soft sensation of this intimacy, but she could not stand it. She began to shiver with heat. Billy's hand brushed her face and throat, cupped her shoulder, then her breast, and he kissed her. Very lightly he pressed himself to her, along the whole length of her body; she was utterly supple under his touch. He traced with his hand the curve of her hip downward, then drew his fingers upward along the inside of her thigh. For what seemed a very long time he conformed his hand to her belly with a delicacy so acute as to set her on edge; she moaned a little. At last he curved his fingers under her belly, between her legs, through the flannel gown, to the wet folds there.

"Uh, Billy, will you—uh, make love to me, please?" she said under her quick breath. Oh, no! Had she said that? Had she put it so? There was a flicker of exasperation. In real life she did not speak in euphemisms. Her senses were reeling again. "I mean, are we going to fuck or what?" she said urgently. She had begun to shiver all over, then to writhe; her whole body had begun to express a profound hunger.

"Yes, ma'am," Billy said.

"Soon?" she gasped.

He rolled her gently on her back, and she helped him gather the gown above her hips. She opened wide her legs, and he placed himself precisely between them. He kissed her deeply on the mouth, and she him, biting his lower lip, and tongued him and tasted of him, of his mouth and teeth, and of his salty, stubbled throat, of his ears and hair. She set her nails into his back. For a long, indeterminate time they touched and tasted and teased each other to the point of desperation. And then, with infinite mercy, he inserted his cock into her cunt, and though it was so gently done she sucked in her breath and stiffened, and then relaxed; and then she felt herself slipping into deeper and deeper currents of sensation, long, ineffable rhythms. She was fulfilled on a great, shuddering eruption of her being. It was appropriate; it was the most natural thing in the world; it was perfect, she thought to herself, when she could think. She opened her eyes. Above her Billy's face was handsome and sublime. In the low light it shone with sweat and ecstasy. She closed her eyes again, tightened her buttocks and spread her toes, and squealed with pleasure.

Then her body and soul were jolted. In an instant her intense pleasure was turned into pain, concentrated and excruciating. A burst of brilliant red light flashed upon her closed eyes. She screamed in pain. Her eyes burst open. The face above her was red and swollen and dripping sweat. In that instant she saw the face of Bob Olinger, but in the next she beheld the huge transported face of Dwight Dicks. His great hands were clenched on her head, pressing her hard into his brutal thrusts. She was nearly blind with rage and desperation and hurt. And already there was in her the seed of sorrow, well below the level of articulate indignation, let alone rage, that would now be with her the rest of her life. In that moment she became almost the personification of hatred, like Olinger, more stricken and diseased with hatred than she could have believed possible. In this unspeakable happening she was forced for the first time to a hatred of the world, of herself, of life itself. She wanted to cry, to lie in her mother's arms, to hold a kitten or a lamb, to hear running water. She wanted to die. In some feeble resistance she thought of Dog, of how Dog would trample into dust the flesh and bones of this despicable, vicious man. In her delirium, because she so needed, she saw Dwight Dicks looking up into the muzzles of the gun in Billy's hands, seeing beyond them the expressionless, nearly colorless, steady, steady eyes. Her arms were scraped and bleeding; there was the taste of blood in her mouth. She was naked and mangled. She must have been deep in shock, she thought, for she could not remember how it happened that she came to this. And it was not over; it was going on, and that realization brought her again to the brink of unconsciousness. No, she must not faint, she had to hold on, to deal straightly with this emergency, horrible and violent and dehumanizing as it was. Even to this she must find the appropriate response.

Dwight Dicks was spent. He raised himself heavily upon his unsteady arms, his chest heaving.

"How was it, Dwight?" she asked, with only the slightest tremor in her voice.

"Uh huh, crackerjack," he said. "Listen, I'm sorry." His breath stank of whiskey.

"Hush, honey," Grey said. "Rest."

A desperate notion of masculinity surged in him.

"Eight inches, uncircumcised," he muttered.

"Don't I know it, honey?" she said.

There was little light in the stall, but enough for Grey to see what was there. The empty bottle glinted beyond her reach.

She tried to summon her strength; she did not know how much of it remained. She, too, was struggling to breathe. After a long moment she said, "Honey, I want to be on top."

Dwight Dicks, who was slowly becoming aware that he had committed a felony, was on his guard. But he was exhausted and drunk.

"Well," he offered. Neither of them knew what he meant.

She had got up on her knees. When he saw her upright, the drape of her black hair and the wonderful disposition of her tilted breasts upon her firm body, how her back curved and was poised upon the flare of her haunches, he said, "Oh, my, yes." She moved into the angle of his pink thighs. And she began to fondle his cock, bringing it slowly to erection, the great, purple glans like the head of a catfish in her hand. He licked his lips and closed his eyes. There was a lull.

Then she took stock of her situation. The dust of the hay and straw was terrible in the air; she was on the verge of suffocation.

Her eyes burned and teared so much that she could barely see. But she saw the things that were in her reach. She rocked upon Dwight's thick, blunt penis and devised her plan. She eased him further into fatigue. Her breasts bobbed above his face.

"Honey," she said, "would you play with my tits?"

Smiling, he brought his meaty hands up and cupped her breasts. "Squeeze them," she said. "Squeeze them a little, honey. Squeeze them together."

He took them in his hands like melons and pressed them together, a mask of sheer contentment on his great round face.

She had the baling wire already in her hands, and though it burned her fingers, she wound it around his wrists as quickly and as deftly as a calf roper winds a pigging string around the hocks of a calf. It happened in a second. Dwight Dicks started. Violently he threw his arms up and bucked against her, grunting in pain as the wire cut into his flesh. But Grey had anticipated him, and she kept her balance, and then she had the fork in her hands. Before he could recover—he lay twisted on his side—she had the tines to his throat. His eyes were wild. Except for his exaggerated breathing he lay still then, sweat welling up in all his pores.

At her command he rolled carefully on his back again, his legs splayed and his red, fleshy arms in an oval frame around his great stomach, wired together at the wrists, his puffed hands reaching almost to his crotch, the tines of the fork in place, gouging his throat to the very point of puncture. He was fixed fast.

"I'd really like to kill you, Dwight," she said. He started to speak, but she pressed the heel of her hand to the handle of the fork, with remarkably little pressure, and spots of blood appeared under his jaw. He held still, rigid with tension.

"If you move," she said as a matter of fact, "you're going to hurt yourself."

Very slowly she drew the tines of the fork from his throat. She drew them over the point of his chin and across his open mouth; he could hear the steel scraping his teeth. The long, curved tines were pointed downward. Her hands were now very steady. She inserted the left outside tine into Dwight Dicks's left nostril; the next tine then came to rest at the outer corner of his left eye, against the ball, between his eyelids. Involuntarily, with all his strength, he pressed his head back, down upon the floor of the stall. The grimace at his mouth and eyes was terrible; his chin jutted up at a grotesque angle.

"Don't move, Dwight," she said. "If you move, the fork will go up your nose and into your eye, perhaps through to your brain."

She entered again into the angle of his thighs. His legs were locked and nearly shapeless, and they were blotched with eczema and indented with numerous little white scars. Settled now in this pronounced stasis, Grey's whole body ached. She would have given anything for a breath of fresh air or a drink of cold water— anything, that is, except this reckoning, this rite of retribution. She must serve her purpose. She took the curved cutting pliers from the top of the bale. It was a handsome and efficient tool. The cutting edges measured an inch and an eighth.

In the long distance, eastward on the plain, dogs were barking. There was a whine of tires on the blacktop, far away.

Grey took between the index and middle fingers of her left hand the generous foreskin of Dwight Dicks's flaccid penis and stretched it toward her. And with the pliers she snipped the foreskin but for a quarter of an inch of its circumference.

Dwight's big body, except for its head, was beyond his control. Its muscles jerked and twitched, its nerves went haywire, its bowels moved.

"Dwight, Dwight, Dwight, Dwight, Dwight," she intoned, "you will have to complete this surgery yourself." The little loop of bunched, bleeding skin sickened her, and she felt tired to the death.

She got to her feet and stumbled to a bucket of foul-smelling syrup, known to her as "calf dope" or "smear," used to seal the wounds of castrated calves. She applied a generous amount to Dwight Dicks's bright, ragged wound. She drew the fork away. His head was relaxed now; he had long since fainted.

Then, still naked, she rode the horse Dog hard to the river and bathed herself for a long time.

There was an orange moon. There was the voice of the grandmother on the water.

20

It all comes to nothing

When Set heard Milo drive away he got up, rubbing his eyes. Because of what had happened in the night he was full of agitation, and he had slept fitfully. He didn't know what to make of things. Who the devil *was* this Grey, anyway, and what right had she to intrude upon him? And what did she mean? What had the old woman, Kope'mah, to give him? Something—medicine—that belonged to him, isn't that what she said? Even if there was a bond between the old woman and his father, why should this presumptuous girl intervene, this woman who was a stranger to everyone except the old man with whom she lived? How was it that she had set herself up as an intermediary, a medium? He had been right about one thing, the apparition in the arbor when he first arrived. The presence there was strange and evasive. It inhabited another world, he thought. But it preyed upon him.

It was early, just past six o'clock. There was no sign of activity in the house, and he supposed that Jessie was not yet up and about. He drew water from the well, washed himself, and shaved. Then he walked rapidly to the creek, following as closely as he could the way he had seen the girl go in the night. And when he reached the bank of Cradle Creek there was a makeshift bridge, a log that lay across the creek, and beyond that a shallow path that led up the opposite bank and through the tangled growth. There were hoofprints on the banks and on the path. Where the plain opened up again he could see the house, Worcester Meat's house, and beyond, where the red land inclined, the sod houses, stark and barren in the morning light. The frame house was in bad repair —the Mottledmare house seemed modern and even grand by comparison. Indeed, it was nothing more than a wooden box with two short sides and two long sides, a door at either end and a window here, another there, four in all. Neither was any sign of life there. He watched for some activity for several minutes, until he became uneasy. He had the sense that he was spying, invading someone's privacy, and was in justice being spied upon. His skin crawled a bit, just as it had the evening before, when the bitch and he had taken notice of something or someone in the dusky brake. The girl Grey had a talent for spy games, he thought, but he had not. And he went up then to the little sagging porch and knocked on the door. There was no answer. He looked through a window. There were clothes and papers and utensils strewn about inside, an unmade bed, empty bottles, particles of dust floating in a trapezoid of light on the floor. But there was no one at home. Suddenly he realized that he was disappointed. Very likely, he thought, he would not see Grey again, and he might never know what it was she meant to give him, if it wasn't all a joke of some kind. Maybe it was a joke, after all. From the telegram on, he had been moved about like a checker on a board. He had been made to appear, pulled out of a hat by a magician, a trickster, a sorceress, and at least he would always wonder, with something like admiration, who she was. *She.* Or what if he had seen a *boy* in the arbor, in the afternoon and in the night? That would be good for a laugh, wouldn't it. He could applaud that; it would cap the act; it would make a finale.

He said nothing of all this to Jessie. They had biscuits and gravy for breakfast, and weak coffee with sugar. In the late morning they left for the dance, and on the way they stopped by the cemetery to visit Kope'mah's grave. Set stood over the mound of fresh red earth and, seeing Jessie weep, put on a solemn face. But in fact he could feel nothing. In his will he had done with this place, this unlikely interlude in his busy life, and he had set himself to return to his familiar world. The old grandmother was dead and buried; his father's spirit had not touched him in the tangles and shadows on Cradle Creek. The girl Grey had made him a promise, but she had not kept it. It all came to nothing. Barring any unforeseen delays, he would be home in time for dinner. The Marina would be cool and misty, and he would walk up to Union Street and lean over a Gibson at Perry's. He would stroll, looking into the shop windows, and afterward he would go to sleep to the foghorns in the Bay. And then he would get back to work. He felt now a keen urgency to paint. His coming away from his work had been to no purpose, and he had nothing to show for it. He had stepped out of bounds. He was out of place in this severe red landscape, among the graves of strangers. Even as he and Jessie stood at the little grave—it was like the grave of a child—the heat grew almost too heavy to bear. There was a crackling in the grass, and great green grasshoppers snapped against them. Kope'mah's grave was conspicuously fresh and bright. The stones in the cemetery seemed random and organic, dark markers of human time. A bird called. The noon was palpable; it could be seen in the distance as wavering columns of burning air. Weeds had grown up long ago on the grave of Catlin Setmaunt.

21

She turns to the painting again

And Set remembered:

Lola Bourne bought one of his paintings, an acrylic on paper entitled "Night Window Man." It was a strange piece, even to Set, and it was powerful. It was a bright green frame, a window, in which was a roiling blue and gray background, a thick, ominous depth; and from this there emerged a figure, a grotesque man with red hair and red dress, approaching. Set had begun it with nothing but color in mind; it had taken form quickly and of itself, as it were. He thought well of it, but he supposed it would not sell. Jason, his agent, had advised him not to show it. "It's not the time for disturbing them," Jason said. "We'll disturb them later, when we're famous."

"It disturbs me," Lola Bourne said when she first saw it. "It is deeply disturbing, and I like it, and I want it." She said it to him. It was the opening of his first show in San Francisco, and he was a bit drunk. He had been mixing, talking, making himself visible, according to Jason's instructions. He had followed Lola Bourne with his eyes from the moment she entered the gallery. She was an attractive woman, and it interested him that she was alone. He had approached and stood beside her.

"Thanks," he said, and he handed her a glass of champagne. "Would you . . . could you tell me why?"

She regarded him for a long moment, as if deciding whether or not to take the question seriously.

"Well, you see," he continued, "I like it too. But I don't think I know why, so help me."

She turned to the painting again.

"The little man, the dwarf," she said, "is intent in the extreme. There is a profound energy and excitement in him."

"Yes," said Set, pleased. "What do you suppose he's up to, the little man?"

"I think he's about to be transformed," she answered.

He comes into the presence of the darkest power

Set parked the car at the base of a grassy knoll; then he and Jessie walked upward along a trail that led into a grove of oak and walnut trees. There were camps all around—numerous tents, several tipis. They made quite a handsome and exotic sight, the white tents with the tremulous, dappled light upon them. And there was a fine tension in the air, an ineffable quality of celebration. Set's spirits began to rise. It felt good to be here somehow. He was excited, as when he was a schoolboy a small circus had come to the Peter and Paul Home. And yet the people in the camps were notably quiet, he observed. He had arrived at a time of pause, of rest. The people he saw were old men or women and children. He supposed that the young men—the "principal dogs," as Jessie called them, for this was a meeting of a soldier society—were engaged in some secret business, off to themselves.

Jessie seemed to know everyone there, and she introduced him as they walked among the camps. "This is your cousin Everett, Everett Gontai. . . . This is your great-aunt Pauline Broken Wing. . . . This is your grandpa, Indian way, grandpa Lone Woman." He tried at first to fix the names in his mind—and indeed some, like Achilles Mad Mother, were unforgettable—but they were too many, and he gave it up. Everywhere he was offered food. "Here, come, we have some tripe and frybread," someone said. "Catfish," said someone else. "Ribs." In the camps, he could see, the first order of the day was an elaborate, incessant preparation of food. It must always have been so, he thought, when there was food to be had. To be satisfied was good; to be hungry was bad. The cooking fires were kept burning, and the aromas were rich and innumerable.

They walked along the edge of the dance ground, a great circle filled with grass. On the east side was a large tipi, decorated with paintings of battle scenes. It was truly impressive, the figures simple and strong like those in ancient rock paintings. Moreover, it was "powerful," according to Jessie, a medicine lodge. Only the leaders of the society could enter there, she said. Set wondered what it would be like to be inside, to sense the sanctity there, to stand in the glow of that translucent cone, inside the light, to breathe the holy, medicinal air. He wondered if Cate had ever been inside.

Already a good many people had gathered on the green apron of the dance ground.

"The men are putting on their costumes," Jessie said. "They take a long time, you know. They have to look good." This she said with some emphasis on the word *good,* and she laughed. "Oh, the women take their time too, you know, but this time it's the men mainly. It's their dance. It's a men's dance." She told him that this was one of two soldier societies in the tribe, the only ones remaining. Its origin was ancient. All the members were veterans of the armed forces; they were warriors.

Set wanted to know when the dance would begin, but apparently there was no telling. "Indian time" was a cliché he had heard before; now it seemed there was something to it. The dancers were not strapped to wristwatches, he hoped. Things happen as they happen, after all. He could live with a concept such as that. But even as he held the thought he glanced twice at his watch. There was not much time now before his flight, an hour and a half at the most, and the drive to the airport would take an hour of that.

The lull grew deeper on the afternoon. The setting seemed an old photograph of summer. Except for the children who were running among the trees, everyone seemed to stand still or at best to go about very slowly, methodically, as in a dream. One could scarcely tell that the air moved; only when it set a glitter on the shifting clusters of leaves overhead. The effect was hypnotic. Still, there was a latent energy just beneath the surface. At any moment something was going to happen. There was going to be, as Jessie had said, "a time." It was going to be real, good, and familiar. Set pondered: It was going to be fortunate, inspiring, appropriate, an aesthetic realization of the human spirit. There was something of the cynic in him, but he was looking forward with interest.

When they came to the Mottledmare camp an elderly man was sitting beside the tent in a plastic folding chair. He commanded attention. He wore braids, a large straw hat, a bright yellow sateen shirt, bib overalls, and black high-topped shoes, all of this apparel obviously brand new. He was very thin, and his bones were prominent in his face and hands. His face was deeply lined and his expression utterly benign. In his right hand, which rested on his lap, was a stripped stick to which was stuck a great billowing cloud of pink cotton candy. He would, Set reckoned, have been more or less out of place in any context; he was an original. Set would have liked him to sit for a painting. In the old man's dim eyes, Set perceived, there was something like arrogance.

"This is Worcester—Worcester Meat," Jessie said, and as Set negotiated to shake Worcester's left hand, she said, "and this is Grey."

Set turned. Grey had just stepped from the tent. Already her hand was extended to him, and she was smiling and looking directly into his eyes. He was taken by surprise, and somehow embarrassed. He knew that he must appear foolish; his mouth was open, but he could find no words to say. It was only that she was beautiful, and he was astonished, for he had been this close to her in the night and had no notion of how she looked. She wore a buckskin dress, richly decorated with beadwork, that reached to her ankles, and buckskin boots. Her heavy hair was fixed in thick braids and beaded braid ties. Two matched eagle feathers were placed at the back of her head; they pointed downward across her right shoulder. Her hair was coal-black and her eyes, just now, violet—the color of clematis. Her skin was darker than the buckskin and shone like sand. The mole at the corner of her mouth was like a dark bead of blood. She wore no makeup other than a thin, black outline at her eyes, and she needed none. Her mouth was generous and precise at once, the corners chiseled. When he took her hand, he was aware of its strength; her hand was nearly hard, its grasp unexpectedly firm. He noticed again how seemingly tall she was, and straight.

"Hello," she said, the last syllable pointed and drawn out, and he remembered her voice from the night.

"Hello, Grey." He held her hand too long, then let go of it abruptly. "You . . . you look . . . I like your dress," he added. It was an inane thing to say, he thought, and he wondered if he were blushing. She continued to look at him directly and smile.

"Mr. Setman, please, will you paint my face?" she asked. "It would honor me."

He was speechless for another long moment, perplexed, and then he understood that she was asking him to apply paint to her face, to paint signs or devices there.

"And me," he answered. "Yes, of course, if you will show me how to do it."

She went into the tent and returned at once with paints and daubs and a drawing on faded brown paper. The drawing was that of a woman's head, the face decorated with colored markings. Under each eye was a very dark blue spot, about a quarter of an inch in diameter, with four radials of the same length proceeding from it: up blue, left yellow, down black, and right red. Above the point of the chin there was an identical blue-black spot but no radials.

"It is good to wear paint, and I like to dance," Grey said. "Only a few of the women paint their faces now. This is how the grandmother painted hers."

Set studied the drawing and applied the paint carefully to Grey's face. His hand was not steady, but he did a reasonably good job under the circumstances. She was standing so close, looking into his eyes, and her skin was so smooth—and she was so beautiful. What he was doing seemed a very honorable and dignified and intimate thing. There was a slight cleft in her chin, and the daub left the impression of two opposing, black half moons. Jessie and Milo were looking on with interest and approval. Milo had emerged from the tent in the full regalia of the society. He wore a roach headdress, a brilliant red and blue cape, and long black stockings. Even in this impressive uniform, he was the comic caricature of a warrior. Like Worcester Meat, Milo was an original.

When Set finished, Grey nodded her thanks to him. *"Ahó."*

"You must see me just before you leave," she said. "I have something to give you. You must take it with you and keep it; it is very important. As I told you last night, it belongs to you alone." Again she looked at him directly, an unmistakable earnestness in her eyes and in her voice. And again he was uneasy. He wanted to protest that he must leave soon, within a matter of minutes, that if they parted company now he might not be able to find her again in time. But he said nothing. He had a strange feeling that she could tell what he was thinking, that in some sense she knew him at this moment better than he knew himself. He could not imagine who she was. He could see nothing of the boy or the tomboy in her now. But for an instant he tried to recollect the apparition in the arbor, the wild eyes that burned in the darkness there. And he tried to see again her lithe, immediate form, her long hair backlighted by the moon.

Then the lull ended. He watched the first dance, a preliminary, a women's dance. All the dancers wore the beautiful buckskin dresses with long fringes and intricate beadwork. They moved clockwise in slow, mincing steps, describing a perfect circle within the circle of the dance ground. The singing rose up steadily and bore the drums upon a long swell of sound. The afternoon seemed poised upon that deep, insistent music.

Grey seemed transported. Her movements were whole and graceful. She stepped to the side with her left foot, flexing her legs all but invisibly beneath the subtle sway of the buckskin, then brought her right foot after in a flow of motion that was as smooth as the slow running of a stream. She seemed to touch the earth so lightly, and yet thunder reverberated and the ground seemed to shake to her steps—hers especially, Set thought. Her hair shone and shimmered in the sunlight. The eagle feathers flared and floated on the wind. As Set watched, fascinated, it occurred to him that the Plainswoman's dress of beaded buckskin was the most becoming costume he had ever seen. He thought of this—it struck him as a revelation—and looked hard at Grey. Had he never seen her before, he would have picked her out of fifty or a hundred women. Never, in a museum or a history book or a fashion magazine or in an opera or on the streets of the great cities of the world, had he ever seen a woman more becomingly attired—or more natural in, or worthy of, her attire. She was more than beautiful. She was infinitely interesting, and she appealed more than anyone else ever had to his painter's eye.

When the dance was over he returned to the Mottledmare camp. His time was up, and he began his farewells. Grey came then and entered the tent. When she came out she was holding a small rolled blanket. It was red in color, though badly faded. It appeared to be very old. It was bound by a single strip of rawhide; this strip looped the roll near either end and formed a kind of carrying strap between. It was bent at a sharp angle. Evidently the roll had long been suspended from a peg or a hook. Grey held it out to him. He took hold of it, but she did not give it up at once. For a moment in which he thought they must have been engaged in ritual, they held the bundle between them. It smelled of smoke, and of some essence he could not identify. Ordinarily, he would have been extremely uncomfortable at such a moment, but in fact he was altogether at ease and at the same time strangely stimulated. He felt a kind of euphoria, as if he had taken a strong drink. But then, though he could not see it, he felt a trembling in his hands. He wanted to remove his hands from the bundle, but he could not. His whole being shivered under his skin, imperceptibly. There was a burning at his eyes, and he had a vision of the grandmother, little and shriveled in her coffin, strangely like a child. And he imagined the mummy of a child in the bundle and felt he had laid his hands to death, that he had come into the presence of the darkest power—until this moment he would have named it "evil"—he had ever known. And he was exhilarated beyond belief.

Does he have a vision and a song?

That night Grey entered the cemetery and lay on the grandmother's grave. She placed her ear to the cool fresh earth and listened. After a long time, when the moon had descended deep in the west, she said, "Yes, Grandmother, I hear you."

Is he the bear, Grandmother? What is it to be the bear? Does he wander in the hills, in the shadows there? Is he lost? Is he free? What is his great pain? Does he know what he is? Can he cry and dance and sing? Does he have a vision and a song? Can he suffer and delight hugely, anciently, with respect and belief? And is he then the bear, Grandmother? Yes. Yes. Yes. Yes.

When at last she lifted her head from the mound she saw the horse standing away on the edge of the cemetery. It was standing still in crystal planes, attending the dead.

This matter of having no name is perhaps the center of the story

---

And Set remembered:

That death shines, that it is crescent-shaped and coldly beautiful. Loki ran ahead, dodging in and out among the people on the wharf. He tripped and nearly fell, would have fallen, in fact, but was caught up in the huge hands of a black man. The black man sat on a bench beside the walk. He wore a white net in his hair, and he was thickly bearded. He smiled until his great lips spanned his whole face, and then he erupted in laughter, strangely high-pitched and shrill. Loki's heart pounded against the hand that nearly encircled his upper body. He regarded the black man timidly, his chin on his chest, his eyes rolled up, and his brow knitted like that of a scrivener peering over his spectacles. Cradled in the black man's right arm was a gleaming horn, a trumpet. The black man had the whitest teeth Loki had ever seen. Cate had caught up. Loki made a funny face and spun away, running on again with glee, hearing the high peal of laughter behind him and Cate's voice calling his name, not angrily, but with alarm, in a tone of paternal and preternatural patience.

He broke into a space circumscribed by onlookers. In the center lay a small shark, the gleam of its body faintly rising and falling like the far inward heaving of the sea itself. Immediately there was quiet, and there was a calm upon the shark's death. All the voices of all the people beyond this intimate circle seemed far away. Loki sank to his knees. Never had he suspected the existence of anything so gravely beautiful as this fish. Then it was dead. The death did not coincide with the cessation of movement—the movement had long since declined beyond perception in any case—but afterward. There was no sign, but Loki knew when the death occurred. It was a thing that even a small boy could know.

And then Cate was gone. Set could not clearly remember the sequence of things. There was Sister Stella Francesca, who appeared to him in his dreams. There was Bent, who adopted him. It had been difficult for him to leave the Peter and Paul Home. Curious. He had not been afraid of Bent, as he had been afraid of Sister Stella Francesca from the first. But he loved her, for he was a child, and there was no one else to love.

And Set remembered:

It is an important story, I think, Cate said, all those years ago. And it is old. The little boy who came one night into the Piegan camp; he must have been about your age. Think of it, Loki. Think of that boy and of that night. There must have been fires in the camp. There were always fires. And the fires shone upon the tipis and dimly on the trees beyond the camp. They made yellow pools on the ground, perhaps, and gave up sparks to the blackness above,

gave them up to the stars. Some of the people were outside, I
suppose. Yes, some were outside tending the fires. And one of
them saw the little boy. The boy came out of the trees, you see,
walking toward the center of the camp. And the man or woman
who first saw him raised an alarm, shouted, probably, and then
everyone came out to see what the matter was. They were suspi-
cious, you see. Some of the men must have drawn arrows to their
bows and set their aim upon the visitor. But then they saw that
it was just a little boy, and they were amazed, and ashamed, maybe.
But you know, I think they were no less afraid. Where did the
boy come from? What might he be bringing into their lives?
Everyone was looking at him, studying him. And he, he greeted
them smiling, spoke to them gladly. But he spoke to them in a
language they did not know. They were afraid of him, I think,
but he was not afraid of them. That is the strangest part of the
story. The little boy seemed to know no fear, or seemed to know,
unaccountably, where he was, to be at home there. He seemed to
delight in the company of the people. He chattered to them, in
the way that a child will babble endlessly to its parents. Some of
the people must have been charmed, maybe the women most of
all, the mothers, you know. How could they resist the little boy?
He was lost, they must have thought, and he was alone, and he
was unafraid. But others must have been wary, you know? How
could they not be? Some must have thought that he had been sent
to disarm them, so that their enemies could come and take them
by surprise. But most of them were charmed. Think of it, Loki.
It must have been like a carnival. There was the little boy, the
actor or performer, standing in the firelight, babbling and gesturing and working a spell. And the performance went on late

into the night. It was a night not to be forgotten. And then, Loki, the next morning the child was gone. Some old man was probably the first to wake up, and he went to the place where the boy had been put to bed. And the boy was not there. And the old man passed the word, and everyone was upset. Where was the little boy? What had happened to him? He had disappeared without a trace. And Loki, the whole Piegan camp was deeply troubled. The boy had somehow become a part of its general life, do you see? From that time on their story must forever contain the story of the boy. The old women began to grieve. And then—then an old wise man came forward and said, "How can we believe in the child?" And the people were somehow waiting to hear such a question. A wise man is always required on such an occasion. "How can we believe in the child?" They had *seen* the little boy, heard his voice; some of them had very likely touched his face and his hands. But the old wise man brought their belief into question, and it was a good thing; it restored them to well-being. Under the circumstances it was better not to believe in the child than to believe. And easier, too. You see, the little boy did not know the language of the Piegan people, and therefore, as far as they were concerned, he knew no language at all. They must have asked him many questions: What is your name? Where did you come from? Who are your parents? Why are you not afraid of us? Any of their own children would have responded in a certain way, would have been afraid, would have been quiet, or would have answered their questions warily. Certainly one of their own children would not have babbled and carried on in this easy, jovial way. And no one of their own children would have appeared and disappeared so suddenly, as if he knew the woods better than they, as if the night and the wilderness were his home. But what little boy knows these things? And what little boy speaks so readily among strangers? Did he have a name, did he speak a name? No matter. As far as the Piegans were concerned, the little boy had no name. And do you see, Loki, this matter of having no name is perhaps the center of the story. Words are names. The old man understood that, and he used his understanding to soothe and console his people. And everyone felt better. But, you know, he could not simply take the little boy away from them. That would have been to deceive them. They could no longer have believed their eyes and ears. So he offered them something in the child's stead, a bear in the boy's place. And they thought: Yes, so it was; it must indeed have been a bear; yes, a little bear came into our camp and babbled to us. Curious and playful it was, a cub. And, Loki, imagine, the little boy must have returned to the woods that same night. Surely he was fed well and given a warm bed. And surely the children of the Piegan camp dreamed of him and of how they would play with him in the morning. Perhaps the women thought of how they would make him handsome shirts and leggings, and of how they would give him a name, for he was an extraordinary being. And then, when it was suggested to them that he was a bear, what must have been their response? Oh, they were relieved, for they had not then to explain a strange and unlikely thing to themselves. But they must have known a sense of loss. And the boy, Loki, what became of him? What brought him to the camp of the Piegans in the first place? And what urged him away? Was it a yearning, a great loneliness, a wild compulsion? In the blackness again, did his tracks become the tracks of a bear? Did his lively, alien tongue fade into the whimper and growl of a beast? In his brain was there something like thought or memory? Did he feed upon his own boy's heart, and did he dream? Was there behind his eyes, like thought, the image of children playing?

The bear comes forth

Set reels and turns inside himself. He applies color to his brain with a knife. Smoke permeates the medicine bundle; a low heat emanates from it. Dancers touch their feet to the earth. A deranged boy glares from the shadows. An ancient woman inhabits the body of a girl. Death displaces the silver, scintillant fish. The bear comes forth. Planes.

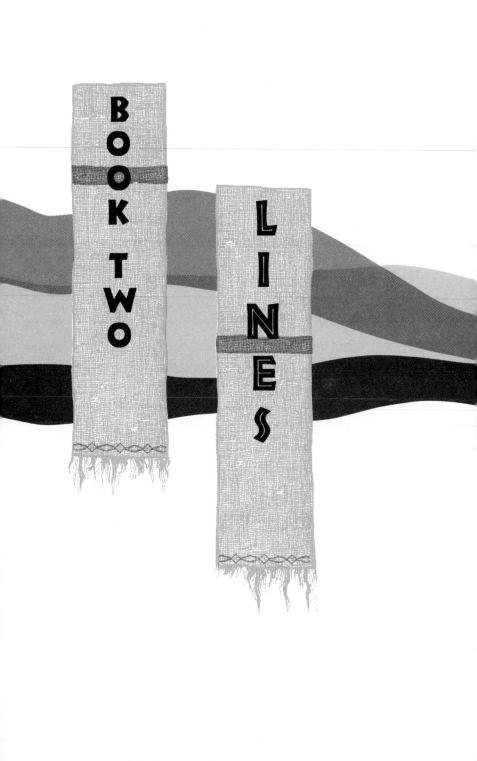

BOOK TWO

LINES

Earth darkens and is beaded
with a sweat of bushes and
the bear comes forth;
the mind, stored with
magnificence, proceeds into
the mystery of time, now
certain of its choice of
passion, but uncertain of the
passion's end.

Yvor Winters,
"Quod Tegit Omnia"

In the hold of such events there is little to be said

No one ever saw the sisters again. Only on the day they left the camp did anyone speak their names. Their names were soon forgotten, though the sisters themselves were remembered, not as individual children, with particular appearances and manners, but collectively. They had become the little sisters to whom it happened. For the first days and weeks after the children disappeared, the people of the camp gathered themselves up in the dusk and waited for the stars to come out. And when the stars came out and flickered on the black wash of the sky, the people were filled with wonder—and a kind of loneliness. Some of them made exclamations, but most remained silent and respectful, reverent even. In the hold of such events there is little to be said. Then a great storm descended on the hills, and the sky roiled for four days and four nights, and there were no stars to be seen. After that, the people did not convene in the same way, for the same purpose. They went on with their lives as if nothing had happened. Even the parents of the lost children went on with their lives, as if nothing *had happened. Of course there was at first the question of whether or not they ought to grieve. It was decided that they ought not, and no one held them up to scorn; no one blamed them in the least. Only old Koi-ehm-toya, one late morning when the snow swirled down and there was a general silence in the camp, emitted a series of sharp tremolo cries and cut off two fingers on her left hand.*

The reflection in the glass is the transparent mask of a man

Set?

He looked into the glass and spoke to himself.

Set?

The reflection in the glass is the transparent mask of a man. I am he. I am that man. It is my face. I love my face. I love it because it is mine and because I have looked at it and touched it with my hands for many years; I have studied and pondered and memorized my face. I love my face because I am an artist. And now I wonder at this ruse of light and shadow, this cold insinuation of myself. After all, there is so little to it, this pale, watered-down image. I cannot see the pores and pockmarks and stubble on my face. No matter, the image is well made. It is clean and essential as a line drawing by Hokusai, as delicate and tentative as the deer of Lascaux. And I wish to God that I had made it, for I am an artist like Hokusai and like the one whose hand described the deer.

Glass. Glass ought not confound the artist. When I was a boy, eight or nine years old, I ran through a glass door, therefore this—but it is not visible in the glass—white line in the brow of the right eye. You, there, your *left* eye.

Are you Set?

The glass seems a block of ice, hard, luminous, translucent, the image fixed deep within like a fossil. Fossil face. Set. Setman. No. It reminds me of . . . yes; I once saw a lithograph by the Dorset artist Jamasie. It was entitled, I think, *Igloo Builders Frightened by Bear.* And in it there were blocks of ice, finely striated, informed with a lucent smoke like this. The bear is lean and lithe, its body long like a weasel's. Ice bear, long and lean, Nanook, dog of God, old man with a fur cloak. *Art* it is, hey, Set? But what is that? Art—drawing, painting—is an intelligence of some kind, the hand and the eye bringing the imagination down upon the picture plane; and in this a nearly perfect understanding of the act of understanding. Ha! Someone looking into a glass at someone looking into a glass—transmitted to the fingertips, an understanding not of ice bears and fright but of these and more, a composed unity of fragments which is a whole. Just now I bring the tips of my fingers together, the thumb and the forefinger and the middle finger of my right hand—your left—and I imagine that I draw water faintly, faintly colored across a porcelain plane with a brush, a very, very fine brush. My father had such brushes. His brushes were soft and sharp, as sharp as needles. Red sable. I used to twirl the sable hair in my fingers and wonder at the soft resiliency of the minute strands, that they should form and hold such a keen point. How, with something of so little resistance as fur, could my father make a line like the trace of a very hard, very sharp pencil along a rule's edge? There is no edge to this image on the glass—but how can that be?—and there is only one eye! Strange. And in it, no spark of life. Yet it is a living eye. See, I can move it in my head; ah, but I cannot *see* that I do so, that's the thing. It isn't funny, I suppose. Then why do I laugh? Why do I lock the joints of my feet, trying to press my weight down into the floor, trying to project my whole face into view?

You, Set?

Yes, I am Set.

And there, on the other side of the glass, is a hallway. The wall opposite is of a rough, darker-than-cream-colored texture, porous as pumice or ancient bone, or so it appears. My focus cannot hold upon my reflected face; suddenly it extends to the wall beyond like a shot; then it snaps back upon the glass, the Cyclops there, the still, vacant eye.

Set, then.

Set.

Nod, damn you! The eye narrows a bit, but it remains fixed, seeming to see. I turn, feeling a resistance in the dank air. And the room darkens directly. The rain, which has been holding off all day—a day, two days, several?—comes down hard and loud, driving, glancing, with wind. When my hearing is adjusted to the sharp, uneven rattle of the rain I realize the telephone has been ringing in the next room, that the ringing has stopped, that the telephone has been ringing for a long time. I look through the crack in the door, and there is the black silence of a cave, a silence dense, almost palpable, enveloped in rain.

The image on the glass dissolves. Night comes with the rain, in the same instant. Everything in the studio is at once indistinct, save for the few canvases that stand about. It's strange; the large one, the one I have only just begun, is more obscure than the others. They stand out. They are bare and almost bright in the vague light, rectangles and squares more or less sharply defined, glowing in the texture of fine white sand or polished rice. That one, though, the large one fixed to the fork of the easel, at eye level, under the skylight—that one is remote. It bewilders me. I ought to see, at least suspect, what is there. Lord, didn't I work on it today, this morning? Was it yesterday? On the skylight an intermittent play of colors from the streetlamps and the traffic lights and the cars below, and the caroms of rain, each drop exploding into color on the white space. There, there are not whorls of color, not now; there are stains, deep and indefinite, in the flashes of yellow, white, blue, green, orange, red light. And I want to believe that there are real forms there, unique, intricate forms straightly related to a deep field of receding grounds, one after another, ranging to a black infinity, the definite forms of definite things, the very things I cannot comprehend by other means.

The telephone is ringing in the next room. No, it has rung. It has been ringing.

Lola?

Bent?

Jason, you?

Hello. Is someone there?

Well, well. Shall I think of going out? I take a tentative—see, this is tentative—step toward the cave. My legs. What? My legs are stiff and sore and nearly numb. I've been far too long here in this large, clinical room. Did I clear my throat? Was that the sound I heard? Was it I? I must be sure, absolutely sure, that I can speak. The phone will ring again, surely. I have not spoken. I have not spoken a word all day, not aloud. Is that possible? Not one word to a living soul. The rain is steady now, unrelenting. The luminous linen planes vibrate, and I take up the telephone —it is dead, stone dead—and I place it to my ear—

Well, what? A moment ago I thought of going out, yes. I don't mind getting out in the rain, the cold, fresh rain. An omelet at Joe's, or a chowder at Scott's. I know I ought to be hungry— when did I last have something to eat?—but I'm not hungry, really. I feel bad, sick; the smell of whiskey is making me sick. God, I've been sick for two days, maybe. I'm sweating through my shirt again. Thirst. I'm terribly thirsty. I need a drink.

Look, what a light show at the skylight! The storm makes brilliant and colored grounds, the successive distances, rising, rising into the night: blinking points of light, wavy lines of light, angles and arcs of light, light of every color and intensity. And . . . closer by it is dark, except the soft, spangled pools in which the rain spatters beneath the streetlamps, and deserted. Only now and then someone steps from a doorway into the roiling rain and vapors. And the Bay is black—

Hello. Set.

My ear is stopped, and there is nothing but a buzzing in my brain. Then, after long moments, the crackle of the storm, then voices so far away as to be unintelligible.

Hello. Set here.

Set here.

Set.

Trees in shadow emerge, and a creeping figure among the trees

---

We need good fathers, Bent. Be my father. I had a strange dream. Oh, Bent, I had strange dreams. In the mornings I awoke with both dread and relief. Something happened to me. Oh, it wasn't the journey to Cradle Creek—the *pilgrimage,* as you call it, to Cate Setman's grave—not that singular, impulsive gesture, anyway (but that figures in too, somehow). No, what happened was something that began a long time before that. I don't understand it. I don't know how I can tell you. There is such a darkness, Bent. The world has so much of the night in it. I didn't know.

Some of my dreams were of my boyhood.

I want to say it is all in the past, but it isn't. It goes on. It isn't that my dreams were; they *are.* When was it that Lukie died, Bent? And Señora Archuleta? I remember when you brought Lukie home; I must have been twelve or thirteen. He was so soft and wobbly, and he had the most wonderful ears! They seemed as warm and thin and translucent as Señora Archuleta's tortillas. When they were trimmed and bandaged he looked for all the world like a religious, like a nun. His eyes so bright and his fine, sharp little teeth so white, flashing. He was the most beautiful puppy I have ever seen, his coat shimmering so; it was the color of sealskin. María Consuelo Ynocencia Archuleta. Once I dared to call her María, or Connie—it was impertinent in the extreme, one grade below mortal sin—and she put on such a frown that I felt like a criminal, a lost soul, for days. I went to confession, to her priest, though I didn't know how. The night you took us to the opera she was lovely, wasn't she?—radiant. Against all the splendor of Seville, concentrated in the brilliant, ranging spots of light. I can see her face, aged and serene and full of dignity—and so excited and so intensely alive! Rapture. En*raptured*, she was. She had the words by heart, Bent, do you remember? She mouthed the words.

> *L'amour est un oiseau rebelle*
> *que nul ne peut apprivoiser,*
> *et c'est bien en vain qu'on l'appelle,*
> *s'il lui convient de refuser!*
> *Rien n'y fait, menace ou prière,*
> *l'un parle bien, l'autre se tait;*
> *et c'est l'autre que je préfère,*
> *il n'a rien dit, mais il me plaît.*

And Micaëla, how she loved Micaëla! She knew the soul of Carmen, but she *was* Micaëla.

Je dis que rien ne m'épouvante,
Je dis, hélas! que je réponds de moi;
mais j'ai beau faire la vaillante,
au fond du coeur, je meurs d'effroi!

Enraptured, that face. I think it was her face when she was a child, when she was a little girl, delicate and wide-eyed, at a Christmas party at Taos.

The thing is, Bent, I am beginning to doubt my mind. I don't mean to suggest insanity, but there are times now when I think I am becoming unhinged, neurotic, obsessive. Yes, obsession, if I understand rightly the meaning of that word. But what I'm obsessed with, I don't know. And that's the aggravating thing. I seem to have become more and more dependent upon my work, but I have a terrible time now keeping my mind on it. I can imagine myself coming to a point where I must work—I love my work, I'm compelled to work—and can't. That frightens me. Last night, trying to sort things out, I thought: I have come to a dangerous place in my life. Something threatens me—middle age, sickness, what? Sometimes I think a disease has been eating at my insides for years, all my life. I find myself struggling with something, and the struggle becomes more and more violent, and I begin to be desperate. I don't like being desperate; I am afraid of desperation. Dear God, Bent, I am ashamed to say these things. It's humiliating. I feel that I am playing a part in a high school melodrama, among properties that are inappropriate, irrelevant, reciting lines that are at best poorly imagined, and I am fighting for my life; that is the definition of my role. And the fight is real; it isn't confined to the stage; and I know that, and I'm the only one who does. Maybe, Bent, I have come to grips with my demon. Didn't you tell me once that that is the most ancient exorcism of all? And yes, you told me something else. You told me that the seventh naval rule is, Never take yourself too damned seriously. Later, about eleven o'clock: I had drunk in four bars, and I was on Scott Street. I hadn't called, but I knew you would be up still, probably poring over some treatise on mysticism that you had read a dozen times before. Mental calisthenics for you, Bent. You are now, let's see, seventy-nine, and your brain is like a muscle; you exercise it to greater and greater strength. We played a game of chess, but it was over by twelve thirty or one o'clock. I couldn't keep my mind on it, and you were disgusted.

"I can't seem to concentrate," I said. "I'm preoccupied."

I hadn't realized until that moment what a pretentious word that is, or can be.

"You're drunk." Then, "Preoccupied with what?"

"I don't know."

"Go to hell, then."

"I really don't know. Jason says I'm preoccupied. It's his word."

"Jason is a fool."

"Well, that may be, but he knows how to sell my paintings." It was a fatuous thing to say. I had become defensive, and I surprised myself. It wasn't like me to defend Jason, especially to Bent, for I despised Jason a little. I did not understand his talent, but he understood mine very well, and so I resented him. So did Bent. The truth is, though, I was quite pleased to pay Jason for what he did, because he did it well. It may even be that he was worth what I paid him. But just now he was put out, frustrated, because I wasn't painting what he wanted me to paint. Jason favored big, bright, expensive canvases; my work had of late become somber, concentrated. I had disappointed him, and he said that I was preoccupied, that I was not painting to my standard. "Standard" was another of Jason's words.

"Jason is a fool," Bent repeated.

I let it go.

But somewhere in the exchange I told Bent that my thoughts (suspicions, instincts, whatever they were) seemed all to point to a time and place in the past, maybe the remote past. It was as if I were trying to bring some crucial memory, deeply buried, to the surface of my mind. Bent listened, and he heard my concern.

Be my father.

I dreamed of woods. There was a darkness beyond successive planes of tangled growth. I was a boy, and I was alone. The air around me was electric; it shone here and there like crushed velvet. I was drawn to the dark interior. I felt myself moving inexorably toward a black point, the very center of the darkness. "Loki!" I heard my name. It was a frantic cry, and strangely the voice was mine, I believe; I could not be certain, and that was what frightened me so. I wasn't in control; I didn't know clearly who or where I was. It seemed that I was trying to find myself, that I had lost my *self!* There was a terrible urgency in me. At last the black density of that place was too much for me. I began to suffocate. And I awoke.

"Helmbrecht Brandt. He wants fifty percent," Jason said, "and he wants to split the cost of framing."

"Out of the question," I said. "Forty percent, and he can take care of the framing." I was kidding. These matters were Jason's responsibility. I knew by the sound of his voice that Brandt's terms were acceptable, but I wanted Jason to sweat a bit.

"Well," Jason said, his voice almost petulant, "we've never shown in Cologne, and Brandt is a force there. He wants to feature us at Basel in July. He's certain that he can sell everything we send him."

"Oh, it's all right then?"

"It's all right," Jason said. He smiled what Lola calls his nine-dollar smile.

Lola, what I did not tell you—probably could not and cannot tell you clearly—is this: that it isn't the same with us. Something has changed. All that time, when we were so close together, I thought I knew who I was; I don't know now. All that time. . . . When I saw you, thought of you, touched you, my mind returned to the beginning, to the night we first met and to the days and weeks following.

Jason's respect for money was transparent. It wasn't the money itself, though, that excited him; it was the making of it. He liked to find ways to attract it to him, like filings to a magnet. He had come to be very good at attracting money. Nothing challenged him so much as that. He was not, I found out, a complicated man, but he could *seem* to be complicated, and he was interesting on that account. There were a good many facets to his character, and some of them I admired. He knew more about painting than most agents do, by a wide margin. His taste was first-rate. It was not only an educated taste but a natural one as well. And he was honest. It was not in him to lie or cheat, and many of those with whom he competed were liars and cheats. I learned early on to trust his judgment where my own work was concerned. He would tell me that something I had done was good or not good, or that I had done something that was not strictly true to myself. And he was right more often than not. His self-confidence was unshakable. I didn't like him. But I believed in him.

He was slightly younger than I, and dapper. He was a Bostonian and an Ivy Leaguer, and he looked out of place in my studio, but he was very much at home in the Financial District, where we often had lunch together. Usually he appeared fit, as if he had just come from a tennis vacation or a week of rock climbing. Only rarely did I see him in shirt sleeves. Habitually he wore dark, expensive suits and exquisite silk ties.

I was working at the large table, where I liked to draw, and he was studying a piece that I had done a while ago, the portrait of a boy I had seen on a boat at Tiburon, acrylic on linen. Lola happened to be there. She was sitting at the smaller table, reading a magazine. She was very pretty in a halter, shorts, and sneakers. I knew that Jason must be very much aware of her presence, agitated by it. He was sexually excited by her, and she knew it and teased him when she pleased, always in a subtle and discreet way. Most often she simply ignored him, to his great consternation. There was a kind of tension between them.

"When will you do some big things again, large canvases, very bright colors?" Jason asked.

"Is that what they're asking for?"

"Always. And especially from you. You remember what a success the Carruth show was?"

"You know, I've fallen in love with paper," I said. This did not please him.

"Yes," he said without conviction, "paper is wonderful, isn't it?"

"I've been drawing, too—ink and graphite with washes."

He winced.

"Color," he said with emphasis, raising a forefinger in the air, as if making a pronouncement of infallible character, stating a law of the universe. I said nothing, but Lola could not help herself, and she spoke up.

"The new drawings are very exciting, aren't they?" she said, giving him no room to disagree. "They are very strong and original. In time they will be as well thought of as the canvases."

"I've been working quickly," I said. "I'm on to something, I think. I've come to a place where spontaneity is a key of some sort. There's very little drafting now, just impressions, very quickly executed line drawings. I've returned to something elemental, and good is coming of it, I think. Look." I was drawing at that moment, and I wanted him and Lola to see.

"What is it?" Jason asked.

"Well, you must look at it closely," I said.

He and Lola both examined the drawing carefully.

"Hmmmm, it's an animal, isn't it?" Jason asked.

I dipped a brush in turpentine and moved the graphite around on the paper. Trees in shadow emerged, and a creeping figure among the trees.

"Yes," Lola said.

"It's a self-portrait," I said, and Jason laughed. But Lola did not. She said "yes" again, and she turned away and stretched her long legs. Jason's attention was then upon her. Flexing her calves, she pointed the white tips of her sneakers to the Avenues. She was teasing Jason again.

There were many of the dark figures in my work now. I didn't know how to account for them. They were a kind of fascination to me. They seemed endlessly vital and mysterious. And they *were* self-portraits in a sense, for they expressed a certain reality in me. I didn't know what it was, but I knew *that* it was, and I knew that it mattered greatly to me in some way. And it was coming closer and closer to the surface of my thoughts; I was going to recognize and understand it sooner or later, and that act of understanding or recognition was going to be of the deepest importance to me.

I went through the usual motions of my life. I painted, I read, I walked. I dined at the restaurants I fancied. I called on Bent regularly—he had slowed down a good deal from the time we took long walks in the Presidio and in Golden Gate Park. I continued to keep the close company of Lola Bourne—to sojourn, to meditate, to dine, to party, and to sleep with her. I visited my galleries and did all the things that were expected of me. But it wasn't the same. A change had come over me. It was even a profound change, I began to see, and it disturbed me considerably, for, as I say, I had begun to lose control over the ordinary events of my life. Always, from the time I was adopted, I had been responsible for myself—Bent had given me that sense of responsibility, that confidence. I determined my actions. I *chose* what to do and what not to do. I did not let the unknown define my existence, intrude upon my purpose, if I could help it. But now there was an intrusion that I could not identify and could not resist. Something seemed to be taking possession of me. It was a subtle and pernicious thing; I wasn't myself. And then others began to see that something was wrong. I had not felt helpless in a long time, but I began to feel helpless now.

Lola Bourne regarded me with suspicion. She turned her large, rather wistful eyes, that expressed her secret self so easily, that always gave her away, directly on me, and I paid attention. She started to say something, cleared her throat, then simply sighed. I had to laugh, but I could see that she was at a loss, that she too was helpless and sad. I understood. I was pulling away from her, or rather I was being drawn away. And she sensed that even as much, maybe more, than I did. And this was another aspect of my confusion, my frustration and guilt. For I did not want to hurt her. In fact I hated not to be completely clear with Lola. We had been very good together—it ought not to have been better. We seemed to bring out the best in each other, and we both knew it, and everyone who saw us together knew it. We had not lost that rapport entirely; we could still excite and sustain each other.

There was a showing of my work on Sutter Street. That was four years ago, and it was there we met. It was my first show in San Francisco, and it was an important occasion for me. I was high; I had the feeling that good things were happening to me, that I was on a streak, a roll. I couldn't imagine what might be next. Well, Lola Bourne walked in, looked closely at my paintings, and bought one. It was a painting I had strong feelings about. I had been reluctant to put a price on it; I thought of adding it to my artist's collection. When she expressed interest in it I was pleased and surprised at once. I wasn't at all sure that anyone would want to buy it. It was provocative, full of strange, even disturbing energy. I thought not many people could live easily with it. Anyway, we talked about it, she and I, and she bought it. Several days later I received a note from her. She invited me to come to tea and to see what she had done with my painting. She lived in a small house on the Peninsula, rather secluded, in a cluster of trees. There was grass, and a stone walk lined with very bright flowers. It was a beautiful place. She met me at the door in a blue shirt, a white skirt, and white sandals. Her hair was loose, and she was gracious and animated: a bit nervous, I thought. At the gallery she had worn pants and a kind of cape, very stylish, but they had concealed her figure. When she led me into her living room, I took real notice of her. Her body was taut and somewhat thin, with small, high breasts and a narrow waist. She was rather angular at the chin and wrists and elbows, but her buttocks and legs were perfect, and she had elegant hands and feet. She might have been a dancer. Her face was pretty, with large, glittering eyes, a very engaging smile, and wonderfully framed by her waves of bright blond hair. Beyond all this, there was a presence about her, a spirit, some intrinsic quality that was apparent in her stance and in her movements. Even at a distance, she caught your eye.

"First, you must have a look at your painting," she said. The adjoining room was a study, richly paneled, with shelves of books, a somewhat cluttered desk, an enormous leather chair, and a fireplace. The painting hung at eye level to one side of the fireplace and close by a window in the adjoining wall, so that there was plenty of natural light upon it and its colors were alive.

"It looks better than it did in the gallery," I said.

"Yes, I think so too. You know, I couldn't be happier with it. I deliberated for two whole days on where it should be. I've spent a lot of time with it already. I find myself coming from outside or from my bedroom just to look at it and admire it, to wonder about it. It has power over me, I believe. It reminds me of a painting by Emil Nolde that I like very much. Do you know the *Sternenwandler?* It is one of the really haunting paintings of the world, isn't it? It is a kind of art that transcends itself. You look at it and you see beyond art—that is the illusion, at least. You see farther into the universe than you have ever seen; you behold the infinite."

"Describe it to me," I said. I was not sure I knew the painting by Nolde.

"Well, in it there is a little man, something like this one of yours, and we don't know who he is. He stands in a black greatcoat and a cap, or headband, among the stars. The void is a wash of grays and blues, and the stars are crude scribblings, stars a child might draw, and they are splotches of yellow. The man's face is green, and the eyes are black holes. His expression is—well . . . it might be anything or nothing; it is not to be named."

"Perhaps it is Nolde's notion of God."

"No. This man, this *Sternenwandler,* is as remote from God as he is from me."

"The *Night Window Man*"—that is what I titled my painting —"is not God either," I said.

"Oh, no. But he is remote too. Essentially unknowable. That

is how I see him. It is *my* window, and through it I see him approaching. There is an awful necessity in him. He approaches a reckoning that cannot be imagined. And it is my window, my view, my reckoning as well as his. You know, when I come into this room now, I half expect him to have changed, to have become something other than he was an hour ago, to have been transformed."

"I don't know if others see in it what you do," I said, somewhat intimidated by her enthusiasm. "It inspires you to eloquence."

"Yes, it *does* inspire me. It moves me deeply. But it's really *your* inspiration that we have here, isn't it?"

She said she had a white Burgundy, a 1966 Montrachet, something she had been saving for a special occasion, and wouldn't I prefer that to tea? We sat in the living room, one end of which was dominated by a grand piano, where there were other paintings and numerous objects of art that defined her taste. The room was bright and cheerful, and Lola Bourne made me feel welcome. But I was far from being at ease. Simply by being herself she kept me in a perpetual state of excitement.

We talked casually over the wine, and then she suggested that we take a walk. The neighborhood in which she lived was pleasant and quiet. The houses were different, one from another, but they were all attractive, set back on spacious lawns, and the streets were broad and lined with lovely old trees. It was a far cry from my studio, which was three stories above Beach and Fillmore streets, with a narrow view of the Bay. I had two apartments, almost identical in floor plan, opposing each other across a hall. In one I worked; that was my studio, and eventually I lived there as well. There was everything I needed to draw, paint, and indeed do almost anything I wanted. It was cluttered and sparely furnished, but it sufficed; it suited me. In the other apartment I furnished, rather expensively, a living room, a bedroom, a study, and a kitchen. It came to be a guest apartment. In the studio I kept a cot, a telephone, a cupboard and refrigerator stocked with survival food, all my materials, an easel and tables, cabinets, dropcloths, a Spanish wall for my models, stools and chairs. It was, as I thought of it, my garret; everything was spattered with paint and reeked of oils and gums and thinners and pastes. I could not have done without it.

Lola and I had made half a circle of the neighborhood, and we paused to watch some children who were playing with a dog, a young Irish setter. They had a ball, about the size of a soccer ball, which they kicked and tossed, rolling, on the grass. It was too big for the dog to take in his mouth, but he fell on it with all his might and knocked it about with his muzzle and his paws in a frenzy—all to the wild delight of the children. At last the dog gave up the game and went off to lie panting beside a duck pond. The children, two girls and a boy, let it be. One of the girls wore very thick glasses, which magnified her eyes out of all proportion to her small, round face. She said hello to us, rather solemnly, as we resumed our walk.

We told each other about ourselves, who we were and what we did. It seemed very natural. She had grown up on the north side of Chicago, had studied music for years with very able teachers, and had taken a degree in librarianship at Berkeley. She had been married and divorced. She had received a sizable inheritance from her maternal grandparents, but on principle she supported herself by giving piano lessons and by cataloging rare books for various dealers and collectors she had come to know. Although she didn't say so, I could tell that she had achieved a good deal of success in both occupations; she was respected and her services were in demand.

For my part, I told her that my parents had died when I was a child. I told her about the Peter and Paul Home, about my adoption, and I told her how I had come to be a painter. She seemed genuinely interested, and she drew me out. Well, I never knew my mother, really; my father, who died when I was still a young boy, was an artist, a painter; my adopted father was a philosopher—a professor who had become disenchanted with the academic world and retired before he was forty—and a man of the world. I couldn't see that there was more to tell.

"Do you like ice cream?" she asked.

"Yes, I do."

"What flavor best?"

"Uh, chocolate, I think. No, vanilla."

"Just plain vanilla?"

"No, vanilla with chocolate in it. Chips, I mean."

She laughed and took hold of my hand and squeezed it.

"When I'm nervous," she said, "I talk about ice cream. It calms me."

"Are you nervous?" I asked.

"Oh, yes."

"So am I."

The sunlight deepened on the lawns and seemed suffused among the limbs and leaves overhead. I had not held hands with anyone in a long time. It was good to hold Lola's hand; it was a particular gratification, like wonder, one that I hadn't known since adolescence, maybe. I had forgotten how good it could be.

"A while ago, when you came, I must have sounded like a schoolgirl," she said. "I wanted to impress you with my knowledge of art."

"I was impressed."

"I can talk more intelligently about music."

I started to confess that I couldn't talk about music at all, but instead I said, "Do you like ice cream?"

"What a strange question," she said. "No, I can't stand it."

"What flavor?" I asked. But she ignored my question.

"Hey, Set, I can do a headstand. Want to see?"

"Well, I—"

"Watch this," she said, and she let go of my hand and removed her sandals. She kneeled and placed her head and hands precisely on the grass. She swung one leg up and then the other. For a moment she made a scissors, her long legs feeling for the balance, and then they were together, placed exactly together, touching at the knees, calves, and ankles, her toes pointed, as in a perfect dive, her slim body arched only three or four degrees from the vertical and stock-still, her muscles stretched taut. Her white crepe de chine skirt tumbled down upon her hips, gathered there. Her panties were blue, light blue with wide diagonal stripes of a lighter blue still, vaguely iridescent. Wisps and coils of crisp pubic hair protruded, a little darker and redder than the hair of her head.

"Well, what do you think?" she asked, upside down.

I cleared my throat and nodded with feeling.

"Good," I said. "Damned good."

"Think you can do it?"

"Not a chance."

"Try."

"No. Even if I could stand on my head—I can't—the aesthetic effect would be, after this performance, a large disappointment."

Then the scissors again. She brought one foot down, then the other, in a wheel of motion, and suddenly she was upright, her body arched and her arms spread up and out in the attitude of a gymnast who has vaulted and planted herself like a javelin into the mat.

Later, by the light of Chinese lanterns hanging from the limbs of trees, over a salad of shredded chicken, she said, "We're going to be in love, aren't we?"

"Yes," I said.

"Then you must spend the night with me."

"Yes," I said again.

That was four years ago, and it was the beginning of an affair to remember, the sort of affair that everyone ought to have once, as a birthright.

We played at everything, especially words, all the time. We were full of banter and rejoinder, puns upon puns. She would say something, and I would make a play upon it, and then she would carry it on, shamelessly, and these games were to us a sheer delight. Together we knew how to take delight in the world. We were glad to be together, glad in the extreme. We might have been a vaudeville act: "Do you say so, Mr. Setman?" "Indeed I do, Miss Bourne." We wadded napkins and threw them at each other across the restaurant tables of San Francisco. We sang duets in the back seats of taxis. We necked in elevators, at the movies, on street corners. We made spectacles of ourselves. Setman and Bourne. But that was four years ago, as I keep feeling it necessary to say. Something happened to us, to me. I became steadily more solemn and morose. Lola and I began to make silences; we began to spend longer and longer times apart. We did not live together, even early on, when we were so crazy about each other. I thought that living together would interfere with my work. I realized soon that she was a social creature, and I liked her for that, but her way of life was diametrically opposed to mine. She enjoyed the company of people day in and day out, and she knew how to make them enjoy themselves, and so everyone adored her. She spent a lot of her time in a crowd of jovial people, it seemed to me, and I had a difficult time dealing with that. She was involved in civic and community affairs, this charity and that campaign; she was forever going to concerts and benefits and poetry readings. And she was always a bit disappointed when I refused to join her. I kept telling her that my work was a solitary thing, that the best that was in me was realized in isolation, in a bright room with bare walls, with no distractions. It was hard for her to understand why this should be so, but she tried. She tried hard, and she made large concessions. I began to feel a tinge of guilt. She was a good sport. One very good thing: she and Bent took a great and immediate liking to each other. I wanted them to be close, close to each other and to me. And they were.

Even after we had begun to break apart, we spent a lot of time together, Lola and I. And we spent a lot of time outdoors. I would paint in the mornings, and in the afternoons she would come to the studio and propose some excursion. We swam and cycled and played tennis, we staged elaborate picnics in Marin, and we read the Sunday *New York Times* on the deck of Sam's Anchor Café in Tiburon. We ventured into the wine country. Sometimes we intruded upon Bent's privacy, but he loved it, especially when Lola cooked from Señora Archuleta's old recipes. We collected dark little bars and restaurants here and there, places with decks and patios, gardens with fountains, nooks that smelled of the sea. And she played for me. She played magnificently. In spite of her numerous commitments, she had a real dedication to her music, and she worked hard at her practice—as hard, I think, as I worked at my painting. This was a great bond between us. The sense of work was something we shared and understood, appreciated and respected.

One day, not long ago, we agreed to meet at Perry's for lunch, and I was early. I was having a stout and talking to Seamus James, the bartender. There was no one else at the bar. Seamus was telling me that he had had a late night; there had been a lady and intricate maneuvers; there had even been a husband somewhere in the picture. He could tell a story well.

"Ah, to tell you the truth, Set, I'm dragging a bit this morning." He shook his head and dusted the bar. His face drooped like a bloodhound's. I could see that he wanted sympathy.

"More than you know," I said. "It's afternoon."

"Holy Mother, is it now? Well, you see what I mean."

"Good God, yes," I said, "you look awful!"

He put a bit of hurt in his face, a bit of the wages of sin, and sighed.

"Well, me second wind will be coming soon."

"Frankly, Seamus, you look like hell."

"Sweet mother of Jesus, get to the point, will you?" Seamus said, rolling his eyes in exasperation. "I *hate* this beating around the bush!"

Lola came in, nearly breathless, and slipped onto the stool beside me. She might have heard our banter, the end of it.

"Set"—she wheezed—"I've just talked to Jason. He's been trying to reach you. You're going to show in New York, then in Paris!"

"That's damned wonderful." It was all I could think of to say. Seamus grunted and winked.

"Yes," Lola said, laughing. "It's damned wonderful. Can I come to the openings?"

"Who's buying lunch?" I said.

"I am," said Seamus. "It's the least I can do."

"The very least," said Lola Bourne, her eyes twinkling. "By the by, Seamus, you ought to knock off early. You look like hell."

I painted furiously, for I wanted new work on view, and in four months we went to New York. Jason and Lola got along, but not famously. Jason stayed at the Algonquin, Lola and I at the St. Moritz. It was January, and New York was cold. Even so, the opening, on Madison Avenue, was well attended. It was, Jason confirmed, a successful opening. Several pieces sold that evening, all of them overpriced, I thought. And we met a good many important (Jason assured us) people, among them Alais Sancerre, who owned the Colombes Gallery in Paris, where I was to show next. She was attractive, and Jason was altogether obsequious in her presence. Lola was cool. Nothing was quite working out, it seemed to me; everyone seemed to be looking at one another, with a kind of critical intensity, rather than at my paintings, and all their remarks were asides, rude and irrelevant, as far as I was concerned. But I was having a professional success. I was amused, and I could see in her eyes that the irony was not lost upon Alais Sancerre. I suggested that we might have lunch the next day, alone.

That night, in celebration of the opening, there was a dinner party at the Russian Tea Room. I sat between Lola and Jason, who got into a fight. It was a tedious evening, and it ended on a sour note.

Later, in the hotel, Lola's mood changed completely. Earlier she had been sullen, even hostile. I was peeved. But now suddenly she was herself, beautiful and engaging and playful. She apologized. As for me, I resisted the temptation to play the party wronged and feel sorry for myself. Besides, my fortunes had improved through the evening. I was self-satisfied, smug, expansive. I called room service for the nightcap, Brandy Alexanders.

Lola had got some rouge and some kohl, and these, together with a vial of pollen and a pale blue salve that I could not identify—something she must have procured from a witch—she brought out for my inspection, and she took off her clothes.

"This morning, in a window on Fifty-second Street, there were two people, a man and a woman, and they were painting their bodies, he hers and she his. It was one of the most exciting things I have ever seen." She had become wistful, dreamy-eyed, and her body was beautiful. I thought to myself: I know this body very well; I know the texture of the skin and the shapes of the bones beneath; I know the tension of the muscles and the thickness of the fat here and there, and there, the spring in the tendons and the pressure of the blood in the veins. But in the light of what she had just said and of the colors she had placed at my hand, I saw her body in a way I had not seen it before.

"They were naked?"

"Practically."

I got out of my clothes, and we applied the paint with great care. She painted a blue mask on my face—it was like a Guerrero dance mask, the face of a Moor—and serpentine stripes, red and black, on my chest and back and on my arms. She painted my penis half red and half yellow. It was terribly exciting to touch the colors to each other. I made yellow spots on her forehead. I painted her mouth and her nipples bright red. Then I described the areolas of her breasts with deep blue circles. I painted crescent moons on her abdomen, and I encircled her navel with a black ring. I drew bright bolts of red and yellow lightning on her thighs and shins, and I placed black stars on her feet. When I had finished, she went to the mirror and beheld herself.

"Oh, I am beautiful!" she exclaimed. And it was true.

In the middle of the night I awoke and she was standing at the window. I got up and took her in my arms, for I sensed a loneliness in her. We said nothing but for a time looked out on the night. It had begun to snow. From a vast black vault, stained with city lights, millions of snowflakes were drifting silently down upon the Avenue of the Americas.

When we had gone back to bed she asked me if I had ever before painted on a woman's body.

"No," I said. Then I remembered, and I said, "But, you know, I once painted a woman's face."

"How do you mean? You made her up, you applied makeup to her face?"

"No, not that. I made emblems, three small designs. They were like shields. I think they must have had a special meaning for her."

"And did you make her beautiful too?"

"Yes."

"Did you love her?"

"No. I barely knew her," I said.

"It seems rather an intimate thing, to touch paint to the face of someone you barely know."

Curiously, it embarrassed me that she said that, as if unwittingly she were intruding upon something very private and personal. I didn't know what to say.

Lola went soon to sleep, but I lay awake for the rest of the night. Somehow the memory of that Oklahoma afternoon preyed upon me. I tried to remember Grey's face exactly, but I didn't have the image whole in my mind. Her face was lovely, and I had made it lovelier, hadn't I? And her voice, and the touch of her hand. And then what came to me, forcefully, with extraordinary clarity, was the medicine bundle. I had not opened it but had placed it on a shelf in the studio, in a kind of closet or storeroom I seldom used. I had been afraid of it. I had told no one about it. I had pretended that it did not exist. But now it seemed to pervade my mind. I had a nearly overwhelming desire to *be* with it, to be wholly in its presence, close to it, to lay my hands upon it. It seemed terribly consequential, *wrong,* even, that I should be away from it. The sensation of touching it for the first time came back to me. I had felt, when Grey and I were holding it, that it was potent and somehow dangerous. Yes, that's it, there was a dark potency, like a strong, thick smoke. Evil. There was something evil about it. How could such a thing have to do with me? What was this sudden and irresistible attraction it bore for me?

One of the paintings that I sold in New York was a watercolor, smaller than the others. It was the likeness of a man on a horse, but the image was indistinct, subliminal. One had to look at the painting closely, steadily, in order to see what was there. The image receded far into the picture plane, which was composed of swirling colors, reds and yellows and browns, each describing a spatial dimension and all a succession of distances from the viewer's eye. To me, the impression was that of the horseman passing from time into timelessness, and indeed I titled it *Venture Beyond Time.*

Alais Sancerre thought it was an interesting piece, and it was one of the things we talked about over lunch. She was happy for me that it sold, she said, but she wished that she might have shown it in Paris.

Her voice was low and her accent rather pronounced. She was fastidious in her dress and in her manner, and rather conservative. She wore a gray suit and black shoes. Her blouse was simple and white, and she wore no jewelry, except earrings, which were pearls. The only color she admitted was a necktie; it was a handsome pattern of blues and purples and greens, all richly dark. Her hands were small and expressive, very feminine, the skin so clear as to seem nearly transparent, and the nails curved down slightly over the tips of her fingers. Her hair was dark and auburn, with a few strands of gray, and she wore it drawn back and fixed in a queue. Her eyes were not hard and bright, like the eyes of a cat, but very soft and glowing. They seemed to hold me softly when she talked; they were lovely and inviting eyes. She was of medium height and neither thick nor thin. I judged her to be in her late thirties.

"Yes, it is a remarkable painting," she said. "I'm having it photographed, with the new owner's permission—and with yours, of course. Then I can at least show the photograph to some of my clients. But, you know, photographs are—how do you say?—unreliable. Let's hope that the mysterious center of the painting comes through. We French love a mystery."

I mistook her meaning.

"I suppose it is the quality of watercolor itself that makes for mystery," I said. "Transparencies, one upon another."

"No, no, no," she corrected me. "The mystery is in you. *You* are the mystery! You are the primary mystery, in any case. If you were not mysterious yourself, you could not create that which is mysterious on paper or on canvas, is it not so? Of course, centaurs are mysterious too, aren't they?"

"Centaurs?"

"Yours," she said, as if I should have known at once what she meant. "The one in your painting, venturing beyond time. I love the concept!"

"Are you so sure it's a centaur?" I asked, intrigued.

"But of course it is a centaur, or it is about to be one."

This she said with such conviction that there was no room for argument. It was a strange moment for me. It seemed that something was rising to the level of my consciousness, a recognition, a truth.

"Perhaps," I said.

"Tell me, Mr. Setman, were you thinking of Kafka, by chance?"

"Kafka? I'm afraid you've lost me."

"Well"—she laughed— "I thought you might have been thinking of Franz Kafka's little description of the centaur. What is it called? *Wunsch, Indianer zu Werden,* as I remember. It describes what must be the sensation of the Red Indian riding his horse very fast, so fast and free that the earth becomes a blur and the horse's head dissolves away. And surely this means that the Red Indian becomes one with the horse, has become himself the head of the horse, you see. Well, I put it badly, but, it is a transformation. Kafka wrote *The Metamorphosis,* you know. He was deeply interested in the subject."

What she said fascinated me. It was as if Alais Sancerre saw very clearly something in me that I had failed to see in myself. Afterward I returned to the gallery and studied for a long while *Venture Beyond Time,* trying to see more deeply into it than I had seen, trying to see what others could perhaps see more clearly than I, what deepest part of me I had imaged.

On the plane back to San Francisco, talking to Lola Bourne, I became ill. It happened quite suddenly; a great dizziness came over me, and my eyes burned. I began to tremble. And then she was talking to me with great concern—I could see the alarm in her face—but I could not make out her words. Then blackness.

The next thing I knew, I was all right; the seizure had passed, but I was wet with sweat. I was holding Lola's hand so tightly that my own seemed locked upon it. I let go with great difficulty, as if my fingers were grafted to her flesh, frozen there. Indeed I had nearly crushed her hand, and my nails left deep impressions on her skin, had nearly drawn blood. There was such pain and fear in her face.

Bent, be my father. Be my father, Bent. I love you.

It marks the passing of an age

In a small, nearly careless hand she wrote:

These figures moving in my rhyme,
Who are they? Death, and death's dog Time.

There had been a great blizzard on the Plains. It had struck Colorado, Nebraska, and Kansas particularly hard, but it had reached Oklahoma too, and it had drawn the earth up hard and fast. The trees on Cradle Creek were brittle and stark on the sky, and there was rime on the dead grass. The wind, driving the snow with deadly force, struck at everything aboveground. Cattle huddled against the cold. Some of them died. The graves of Kope'mah and Catlin Setman were bare, barren.

Then there had come, incredibly, a warmth like summer. For a time the earth was soft, run through with melt and the heat of the sun. And the grass was restored to life, and the trees seemed about to bud, and the water ran fast. Then the land was firm again, and vital. Birds appeared everywhere. It was like spring.

The Mayor of Bote, Oklahoma, sat in the arbor of the Mottledmare homestead, hunched over a book on her left and a notebook on her right. She read, and she made notes, and she composed poems and prose pieces. It was the middle of the morning. She had slept soundly, she had made a prayer to the sun, she had eaten a breakfast of hardtack and potted meat, and she had drunk large quantities of Earl Grey tea, in which she stirred a considerable amount of raw milk from a Jersey in the Dicks herd. Now she was gulping yet another mug of tea and peering intently into the printed page.

"Author! Author!" she called, clapping her hands. "Hey, all *right!* Why, you must be talking about one of the Yazzies, the Low Mountain Yazzies—one of the sisters. Hey, my Uncle Ashkii knew those ladies . . . there were three of them, could ride like hell, could outride a man, any one of them. What was the oldest one's name? Not Desbah—*Bertha.* Bertha Yazzie. My uncle said that lady could *ride.* But she could show off better than she could ride, my uncle said. She was a gambler, my uncle said. She had beautiful jewelry, my uncle said. *Nizhóní yei!"*

She read the passage again:

> Some of the men of Jemez rode out to meet the Navajos. John Cajero was one of them. He was then a man in his prime, a Tanoan man, agile and strong in his mind and body, and he was a first-rate horseman. He was mounted on a good-looking gray

quarter horse, which he handled closely and well, and he cut a fine figure upon it in his blue shirt and red headband, his manner easy and confident. He singled out old friends among the Navajos, and soon there was a cluster of riders holding up on the side of the road, convened in a high mood of fellowship and good humor—and a certain rivalry. Then John Cajero was holding the coils of a rope in his hands, shaking out a loop. Suddenly he leaned forward and his horse bolted into the road between two of the wagons, nearly trampling over a dog; the dog lunged away with a yelp and ran at full speed, but the horse was right upon it, bunched in motion, and the rope flashed down and caught the dog up around its hips and set it rolling and twisting in the sand, jerking it up then into the air and slamming it down hard, as the horse squatted, jamming its hooves in the earth, its whole weight cracking against the bit. And John Cajero played out a little of the rope from his saddle, and the dog slithered out of the noose and ran ahead, its tail between its legs, and went crouching and wary under its wagon. John Cajero laughed, and the others, too, though their laughter was brittle, I thought, and the Navajos watched evenly the performance, the enactment of a hard joke, and considered precisely what it was worth. There was a kind of trade in this, a bartering of nerve and arrogance and skill, of elemental pride. Then, getting down from his horse, John Cajero drew a dollar bill from his pocket, folded it once lengthwise, and stuck it down in the sand. He gestured to the others; it was a beckoning, an invitation, but I did not understand at first what he meant them to do. He swung himself up into the saddle and gestured again, pointing down to the money on the ground. No one moved; only they were watchful, and he urged his horse away, prancing, a little distance. Then he turned the horse around and set it running—or loping, rather, not fast, but easily, evenly—and reached down from the saddle for the dollar bill. It seemed that his fingers brushed it, but he could not take hold of it, for the stride of the horse was broken slightly at the crucial moment. It was the barest miss—and a beautiful, thrilling thing to see—and he was upright in the saddle again, his motion and the motion of the horse all of a piece. I was watching him so intently that I did not at first see the girl. She came from nowhere, a lithe, lovely Navajo girl on a black horse. She was coming up fast in John Cajero's dust, faster than he had come, and her horse was holding steady in a long, loping stride, level and low. When I saw her she was already hanging down nearly the whole length of her arm from the saddle horn, her knee cocked and her long back curved like a bow, her shoulders close against the deep chest of the horse; she swung her left arm down like a scythe, and up, holding the dollar bill with the tips of her fingers until it was

high over her head, and she was standing straight
in the stirrups, and her horse did not break stride.
And in that way she rode on, past John Cajero,
along the wagon train and into the village, having
stolen the show and the money, too, going in
beauty, trailing laughter. Later I looked for her among
the camps, but I did not find her. I imagined that
her name was Desbah Yazzie and that she looked
out for me from the shadows.

"For you, for anyone, my uncle said," Grey muttered. She looked
up, through the crystalline air, at Dog, with a glint in her eye.
He stood just off, maybe thirty yards away, on the apron of the
great pasture. He had come through the hard days of the storm
unharmed. Now he stood, lethargic, in his winter coat, in the
brilliant light, his head held nearly perpendicular to his spine,
basking in the sun. He was napping. She called, and he raised his
head abruptly, jerked it up high, his ears black and erect. She
took down her bridle, made of braided horsehair, from a nail on
one of the corner posts of the arbor and walked slowly toward him.
Sometimes he allowed her to approach him with no resistance
whatsoever; at other times he shied, pretending to a wildness, and
dashed away, mischievous and full of insolence and play. Therefore
she approached him stealthily. She had not ridden him for twelve
days. This time he stood still, even turned to her and opened his
teeth for the bit. She was understandably wary, and she explained
to him very carefully what he must do.

She led him to a long, level reach of ground that suited her
purpose. She took a matchstick, one she had been using as a

bookmark, and planted it in the ground. Then she leapt lightly upon Dog's back, rode away a few yards, and turned. She had to study the matter for a moment. The matchstick was clearly visible; its red and white tip was an inch and a half above the swelling of red earth. The distance, she reckoned, was a hundred feet.

"Now, Dog, the problem here is clear enough; it involves the elements of speed, accuracy, and cooperation," she said. "The speed must be less than breakneck, the progress must be consistent, and the aim must be true. The collaboration must be fortunate in the extreme. We have not done this before, so our first try is going to be of great importance to us, critical. I know precisely what I have to do, but do you know what *you* have to do? Dog, you must run steadily; you must not break your stride. You must not mind my movements, no matter how sudden and unfamiliar they may seem to you. You must carry me within reach of the matchstick. We are talking about inches, Dog, *fractions* of an inch, perhaps. You must run smoothly; absolutely level, your run must be. Do you understand? If we screw up, it will certainly not be my fault, if you catch my meaning. Are you ready?"

On the first pass Dog, not expecting her to lean, broke his stride and nearly spilled her. With remarkable balance and agility she kept her seating, like a trick rider. On the second pass she didn't plant her heels surely enough, and she *was* spilled. She tumbled upon her left shoulder and rolled, and she was unhurt. On the third she touched the matchstick but could not grasp it. On the fourth, fifth, sixth, and seventh everything went wrong. They were not coordinated, she and the horse, and she was spilled twice again. On the eighth, she took the match from the ground, and she was elated. She was somewhat battered and bruised, but she was triumphant. She rewarded Dog with sugar, after scolding him for the misses. And she said to him, "Bertha Yazzie needed a saddle, and her horse had bad breath, my uncle said."

She went every day to the grandmother's grave and spoke to her, though she had not need, for the grandmother's spirit was here and there; it was frequently in the room where she had died, and there Grey spent much of her time now. Jessie and Milo did not stand in her way; they knew that she was becoming a medicine woman, so they stood off and tendered their respect. Jessie, besides, was a woman very generous of spirit, and she held a great affection for Grey. She thought of Grey as a sister. Milo too, who, had he dared, would have approached Grey with dubious intentions, was afraid of her growing power; she had already become somehow inviolable. So did Worcester Meat know. Grey no longer lived in his little house, and Worcester found it almost unbearable without her. But he was an old man, and he had long ago learned how to live with his losses. In his frame of reference, it was simply appropriate that she hold on to his mother's spirit, however she must do it. He had never had any claim upon her; no one had. There was nothing to give up, but much was lost.

Grey was still a girl, and her fantasies were still dear to her. But in fact she was aware that her destiny was singular and that she must accept certain very serious responsibilities. Notwithstanding, for the time being, she persisted in seeing herself so:

"**N**ow, I tell you what," Billy said. "Here's what you done wrong.
You didn't point. You got to point. You know how, when some
body asks you where the saloon is, you point? You say, "Well,
it's over yonder,' or, "It's down thataway, past the stable,' and
you point with your finger? Well, that's how you do it, and that's
how you should have done with that horse of yours. That's how I
do it with my guns."

When he said such things, she listened with deep respect and
even reverence, as if he were intoning prayer. How could he know
such things, she wondered. How could a boy of a man, twenty-
one years old, have acquired such knowledge? *Ah, what sagacity
perished here!*

It was April Fool's Day, morning. Billy was at the Tunstall
store with some of the other Regulators. She looked down the
street, but nothing seemed out of place. Squire Wilson had begun
hoeing in his onion patch. A heavy woman in a sunbonnet came
out of one house and entered another; she carried a basket. Some
children were playing tag at the far end of the town. Grey shivered;
although the sun was high now, there remained a faint breeze of
the dawn. But for that, there was a stillness on the scene.

She sat very still on the stallion. Dog, too, was still, standing
at an angle to the street, in the street, his head high and his ears
cocked. Grey was wearing the long white dress, draped upon her
thighs and reaching to her feet, which were encased in small beaded
moccasins of softest doeskin. Her hair, her skin, the dress and
moccasins, the dark hide of the great horse, were touched with
the brilliance of the spring morning. The girl and the horse were

statuesque, elegant, noble, ineffably graceful, full of grace. She would have seemed in place before a white-columned courthouse in the square of an Alabama hamlet, or before the battlements of Patay.

At precisely nine o'clock Grey raised her right hand and brought it sharply down. Then, from the Dolan store, five men stepped out into the street and began walking slowly, cautiously, toward her. They were Sheriff William Brady, George Hindman, John Long, George W. "Dad" Peppin, and Billy Matthews. They were heavily armed. Brady, in fact, carried the rifle that he had confiscated from Billy the Kid on February 20, in connection with the murder of John Tunstall.

When the five men were opposite the Tunstall store, shots were fired, a great many of them. To Grey the sounds seemed farther away than they actually were, and what she saw seemed dreamlike. With the first volley Brady fell dead; he had been shot eight times. Hindman, struck only once, staggered a few feet and fell. Long was wounded. Squire Wilson, tending his onions, received flesh wounds in both his legs. Billy the Kid must have shot Brady at least once—with all the gunfire, it was impossible to say (Grey could not say)—and surely he tried to shoot his hated enemy Billy Matthews, who took refuge immediately in the Cisneros house.

Grey watched, holding her breath. There, in the middle distance, in the center of the little town of Lincoln, there was chaos. Already, a smoke lay out on the April air. There was utter confusion. The children of Lincoln must be delivered to their rooms, she thought. The mothers must be comforted, tranquilized. Decent men—good, hard-working, churchgoing, law-abiding men—must be encouraged, reassured that they were in control of their

destinies. But men, women, and children were terrified and sickened, lost and helpless in this hellish eruption of violence.

Then Grey saw something that caused her to gasp. From the
gate of the Tunstall yard, Billy—her Billy—raced into the street
to fetch his rifle, which lay next to the body of Sheriff Brady. From
the moment he appeared she held her breath. He ran, his pistol
wagging in his hand. It was only a few yards, but it seemed to
her an immeasurable distance. He ran slowly, slowly, and the
sound of gunfire was going on randomly, distantly, as if in another
town, another country. He bent over to pick up the rifle, and
there came a shot from the Cisneros house. For a moment of
impossible duration, Billy the Kid staggered and clutched at the
inside of his left thigh. With the rifle he then ran, as he could,
to safety. Grey did not know how badly he was wounded, and she
knew she would not soon find out. He would have to hide; perhaps
he would require medical attention. And could he ride? Clearly
he was wounded in such a place as to make riding difficult if not
impossible. With Billy the Kid's brave, reckless act, the war
seemed to end. The smoke of the gunfire rose away out of sight,
and an awful quiet descended on Lincoln town.

She walked the horse about, set it on the way north. There were
deep hoofprints in the road; it was well traveled. Birds called in
the branches. Somewhere off to one side was the voice of a trou-
badour, a young man singing a lament. The song was not familiar,
but it touched her nonetheless, and her blood rose to it. It was
about a young man whose love was lost in the Valley of the Fires.
She listened, and the strains brought tears to her eyes. When she
was out of earshot, she set Dog running. They thundered by an
Apache family on the trail, in a covered wagon. The Indians looked

after her with sullen wonder and great goodwill. She was beautiful, and she rode a beautiful horse.

Grey was still a girl, but there stirred in her now the deepest feelings of womanhood. Her fantasies sustained her; she required them absolutely. They were hers alone; they expressed *her* spirit, *her* imagination. But there lay before her now realities that would define her whole life. Her resources were plentiful. She had been born with extraordinary intelligence, health, energy, stamina, and will. Her capacities were barely exceeded by her appetites; she was intensely in love with life and could not get enough of it. Above all, she had been born to dream. It was this, more than anything else, that set her apart and enabled her to have and to create singular moments. There was in her tremendous respect for herself and for the earth and its creatures. Wonder and delight informed her whole being. To dream—that was at the center of life, hers anyway.

She had not decided to be a medicine woman. Such things are not decided, after all. She was becoming a medicine woman because it was in her to do so; it was her purpose, her reason for being; she *dreamed* it.

Already she had considerable power, but she would have more, as she learned more of the world. In her dreams the grandmother instructed her. In her dreams the earth, eagles, fishes, coyotes, tortoises, mice, and spiders instructed her. In her dreams she knew of things that had long since been lost to others. She knew of things that lay in remote distances of time and space. She knew of winter impending upon the top of the world, of sheer glacial vastnesses, of huddled ancients, walking like bears through the mists. And she knew of the ancient child, the boy who turned into a bear.

To the grave of the grandmother she would take pollens and herbs and teas, and she would anoint the earthen mound and speak over it words that were sacred. And she spoke, too, over Catlin Setman's grave. It was as a kind of intermediary that she thought of Catlin Setman. She had not known him, of course, but she had *known* him, dreamed him. His voice was of a different character from that of the grandmother's in her dreams. His place in the story was strategic; he stood in crucial relation to the grandmother and to the indefinite line of ancestors on the one hand, and to his son, Locke Setman, on the other, who was to be important in her life. Indeed, the beginning of this digression had been made; she had passed to Locke Setman the bear medicine. In that initial moment had been power and mystery and meaning; the proprieties had been observed, the giveaway had been accomplished, a marriage had been made. Locke Setman, Set, was a name she spoke often to herself now. It was the name of the man who would require her strength and wisdom and spirit, whose consummate need would be her need.

She was still a girl, and in the day she dreamed of Billy the Kid and gave herself up to the ordinary occupations of her life. She looked after Worcester Meat, she assisted Jessie in this way and that, she saw to the well-being of Dog. And she looked after herself. She read and listened to music—and she worked on the "memorial," as she called it. It occurred to her that Billy the Kid, companion, lover, confidant, and hero of her girlhood, who had drawn her into the deepest mythic currents of the Wild West, was deserving of commemoration, hers especially. She had begun therefore to write an elegy and farewell, a "memorial," which otherwise bore the title "The Strange and True Story of My Life with Billy the Kid." It was to be composed of twenty-one poems and prose pieces, one for each year of Billy's life, and it would reflect him in both his human and legendary dimensions. And in some sense it would be a memorial to her own childhood.

She wrote:

> Ride, Billy, Billy,
> Ride, Billy, ride;
> Ride about the countryside.
>
> Sing, Billy, Billy,
> Sing, Billy, sing;
> Sing a song of galloping.
>
> Whoa, Billy, Billy,
> Whoa, Billy, whoa;
> Hold your horse and let him
> blow.
>
> Sleep, Billy, Billy,
> Sleep, Billy, sleep;
> May your sleep be dark and deep.

But in the night she let herself into the presence of the grandmother. She put aside everything but the medicine way. She placed herself wholly in the deep currents of the grandmother's voice. Every night, from the time of the grandmother's death, Grey had gone into the old woman's room, to the deathbed, and had remained there for hours, sometimes the whole night. She sat in the darkness, or she lighted a candle, and listened. Sometimes she spoke, in order to question, to take hold of the meanings and mysteries, to fix the holy words firmly in her own voice. Sometimes she sang, and Jessie and Milo would hear her and be filled with wonder and fear, for it was not Grey's voice they heard, but the grandmother's. But mostly she listened. And she touched the grandmother's possessions. She would put on the grandmother's moccasins and aprons and shawls. She would touch the walking stick, the comb, the beaded pouch that had belonged to the grandmother. And she began to make masks. She made them out of paper and cloth and leather. They were the faces of animals and humans and spirits. And when she put on a certain mask, it was as if she put on the power of the spirit it represented, too. She made them only at night, in the grandmother's room, and there only did she wear them. They were crude at first, but each one was better than the one before, and in time they would be made in the proper way, with deep belief, and they would be not only objects of art but sacred objects, objects of power. And she would wear them abroad, according to her voices and signs.

In the days and nights, she bided her time. There need be no hurry. Everything would come about, as it must, in the fullness of time. Her preparation would be made in the rhythms of the natural world, as Set's must be. Even if she could, she would not oppose the motion of the days, the seasons, the sun and moon. Her time would come. She would grow older, wiser, ever more closely involved in the wide world. Her body would find the rhythms of the rivers and the winds and harvests. Her appetites would not diminish but would come perfectly under her control.

Her passion would not subside but would be defined by her power of discrimination; it would be more definitive of her. Her whole being would become more sensitive and alive.

Sometimes in the candlelight she stripped and examined her body, looking for the changes that must come about. Her body was growing softer, more womanly. Her breasts were becoming rounder, heavier. Her shoulders had begun ever so little to slope. Her skin was no longer so tight with the tension of adolescence; it was becoming steadily more supple and resilient. And she would excite her woman's skin with her fingers. She fondled her breasts and teased her nipples. She stroked the insides of her thighs. And she masturbated. Her desire was becoming deeper. It was no longer a physical thing, entirely, but there were new emotional intensities to it. This was initiation far beyond puberty. She was becoming a woman in every way.

There was almost an urgency to her finishing the chapbook on Billy. It had become a work of real dedication and a landmark in the journey of her growing up. It would, as she thought of it, mark the passing of an age. On this side of it there was all that she had been in her girlhood; on the other there was all that she would be. It was then a rite of passage, and she was pleased to perform it.

She wrote:

> Riding is an exercise of the mind. I dreamed a good deal on the back of my horse, going out into the hills alone. Desperadoes were everywhere in the brush. More than once I came upon roving bands of hostile Indians and had, on the spur of

the moment, to put down an uprising. Now and
then I found a wagon train in trouble, and always
among the settlers there was a pale, handsome boy
from Charleston or Philadelphia who needed simply
and more than anything else in the world to be
saved. I saved him.

After a time Billy the Kid was with me on most
of those adventures. He rode on my right side and
a couple of steps behind. I watched him out of the
corner of my eye, for he bore watching. We got on
well together in the main, and he was a good man
to have along in a fight. We had to be careful of
glory-seeking punks. Incredibly there were those in
the world who were foolish enough to oppose us,
merely for the sake of gaining a certain reputation.

The words, visible in tight formation, thrilled her, even in her
unlovely scrawl. She imagined them in crisp print upon bound
white leaves, the margins justified, the spacing even, snowy webs
running among the fabulous words. She played with the words in
her mouth, tasted them, rolled and fondled and savored them in
the groove of her tongue. The words rang and rippled and tripped
and rumbled at her ear. They described, quite apart from their
meanings, a flow, an endless rising and falling, a soaring, a wheeling around the sun, a trembling plane of infinite possibility, a
sunrise, a sunset, an ecstasy.

Already, in the sultry streets,
the mean quotient of suspicion

> settles at his crooked mouth, but
> just inside himself he perceives,
> in the still landscape of legend,
> the cold of his dark destiny;
> already, in the sultry streets,
> he resembles himself in death.

Who but you, Billy, would have the real name of Henry McCarty? Grey said to herself. It isn't a likely name for a reprobate like you. Your name ought to be Jack Black, or Hunter Dark, or Judas Night. And my name is Grey, Billy; Billy, Grey, Billy, Grey. And it ought to be Belle, or Blanche, or Ynocencia, or Dolores —yes, Billy, *Dolores*. Paulita, her name should have been Dolores. Your mother, Catherine; her name should have been Dolores. Was she beautiful, Billy, your mother? She was frail and sick, and she died a young woman. Did you dream of her, Billy? In the terrible times, the times when there was little hope, when you were caged like an animal in a circus, when Billy Matthews and Bob Olinger looked at you with hatred in their eyes and said things to you that no human being should say to another—unspeakable, unforgivable things—did you dream of your mother? Did you remember her voice as it was when you were little? Did you remember that she laid her hand on your head when you were hurt and crying. Was she beautiful?

> She is pale, lovely, and lithe.
> Her sons are stiff and homely,
> and they make hard witnesses.
> Joe is careless, distant, dumb;

Henry imagines marriage,
the remorse and agonies
of age. He looks upon her,
his mother, and his mind turns
upon him, the beautiful
his example of despair.

Isn't despair a mighty thing, Billy? Isn't it? You know, I used to glory in those adventures of ours. I loved it when we shot our way out of all those scrapes. God, we got ourselves into some tight spots, didn't we? But we got ourselves out, too. Well, until. . . . But you know, Billy, there is a sadness in me now, when I think about those times. There was so much hurt, so much death and dying. Death and hurt followed you like little quails. I remember you running to pick up your rifle, the one Sheriff Brady carried when he went down. And Billy Matthews shooting you—I thought you had been killed!

The wound gaped open;
it was remarkably like the wedge of an orange
when it is split, spurting.
He wanted to close the wound with a kiss,
to graft his mouth to the warm, wet tissue.
He kept about the wound, waiting
and deeply disturbed,
his fascination
like the inside of the wound itself,
deep, as deep almost as the life principle,

the irresistible force of being.
The force lay there in the rupture of the flesh,
there in the center of the wound.

Had he been God,
he should himself have inflicted the wound;
and he should have taken the wound gently,
gently in his hands, and placed it
among the most brilliant wildflowers
in the meadows of the mountains.

It was awful, the shooting, the killing. You really wanted your rifle back, didn't you? Why? Why so much? Why on earth would you risk your *life* for that deadly bit of metal and wood? You know, Billy, I've thought about that. I hear you saying, "Well, ma'am, it was *mine,* let alone it was a pretty good gun." It was a principle, wasn't it? I've wondered a lot about it. And once I thought I understood, but I'm no longer sure I do. There's more to it than the principle. It has something to do with legend, and with the way we must think of ourselves, we cowboys and Indians, we roughriders of the world. We are lovers of violence, aren't we? You must have loved it; your life was centered upon it. I must love it, for I love you. When you killed Bob Olinger, I thrilled to the killing. But now it saddens me; there is such a sorrow in my heart, Billy. I think of Pat Garrett's gun, the gun with which he shot you dead. If I could, Billy, I would take that gun out of history. I would erase it forever from human memory. And I would erase too the gun with which you killed J. W. Bell, and I would erase even Olinger's shotgun. I would do away with all the guns in the world, I guess. What is it to pass into legend? What do you inspire in me?

She wrote:

> I rode across the snowfields in the moonlight, holding myself in steady relation to the stars. The black timber on either side lay flat against the slopes, running down before me into the bottom of the night. In the dusk I had seen rabbits—and once a fox, like the point of a flame, flickering among the trees. But now for miles I had seen nothing but the night. There were wolves about; I believed in them, for the near edge of their presence cut into the nerves of my horse, and our going on was quiet and cautious. And it was cold; the cold was absolute. At length nothing mattered, not even the wolves, because of the cold. At nine o'clock, perhaps, I saw the lights at Arroyo Seco.
>
> The man sitting across the table from me was slight of build and rather unseemly in appearance. He affected the wearing of black, which in another, more imposing figure might have been dramatic, even ominous; but in this man it was an unremarkable aspect, save that it accentuated something that lay deeper than his appearance, a certain somberness, a touch of grief. It was as if the Angel of Death had long ago found out his name. His skin was nearly colorless, and his front teeth protruded to such an

extent that his thin lips seemed never to come together. His eyes were blue, just the blue of water
in milk, and devoid of expression, so that it was
impossible to say what he was thinking—or indeed
that he was thinking. Thought seemed somehow
irrelevant to his real being, apart from his true nature.
I have heard that certain organisms—sharks, for
example—are virtually mindless, that they are creatures of pure instinct. So it was with this man, I
believe. If a rational thought, or a whole emotion,
had ever grown up inside of him, he should have
suffered a great dislocation of himself in his mind
and soul. Such was my impression; he should have
been like a plate of glass that is shattered upon a
stone. But at the same time I had the sense that his
instincts were nearly infallible. Nothing would ever
take him by surprise—and no one, except perhaps
himself. Only one principle motivated him, that of
survival—his own mean and exclusive survival. For
him there was no morality in the universe but that,
neither choice nor question. And for that reason he
was among the deadliest creatures on the face of
the earth.

His hands were remarkably small and delicately
formed. I have heard it said that they were like a
woman's hands, and with respect to size and shape
that is true. But they were rough, too, and marked
by hard use. There was something like propriety in
all their attitudes—and great utility; you looked at

them and you thought at once of fine tools, precision instruments. They were steady and extraordinarily expressive. You could read this man in his hands as you could never read him in his eyes. His hands articulated him in the way that a leaf articulates the wind or the current of a stream. And yet they were nearly evasive, too, in their propriety.

There was no resonance in his voice; it was thin and hard and flat—wood clacking lightly upon wood. He was ill at ease within the element of language. I believe that silence was his natural habitat. Notwithstanding, his speech was plain and direct—and disarmingly polite.

"Thank you for coming," he said.

"I will go with you," I replied.

And this is how it began; and this is the strange and true story of my life with Billy the Kid.

The writing of the chapbook had become for Grey a kind of mystical experience. At first she thought the writing would be easy. She was supremely confident in her ability to dream, to imagine, and she supposed that expressing her dreams in words, in writing, would be entirely natural, like drawing breath. She had read widely from the time she was a child, and she knew how to recognize something that was well written. She admired certain lines and passages so much that she had taken complete possession of them and committed them to memory. She could recite "The Gettysburg Address" and "The Twenty-third Psalm." She could recite "Jabberwocky" and Emily Dickinson's "Further in summer than the birds" and Wallace Stevens's "Sunday Morning." She knew by heart the final paragraph of Joyce's "The Dead," and if challenged she could say in whole the parts of both Romeo and Juliet. And she knew many Kiowa stories and many long prayers in Navajo. These were not feats of memory in the ordinary sense; it was simply that she attended to these things so closely that they became a part of her most personal experience. She had assumed them, appropriated them to her being.

But to write! She discovered that was something else again. For the first time, words failed her. She knew what she wanted to say, but she could not say it in writing. She wrote a line, the line of a poem, as she dared to think, but it was not the line she heard in her heart. She wrote it again—and again and again—but she could not make it the perfect thing she wanted.

She brought to her writing the same positive and unquestioned attitudes that she brought to her horsemanship. It was, she said to herself, merely a matter of mastery. She mastered the art of riding. There were no mysteries, no elements of genius, no gifts of God about it. Riding was not a talent or an instinct; it was an accomplishment, plain and simple. In physical terms she knew what she could do on a horse, and she knew what the horse could do. She must control this collaboration, this equation; it was a matter of understanding and realizing the possibilities of this union. When from the back of the running Dog she had reached down and plucked the matchstick from the ground, it was not a question of whether she could do it or not; it was only a question of how and when, a question of control, coordination, mastery: how to bring her body and the body of the horse into concert, to bear together and precisely upon the realization of the desired result. It required practice; it involved trial and error; it demanded some acquired knowledge on the part of each animal of the other, some horse sense, some highly sophisticated communication. But in the end it would be realized, achieved, finished. At least that is how she thought of it. It was difficult, but it was more than possible. *You got to point.*

But this confidence did not serve where writing was concerned. There were no limits to the power of words. She could not look at a word and say, "This is what this word is and does; these are its possibilities, no more, no less." Every time she set a word down on paper she became aware of another use, other uses, another effect, another meaning—something she had never seen before. It had been thrilling and natural to bring her imagination into the presence of words as a reader. But when she tried to choose and arrange the words herself, to fix them forever in relation to each other on paper, she found it laborious, confusing, frustrating— maddening, in short. Sometimes she would sit over her notebook for hours, and nothing would come of it, and tears would fill her eyes. She would then have to turn her mind away. She would have to return to the simple joy of watching scissortails darting in the sky and magpies fluttering in the tree limbs, the blue-black sheen of their backs like oil on water. Or she would have to race her horse mindlessly toward the river or the cemetery or the horizon.

But once in a while she would write something that pleased her, that seemed very close to what she wanted, and that satisfaction was like no other that she knew. It was the satisfaction of having done what it was in her to do, of having reached the best that was in her, of having been true to her purpose, to herself.

The sequence of poems was difficult to write, and yet it came to be; the syllables appeared under her eyes, one by one.

> He finds a fossil fish
> there in the riverbed.
> He wonders about it;
> it is a long time dead.
>
> The fish descends in rock,
> as if the sheer incline
> might slant its destiny
> according to some sign.
>
> So Sagittarius
> must swim against the tide.
> He reckons upon time,
> and time is on his side.
>
> His legend is secure;
> he bodies resistance.
> The fossil is himself,
> his own indifference.

Looking for him, she questioned an old man, a prospector, at Las Cruces. Billy had been seen in the Doña Anas. She turned Dog toward the Organ Mountains, remembering what the old man had said.

> He wanders in the high desert
> like a coyote. The wind burns him.

His spirit is a brittle limb,
his instincts languor and alert.

And there was in Grey a certain streak of jealousy. She was keenly aware of the Paulita Maxwells and Celsa Gutiérrezes in Billy's life, and of more casual encounters as well.

She wrote:

They say the whores
are indolent
at the Doll House,
where he has been

a sometime guest.
He remembers
a girl whose hands
distracted him.

Her hands were long,
soft and supple;
nor were they drawn
with dread. She said,

"Will you come back?"
And he answered,
"No." Nonetheless
he remembers:

Indolence lay
cold and benign

in her white hands
and hardened there.

She suspected Billy of making love to an Indian woman, a weaver, Anacita Chacon, whose husband was said to have killed four men on her account.

In Mesilla he sees a woman weave;
he loves her, and his heart is on his sleeve.

But she is lost to him. Her husband stands
between them, holding vengeance in his hands.

And she saw more deeply than most into that side of Billy that was kind and gentle, that part of him that secured his legend beyond time. It is, she knew, the admixture of the violent and the benign that seems so central to the American experience and so powerful in the American imagination. When she dreamed of Billy, it was often to the strains of Aaron Copland's great ballet. Sometimes she saw Billy as Marlon Brando or Paul Newman or Kris Kristofferson, for each of these men had in his own way reflected some vital truth at the core of the myth. But most often she thought of Audie Murphy, slight, good-looking, soft-spoken, jovial, and deadly. How appropriate to the course of the legend that Billy (Audie) should have been the most decorated American soldier of World War II. Gracious me, she thought, how's *that* for irony? How is that for the marriage of history and myth?
She wrote:

He was a broken-down old man, a twist of rawhide. When you looked at him you had the sense that you were looking at a ruin, something of prehistoric character, like a shard of pottery or the remnant of an ancient wall. His face, especially, was an archaeology in itself. The shadows of epochs come and go in such a face.

He was a cowboy, he allowed. He had broken horses all his life, and not a few of them had broken him. And he had known men and women, good and bad—singular men and singular women. He was more than willing to talk about these and other things. We listened, Billy and I. The old man's real existence was at last invested in his stories; there he lived and not elsewhere. He was nothing so much as the story of himself, the telling of a tale to which flesh was gathered incidentally. It was no wonder Billy liked him.

We passed the time of day with him, and he created us over and over again in his stories, fashioned us into a myriad wonderful things that we should not otherwise have been. Now we were trick-shot artists in a Wild West show, and the old man, his guns blazing, shot the buttons off our vests. Again we dined on the exotic and delicious fruits in the golden palaces of the Orient. We were there at the Battle of the Wilderness, at the very point of the Bloody Angle, following the old man into legend. Christmas was coming on, and we were the

Magi, the old man said. Laughing, we half believed him. And then it was time to go.

Billy fetched a plug of tobacco from his coat pocket, cut it in two with a jackknife, and gave the old man half. We said goodbye and left the old man there at Glorieta, before his fire. The leading edge of a dream was moving like a distant, migrant bird across his eyes.

Later, on the way to Santa Fe, I said to Billy:

"Say, Billy, I have never known you to chew tobacco."

"No, and it isn't very likely that you ever will," he said. "I don't have any use for the weed." Then, seeing that I was perplexed, he went on:

"I bought the tobacco at La Junta because I knew that we were coming this way, and I hoped to see the old man, who is my true friend. He has a taste for it. And I offered him the half instead of the whole because he would prefer that I didn't give him something outright; it pleased him to think that I would share something of my own with him. As it happens, I've thrown away my share, in which the ownership consists—it lies back there in a snow-drift. But that is an unimportant matter, a trivial conceit—and this the old man understands and appreciates more even than the tobacco itself."

He started to say something more, but apparently he thought better of it and fell silent. He seemed lost in thought, but it was impossible to say. This brief sojourn into language had been for him extraordinary, and he seemed spent, and indeed almost remorseful and contrite, as if he had squandered something of which he had too little in store. His eyes were precisely equal in color to the sky at that moment, and the sky was curdled with snow.

"Indeed we are the Magi," I said, but I said it softly, that his thoughts, whatever they were, should not be disturbed.

Was it Billy who was articulate, or was it she? He was literate; she was verging upon the literary. And where better to begin than here, with the venerable ballad of the dying cowboy? Billy's death at the hands of Patrick Floyd Garrett was among the most vivid scenes in her imagination. When she thought of Pat Garrett, it was not with rage or contempt—though she could sympathize well enough with her kinswoman, Deluvina Maxwell, the old Navajo servant who loved Billy and who heaped verbal abuse upon Garrett's head after the killing—but with a kind of infinite sadness. Billy's death devastated her so that she had not the strength to hate. When Garrett pulled the trigger in the dark room, it was an act so decisive, so completely final and irrevocable, that it reduced all her feelings to simple grief. Other emotions were irrelevant and indeed unavailable. It was even possible for her to imagine that Garrett might have been a decent man in the main, that he did only what he had to do. Garrett had written *The Authentic Life of Billy, the Kid* (actually it was written by Marshall Ashmun Upson), more nearly a dime novel than a biography. She had of course read it dutifully, had even tried to take it seriously, as in fact she tried to take seriously everything that had been written about her lover. Finally the thing that fascinated her was Garrett's pose as the author, that he was supposed to have written the life of the man whose life he ended. Another irony. The book was the mean and desperate document of Garrett's own self-made immortality, his own quest after legend. Was then "The Strange and True Story of My Life with Billy the Kid" the document of hers? And like her, Pat Garrett had been in some trick of fate a merchant of words.

> Come down, Billy, to Lincoln town;
> come down, you kid of great renown.
> *All right, Patrick, I'll come with you,*
> *and then, pray tell, what will we do?*
> We'll dance a jig and dine on shoat,
> and you shall be my billy goat.

It was wonderful, she thought, that Pat Garrett and Billy the Kid had been friends. They had joked and gambled together. More likely than not they had traded horses and women and confidences. It was wonderful that there came a moment when their friendship ended—each man could probably fix the moment on a calendar or a clock—and from that moment on they were deadly enemies. And each man knew, surely, as surely as he knew anything at all, that he would kill the other if he could. Death became a bond between them stronger than friendship. For Pat Garrett and Billy the Kid, death was a covenant.

And Grey often thought of Sister Blandina Segale, who was

born in Cicagna, Italy, in the Ligurian hills above Genoa, in 1850, and who had come to America as a child and had entered the motherhouse of the Sisters of Charity in Cincinnati, Ohio, in 1866. She was missioned to the West in 1872, and she had two gratuitous and unforgettable meetings with Billy the Kid, one at Trinidad, Colorado, and the other at Santa Fe, New Mexico Territory, both recorded with care in her diary. Grey imagined Sister Blandina through her long life. It was a life that attracted Grey strongly. She thought of the little Italian girl leaving her homeland to come to the New World, of the child giving her life over to God, of the young woman venturing into the wilderness, of her encounters with outlaws and men of the frontier, of her deep determination to live strictly according to her Christian conscience and to record her life as truly as she could. Grey could appreciate all of this, and although she was not herself a Christian, she was drawn to Sister Blandina's example. To be a nun, she thought, that was to be in love; that was to be dedicated; that was to be spiritually alive. Had she not been Billy the Kid's companion and lover, had she not been the daughter of Walker (Spotted Horse Walking), had she not been a mask maker and the grandmother's chosen one, had she not been so clearly on the other side of the fence, as it were, she might easily have imagined herself Sister Blandina or Saint Theresa of Lisieux or Joan of Arc. Her imagination might have taken another turn, that is. And sometimes, when she looked into her mind to see the face of the grandmother, Kope'mah, she saw instead the face of Annie Oakley or that of Emily Dickinson.

In the lamplight she looked at her hands, closely. They were small in proportion to her body, but they were finely formed. They were not the hands of a pianist, she thought, but of a violinist, perhaps. Or of a botanist. They were made to touch the petals of flowers and the leaves of trees. Were they the hands of a nun? No. They were made also to hold great, heavy horses by leather strings, and to touch things of great, dark power. They were the hands of a medicine woman. And she looked at her feet. Her feet were hard and sculptured. The soles were tough, and the flesh at the toes and balls and heels was hard. Her toes were long and the nails were painted a bright Chinese red. These were not the feet of a nun, decidedly. She brushed an eagle feather across her toenails and thought of the talons of great birds and the claws of bears. She chanted in Navajo.

Sister Blandina, sitting on a small ax-hewn wooden chair, regarded her delicate white hands, in which she held her breviary. They were always cold now, in this high country, in winter. She turned the leaves of the book unsteadily, shivering. She thought of the thousands of rosaries she had said, would say, with these small hands.

Then she began to prepare herself for her appointment. It wasn't an appointment, really, but she liked to think of it as having some aspect of public importance. It was a personal mission, in fact, a small private pilgrimage, but it was a thing to fill her heart.

Sister Blandina washed, then examined her feet. They were little and pale. She could not remember that they had ever been other than pale, seemingly bloodless. They were like the alabaster of Volterra. She tried to see the bare feet of the little girl at Cicagna, browned by the sun of northern Italy, but she could not. The nails on her toes had turned a pale yellow, like the leaves of old books, and her toes had been cramped so long in narrow black shoes that they were impressed, one upon another, and she could not spread them apart. The nails of the great toes had become ingrown and painful. She massaged the soles of her feet. Her feet were very soft to the touch. They were like a baby's feet in their softness.

She was not yet an old woman, but signs of age had come upon her. She would become old in the most natural and graceful way, and at last she would be beautiful in her old age. Already her eyes had begun to deepen and the corners of her mouth ever so slightly to turn down. Her passion, her spiritual ardor, would grow steadily in her until it should be apparent to all who beheld her. She would be saintly. But of all this she was unaware, would always be unaware, for her humility was profound. It disturbed her at times that she loved her life, that the things of the world excited her.

Now, on this bright day in the Royal City of the Holy Faith of Saint Francis of Assisi, she was going to have an adventure. There was a general excitement in the city. Some days before, Billy the Kid had been captured at Stinking Springs, and now he had been brought to Santa Fe in chains. His presence made a kind of brightness on the air; all the people were talking about their infamous guest.

Sister Blandina drew a shawl about her and went out into the raw March day. She walked quickly through the narrow streets, looking down into the ridges of hard, dry mud, careful of her footing. Children, and old men and women dressed in black, like her, greeted her, and she returned their greetings with shy good-will. She walked briskly, to keep warm. Here and there she caught the scents of animals and wood smoke and food cooking. And she felt the bite of a little wind. It was all very good to her, and she tried again to remember the air of Italy. She must have relatives, she thought, who were even now walking in the streets of Cicagna, tasting the air, inhaling the smells of kitchens and stables too. And she thought also of the broad avenues of Cincinnati and of the deep-rutted wagon roads of Trinidad. She was a little surprised to find herself humming a song under her breath.

The door opened, and someone admitted her. The room was very dimly lighted, and for a moment she could not see. And then what she saw appalled her, and she brought one of her hands to her open mouth and gasped. Not only was Billy the Kid shackled, hands and feet, but he had been nailed to the floor. He could not stand or even sit up. She was shocked and terribly saddened to see him so. She felt what later she realized was shame. She was utterly embarrassed, humiliated. She wanted to apologize to him, but she had no voice. She wanted desperately to say something to him.

Looking directly into her eyes, he said evenly, "I wish I could place a chair for you, Sister."

> They had met at Trinidad,
> the nun and the renegade;
> they had measured each other
> and exchanged confidences.
> He was simply chivalrous,
> she thought; she prudent, he thought.
> Precisely, they got on well.
>
> And now, in her charity,
> after years, she comes to him
> at the jail in Santa Fe.

There is nothing in his eyes;
he is shackled, hand and foot.
Still, he regards her. "I wish
I could place a chair for you,
Sister." And she regards him.
Later she will weep for him.

Murphy Dicks had gone off to Stillwater to school, and Grey missed him. Now and then they exchanged letters with many x's and o's. In them they recollected their giggling, behind-the-barn sessions with cigarettes and bootleg, their ventures into sex and philosophy. "Hey, remember that time . . . ?" She teased him about wanting to become a "cow and sow surgeon," but she truly wished him well. In his most recent letter he had told her of his girlfriend, Ida Mae Teeter. She was from Kansas, he said, and she was pretty and shy, and she had a tiny birthmark on her forehead; it was remarkably like a morning glory.

One afternoon, having worked late into the night, then half the morning on a mask, she decided that she wanted to show it off. It was the head—the skull, rather—of a great turtle, made of papier mâché. It fitted her head perfectly, so that it seemed indeed to be *her* head, *her* skull, well beyond the effect of most masks. It was wonderfully large and reptilian, simple in its smooth, sun-bleached appearance, but sinister too. There was an aspect of evil in it. She had fixed to the top of the skull scissortail and red-tailed hawk feathers. It was the most impressive mask she had yet made.

She needed a lance, she allowed. From the brush arbor she took a long willow limb and worked at it with a jackknife until it suited her. She painted it with very bright colors and fixed turkey feathers to it. Then she took off all her clothes, adjusted the mask before a mirror in the arbor, went outside, and, with only a bridle and a saddle blanket, mounted her stallion, Dog. She raised the lance above her head and struck her bare heels hard into Dog's belly, and he bolted across the yard of the Mottledmare house, beating his hooves into the grass, throwing up great clods of earth. And Grey emitted terrible sounds, war whoops, at the top of her lungs, and brandished her lance. She made an appearance of great color and motion and moment, truly a sight to behold, to take the breath away.

The Reverend Milo Mottledmare, sitting at the kitchen table, looked up through the window and ejected himself from his chair, spilling a dish of chili and eggs across the front of his new four-dollar shirt.

In this incredible manner, in her terrible holy mask, the Mayor of Bote, Oklahoma, raced out of the yard and along the south side of the property into the plain, along a fence, past a melon patch in which Worcester Meat was hoeing. Worcester cringed when he saw her coming, and when she hurtled by he began to laugh, and then he began to dance. In his heavy brass-eyed and cleated work shoes, in his baggy patched pants, with elegant suspenders crossed upon his scrawny bare back, Worcester Meat danced a two-step in the melon patch, a crackling laughter rising from his nearly toothless mouth.

In the distance, in a cloud of dust, Grey reined in, and Dog squatted on his haunches, his hooves cutting furrows in the earth. She turned him sharply and set him racing back. She stretched out at full speed, and she leaned her lithe, naked body forward, her hair flowing beneath the mask, her thighs taut, her toes curled, her breasts bobbing in the wind. And she screamed and held the lance high.

Dwight Dicks, who was beside the barn, shoeing a blue mule, was struck dumb. He dropped the mule's foot and stood up, rigid, his eyes and mouth open wide. Grey reined in again, and Dog came to a skidding halt. Then she walked him up close to Dwight. She sat naked above the great, red, dumbfounded man, her coppery body glowing with sweat, her breasts heaving, the unearthly turtle mask tilted downward, looking into his stricken soul.

"Hey, Dwight."

"Hey, Miz Grey," said Dwight, faintly.

"Nice day, ain't it?" the turtle said.

"Yes'm, shore is," Dwight said, trying hard to smile, smiling feebly.

"Say, Dwight, how's your injured member?" the turtle inquired.

"Please, ma'am?"

"Your cock, Dwight."

"Oh, it's fine, Miz Grey, thank you."

The mask nodded to him, and Grey turned her horse and walked away, her round buttocks jiggling above the sheen of Dog's long black tail.

She wrote:

> One day Billy and I were riding down from the high country south of the Hondo Valley. It was getting on toward evening, and the light was failing fast. Far below we could see the pale geometry of a village, Arroyo Corvo, as I recall, and we made

straight for the cantina there. Night came on as we stood, without talking, at the bar. An hour passed, and another; then:

"Move over, friend."

A thick, bearded man stepped between us, facing Billy. Quite apart from the fact that he was obviously drunk, there was something repulsive in his manner. You could see at once that there was no steel in him—and not a glimmer of the doom that was about to fall on him. I caught my breath. Over the intruder's shoulder I saw Billy raise his eyes, slowly. He said nothing, nor did he give so much as an inch, but for a moment his eyes lay upon the man like a shroud, and he returned to his drink. The man withered away. I had never seen Billy fix a man in his gaze before. For years now I have tried to understand what it was that I saw in his eyes at that moment. There are times when it seems surely to have been something like sorrow, a faintest sadness. But at other times I realize there was nothing, nothing at all; Billy was the only man I have ever seen in whose eyes there was no expression whatsoever.

Moonlight poured in the window of the grandmother's room. Grey lay asleep on the bed, one of the grandmother's shawls across her legs. On the little table near her head, gleaming in the moonlight, was the turtle-skull mask. It seemed phosphorescent. The sockets of its eyes were black beyond depth. Grey's breathing was even, scarcely audible. What *was* audible was the grandmother's voice, low and persistent, monotonous. The room was full of words, softly spoken in the intonation of prayer. Grey's eyes fluttered. At the cemetery the grandmother's grave shone in the blue light. The grasses were silver-tipped, and the night had taken hold of the long, rolling plain. There seemed a deep silence. But the sound of the night was made of innumerable voices on the earth and in the far reaches of the universe. They were the voices of animals and birds and insects, of leaves rustling and water running, of the endless wind. And they were the voices of the dead.

Even on the verge of madness there are times of profound lucidity

On the day of Set's opening at the Colombes Gallery, Paris was dark and rainy. The Seine was shrouded in a thick mist, and the towers of Notre Dame were vague as shadows against the roiling sky. Throughout the afternoon the sky thickened, and by five o'clock it seemed as if it were night. At that hour the traffic was heavy in any weather. Now, as it began to pour, it was hazardous. Hordes of people, coming from work, jammed the streets and the stairs of the metro stations. It was taking Jason and Set more than half a hour to go from the Grand Hotel to the Colombes Gallery in a taxi. Jason was very tense, and he grated on Set's nerves. Set wished Lola were there; she was so good at parties, she would have taken a lot of the strain off him and Jason too. But she had remained in San Francisco. She would perhaps be able to join him in two or three days, depending on Bent's condition. Bent was taken suddenly ill on the preceding Sunday, and it was agreed that Lola should stay with him, at least until the doctors could be sure that he was out of danger. It appeared that he had suffered a minor stroke. Set had talked to Lola Bourne in the early morning, Paris time. Bent was alert and complaining, belligerent even, and the doctors were optimistic. But there would have to be more tests.

"Nothing like the rain to make an opening," Jason said, and he cracked his knuckles.

"Don't worry," Set said. "There will be a good turnout."

"Easy for you to say. How do you know? Would *you* go out on a night like this?"

"I *am* out on a night like this. The answer is yes. I *like* the rain, I like to hear the tires on the wet streets and see the reflections of the lights on the pavement, the rain streaming at the windows, and I like to shake my umbrella in museums and department stores and medieval places of worship. Besides, Alais says it happens all the time. The Parisians are used to it."

Jason closed his eyes and shook his head.

Turning into the avenue des Champs-Élysées the taxi driver very nearly swerved into a Mercedes. He was entirely at fault; nonetheless, for the benefit of his passengers, he went into a harangue in broken English in which he consigned all the drivers of Paris to hell.

As it happened, the rain lifted an hour later, and the gallery was crowded. Jason was in his element. All evening long he was in constant motion, gesturing expansively and chattering in French, dealing business cards all around. Set, who could not speak French, stationed himself first here, then there, and tried to appear amiable and at ease. As always, it was not as difficult as he thought it was going to be, and he relaxed with the champagne that was offered him every few minutes. The time passed quickly. Alais Sancerre presented him to a great many people, it seemed to him, whom she obviously knew very well. Most of them were respectable, well-spoken, even distinguished men and women who asked interesting and informed questions. Sometimes Alais translated their questions and remarks, but most of the time she hadn't need; they spoke English as well as she. In his life as a painter Set had learned something about gallery owners and their qualifications. Alais Sancerre was impressive. She knew her business, and she excelled in it. She had established herself solidly in the art world, and she had attracted a first-rate clientele. But she was more than a businesswoman. Unlike Jason, who was also impressive in his way, she was—what was the word Set wanted?—*inclusive* in her interests and abilities, a woman of parts, facets, splendors. The more he saw of her the more he admired her—and the more he was attracted to her. When they met for the first time, in New York, Set had enjoyed talking to her, had found her to be extremely perceptive where painting was concerned, not only perceptive but enthusiastic, passionate. But as a woman she had seemed to him somewhat reserved, somewhat confined to the necessities of her professional life. Here on her own ground she seemed otherwise. In New York she had dressed smartly, appropriately, according to her station. She had, Set decided, put on an appearance; there were others, beneath the one. Tonight she was *très chic,* vivacious, charming. Again her hair was drawn back, arranged in a bun. Her blouse was again white and closed at the throat, and she wore a dark blue velvet blazer. But her eyes had been carefully, expertly shadowed;

she wore large turquoise earrings and a necklace of matching turquoise stones on a silver chain, and a long patchwork skirt of many colors. And she wore blue suede high-heeled pumps. Set enjoyed watching her come and go, glide and mingle. In the presence of her many friends and associates she was lively, gracious, completely engaging. As was everyone, he was completely taken with her, charmed, enchanted.

At nine o'clock the lights blinked, and the opening was concluded. For another half hour there were farewells, and in that time Set drank four more glasses of champagne. Alais stood at the door and said good night to her guests, one by one, according them the formal courtesy they expected. Her patience was inexhaustible, Set thought. He on the other hand was restless. He felt good—light-headed, jovial.

It had been arranged that Jason would remain at the gallery in conference with Alais Sancerre's assistant, Françoise Hubert. Already Jason had cornered her at her desk and was leaning over her closely, speaking into her ear in an attitude of great confidentiality while they examined papers in the concentrated light of a desk lamp with a green shade. Set laughed, for never had he seen Jason as a predator. Françoise was pretty and plump, with heavily lined Egyptian eyes. Set looked for Alais, who had slipped from his sight.

She had draped a blue fishnet shawl over her shoulders. She smiled at him. The lights had gone down in the gallery.

"Where are we going?" he asked.

"Come," she said.

They went out into the Paris night, into the rain-fragrant street, and got into her red Citroen. She drove slowly through the night, through a maze of ancient alleys, and they listened to Jacques Brel on the car stereo.

> *Laisse-moi devenir*
> *L'ombre de ton ombre*
> *L'ombre de ta main*
> *L'ombre de ton chien*
> *Ne me quitte pas*
> *Ne me quitte pas*
> *Ne me quitte pas*
> *Ne me quitte pas*

"**O**h, it is so beautiful, this song—how do you say?—heartrending," Alais said.

"Yes."

"He says, 'Let me become the shadow of your shadow. Don't leave me.' You do not speak French, I think."

"*Allons donc! Il n'y a pas un mot de vrai. Vos yeux, votre bouche, tout vous dit bohémienne.*" He was giddy with champagne.

"What?" For a moment her face was frozen in surprise; then she burst into laughter.

"*Bohémienne, tu crois? J'en suis sûr! Eh oui, je suis bohémienne, mais tu n'en feras pas moins ce que je te demande, tu le feras, parce que tu m'aimes. Moi! t'aimer! allons donc!*"

"Why, it's . . . it's *Carmen,* isn't it?" she managed. She was laughing so hard that she had difficulty speaking, driving.

"Yes, yes," he admitted, signaling her to watch where she was going. "*Carmen* is the totality of my French. An old lady taught me. My French is Bizet."

"Your French is *bizarre*," she said, laughing.

At ten o'clock they arrived at La Marée. Everyone greeted her; they were received with great favor. When they were seated she asked him if she might please place the order in consultation with the chef, a personal friend, whom she summoned to their table. She ordered *soupe de truffes, loup de la Méditerranée en croûte, salade de champignons, fromages,* and *apricots flambés au Grand Marnier.* And she ordered three splendid wines, including a 1926 Roederer champagne. After coffee they were offered cigars. Set declined, but Alais Sancerre selected a Macanudo Imperial, and she smoked it with delight, telling stories over the *fine maison.*

"When we come here again," said Alais, "I shall wear a red sequined bandeau and a matching headband, and I shall—how do you say?—go barefoot. You will like me, I think. Everyone will take notice." She spoke slowly and handled the cigar with exaggeration.

"I have no doubt," Set said. "I like you already." He imagined her bare shoulders, which he had never seen. He imagined that they were creamy, like her throat, round and smooth, perfectly fitted to his hands.

In the red Citroen they drove to her house at Rambouillet. Very late, at an open window in her bedroom, which overlooked the garden, she came to him dressed only in panties and sat on his lap, her arms around his neck. The soft light of a Lalique *monnaie du pape* lamp shone upon them, and he wondered who might be observing them in this set piece, this rich composition that was worthy of Gauguin. Her shoulders were indeed smooth and round and lovely. Her breasts were full and firm, the nipples blushed and extended. She had let down her hair. It was long and thick, luxurious, very soft to the touch. Her hands were very firm on his arms, his shoulders, his head.

He kissed her hair, her eyes, her mouth, her breasts. His hands traced the rounds of her body. Her body was firmer than it appeared, warm and responsive to his touch, perfectly congenial. He could not have imagined the luxuriance of her hair, let down. It shimmered and sprang; it tumbled on her shoulders and her back, on his hands and chest; it was alive in his fingers. She unbuttoned his shirt and placed her hand on his chest, her fingers spread wide.

"Ah, I have made your nipples hard," she said.

"And I yours," he answered.

Laughing, she fitted her mouth to his and they kissed for a long time, their mouths and tongues engaged and moving around, over, under, in and out. Their mouths were wet and delicious to each other. At last, when they parted, she shivered and sighed.

"What do they say in America that we are doing?" she asked suddenly, tossing her hair back and looking at him with curiosity.

"What are we doing?"

"But yes," she said, "exactly, this very thing that we do now, that we are doing just now, here on this chair, in the window of my boudoir. How is it called in America?"

He thought for a long moment.

"Cuddling," he said. "We are cuddling."

She burst out in delighted laughter.

When they kissed again he stood up, lifting her in his arms, and carried her to the bed. He laid her down on her back and removed her panties. She watched him, though her eyes were half closed. He removed his clothes.

"Why, you are . . . you are *pretty*," she said.

He lay down beside her and caressed her, fondled her. He stroked her belly and her thighs. Then, after what seemed a very long time, he brought his hand between her legs and placed a finger in her cunt and drew it back and up the wet folds to her clitoris. She moaned and, very lightly, somehow bashfully, she took hold of his cock and fondled it. It was hot and hard to her touch.

"What do they say in French we are doing?" he asked.

"*On se prépare à l'amour, monsieur.* Foreplay. We are engaged in foreplay."

He set himself above her, looking into her face. She had closed her eyes. Her face was beautiful and beatific. He imagined her in a sequined headband, but he could not bring himself to imagine the bandeau. Her breasts were wonderfully white and pink-tipped and expanded on her body. They settled under their own weight, curving over her arms and underarms. He brought his knee into her crotch and sucked each nipple for a long moment, biting very gently, blowing, pulling.

In her playfulness, which was on the very edge of ecstasy, she resisted him, and he was surprised by her strength. She was very tight when he entered her, and then she let go, and her whole body became supple and rhythmical, as yielding as water. They rocked, as in water, for a long time.

And in the morning, late, while he was standing at a mirror, shaving, Alais came up behind him and kneaded the cords of muscle below his nape.

"I like you because you are hairy," she said, "like a dog, a big dog. You have hair on your head and on your shoulders and on your chest and back, on your arms and legs, even on your hands and feet. It is quite remarkable, really."

He laughed. In the mirror he saw that it was true. Although he shaved closely, his beard was a dark shadow on his skin.

When he returned to the Grand Hotel, the girl at the reception desk handed him a message with his key. "I believe there is some urgency," she said.

He telephoned Lola at once, and her answering service told him to call the hospital. It was just past seven in the morning in San Francisco.

"I've been trying to reach you for . . . *seventeen hours!*" Lola said, her voice shrill and breaking. "It's Bent. He had another stroke, massive. He's *dying,* Set!"

For a moment he was dumb. Then he said, "I'll come as soon as I can, the next plane."

"Didn't Jason *tell* you?" she asked.

"I haven't seen Jason," he said.

There was a pause.

"Where were you?"

"It doesn't matter," he answered, and hung up.

When he arrived in San Francisco, Bent Sandridge was dead. Lola was at the airport, and he knew by looking at her what she had to tell him. She wanted desperately to console him, and she wanted to be consoled by him. But he had nothing to give, and he wanted nothing given just now. He knew it was a betrayal of some kind, but he had to be alone.

That night Lola Bourne went to her piano and played. She played Chopin's Piano Sonata No. 2, over and over. She played well, better each time, it seemed, until she was overtaken with fatigue.

And still she played on, until the piece was destroyed at her hands, and her hands were like stone.

Late in the night Set walked from the studio to the house on Scott Street. He stood in front of it for a long time, an hour or more, until a police car approached and stopped. A policeman got out of the car and trained a flashlight on Set's face.

"What are you doing here?" the policeman said.

"Nothing," Set said. "Just taking a walk."

"This time of day? We got a call. Seems you been standing here quite a while."

"I used to live here," Set said.

"Oh, yeah? Let's see some ID."

Set still had his passport in his jacket pocket. He handed it over. The policeman examined it carefully, moving the flashlight back and forth from Set's face to the photograph in the passport several times.

"Are you all right?" the policeman asked, handing back the passport.

"My father died," Set said.

"What?"

"My father died again."

"Oh, shit," the policeman said. "Get out of here, will you? Go home. If I see you again tonight, I'm taking you in."

In the studio he sat on the floor in the dark, staring at the various papers and canvases. They were barely luminous in the glow of the streetlamps below the windows, and like living things they throbbed faintly with light when an occasional car passed in the street. It seemed wrong to him that the surfaces of these rectangles should be bare. This conviction grew up in him until it was the only thing on his mind.

Tormented, he slept almost not at all. At first light he got to his feet—he was cold, and his legs were painfully cramped—and prepared his palette. He placed a large canvas on the easel and began to paint. He painted quickly. He filled the white expanse with color, whorls, streaks, gradations of color. And as soon as he had filled one canvas, he took up another. He painted all day and late into the night, until he was spent, almost helpless at the easel. He thought that he would drop, and he wanted to. On the floor at his feet were paintings, shining up like great facets, still shining wet. They did not express his understanding of the world. Indeed they expressed nothing, only his acknowledgment of the unknown. They were not the productions he had been taught by his instructors to make as a serious artist, but they stood for his grief. And more closely than anything he had ever done before, they stood for the condition of his mind and soul. They were crude and tentative, but they were his; they were somehow related to his spirit. He looked with fascination at the nearest of the dark abstractions, set in bright, whirling depths, mysterious and profound as ancient rock paintings, beasts and anthropomorphic forms proceeding from the far reaches of time.

And, perhaps by virtue of the medicine bundle, there was insinuated upon his consciousness and subconsciousness the power of the bear. It was *his* bear power, but he did not yet have real knowledge of it, only a vague, instinctive awareness, a sense he could neither own nor dispel. He was afflicted. He was losing his physical strength steadily, he believed, or he was losing control over the strength within him, physical and more than physical. He wanted to hide himself away, for he felt that his sickness must be apparent. He would have gone willingly enough to doctors of medicine. But this affliction was not pneumonia or malaria or tuberculosis. This was a sickness of the mind and soul. He could not tell anyone what was wrong, for he did not know. At times he seemed all right. He wanted to work, to be with others, to walk beside the Bay. But he was more and more powerless to do these things. He suffered deep depressions, and these he anticipated with an overwhelming dread. He no longer answered the telephone. He had told Jason to leave him alone; he was not working and there was nothing to do about it.

Bent's death had come as a terrible blow to him, and Jason and Lola attributed to that Set's strange, almost hostile behavior. But in fact it was only part of a larger disorder; he knew it and they did not, and there was no way he could make them or himself understand. Better not even to try. In the nights he sat up till all hours in the darkness and clutched the medicine bundle to his head, and he wept.

To Lola and Jason, who were both angry and concerned, it seemed that Set was suffering what, for want of a better term, they called a nervous breakdown.

Set thought he must be going mad; there were moments when he was absolutely convinced of it; there were such strange and disturbing visions in his head, such impulses to violence, such pain. No one else questioned his sanity as far as he knew, had yet enough reason to do so. But that did not console him; it frightened him.

What he saw, not once but recurrently, was a dark, impending shape on a dark field of the sky. It seemed very slowly to revolve and approach. At a certain distance it was seen to be a beast, massive and indefinite. It was disintegrated, distorted, changing. The head was twisted in a severe, unnatural attitude, as if the neck were broken. It described a terrible mutation and suffering, a pain so great as to have become desperation and rage, and profound helplessness. There were faint blue facets upon the grotesque head and limbs, elongated like the quick strokes of a brush. But these only intensified the darkness of the thing and gave to it the illusion of light within, of a deep, steady, central life. The sky beyond was murky and splotched with light, not points of clear bright light, but random forms like beads of amber in which were ancient and delicate debris. And closer, the eyes of the beast glinted and were pierced with dull opalescence, and the great misshapen mouth gaped and flamed. Set had the terrifying conviction that when the beast drew near to him, within reach, it would crack open with pain and all its shining, ulcerous insides, its raveled strings and organs, its slime and blood and bile would fall and splash upon him, and he would dissolve in the hot contamination of the beast and become in some extreme and unholy amalgamation one with the beast. The infinite milky sky, glittering with amber stars, consoled him barely.

In his desperation he became steadily more self-destructive. There was no longer a design to his existence. His life was coming apart, disintegrating. He drank heavily, and he did not eat or sleep for long periods—until he was staggered with hunger or fatigue, and then he ate ravenously and slept for days on end. He began to shake, and a terrible cold came upon his extremities. His whole being suffered a numbness, a kind of paralysis.

But at the same time there were periods of great calm and creativity. Even on the verge of madness there were times of profound lucidity. The dissolution of his life seemed an illusion, and he was filled with purpose and confidence. He knew what others, in their ordinary perceptions, did not know. He painted with great energy and clarity and assurance. Never had his paintings been so true to his vision and his capacities. The coordination of his hand and eye was as precise as it was possible to be, he felt. His sense of proportion was extraordinary. He understood color, and his placement of colors, and his blending of colors, were nearly perfect. He understood the factors of composition; he knew exactly how to achieve the balance between appearance and reality. And his subjects were worthy, primary, serious. His paintings reflected, as art must strive to do, a great and true story of the world, he believed. But this clarity, this lucidity, this principal work, was his alone, and he did not want to trade in it. He wanted to keep it to himself, as it were, for it was as personal to him as thought. Yes, he believed, there is only one story, after all, and it is about the pursuit of man by God, and it is about a man who ventures out to the edge of the world, and it is about his holy quest, and it is about his faithful or unfaithful wife, and it is about the hunting of a great beast. In his paintings others might have seen confusion and chaos, but Set saw the pure elements of the story, and he must be true to the story at all costs. To fail in this would be to lose himself forever. He must be true to the story. *He must be true to the story.*

The unknown is the largest part of the universe

She must be true to the story. There is one story, Grey thought, and we tell it endlessly because we must; it is the definition of our being.

She wrote:

> He saw the black trees leaning
> in different ways, their limbs
> tangled in the mottled clouds,
> the clouds rolling on themselves;
> a wide belt of four colors,
> yellow, orange, red, and black;
> and stars in the tangled limbs.

The morning of December 23, 1880, was clear and cold, and she sat huddled in the saddle, peering through the trees. She wore a greatcoat over the long white dress, and a black scarf over her head, under a black beaver hat. Her hands were gloved in fringed and beaded gauntlets, and her feet were encased in black boots of English calf. The rock house at Stinking Springs was clearly visible in the sunlit distance. Three horses were tied outside. Closer were Pat Garrett and his men; they had taken cover and were studying the front door, their guns at the ready. Farther away, some Texas cowboys, temporarily enlisted by Garrett, were covering the back entrance. Billy the Kid and four other men were inside the house. Moreover, Billy's horse must have been inside, for it was not one of the three outside. Perhaps there were two horses inside, three. This was a clever thing, she said to herself. If it came to that, Billy could make a break on his fast bay mare; he could at least have a fighting chance.

Suddenly the front door burst open, and Charlie Bowdre ran out. Garrett raised his rifle and shot Bowdre dead. Then, methodically, he shot the three horses dead. One of them fell across the front door, effectively cutting off any possibility of escape on the back of the horse from inside. It was finished. She watched with deep, fearful interest as two or three members of the posse crept close to the house. They were waving to each other to be still, and she knew they must be talking to Billy, must be engaged in a deadly serious parley with him. There was no hope; his situation was absolutely desperate. They would starve him out if they had to. They could station an army around the rock house. She could not hear the exchange, but she could imagine it.

"Billy?"

"Hello, Pat."

"Billy, come on out and have some coffee with us. We got plenty." Garrett, who was from Alabama, spoke in a drawl.

"I sure would like some coffee, Pat, and some breakfast, too. We ain't et in a while."

"These winter mornings a man has got to have some coffee and bacon, Billy."

"The whiskey's run out, too."

"Just happen to have some," Garrett said. "Come on out, and we'll have a couple of swigs for old times' sake, Billy."

"Well, Pat, ol' Charlie come out," Billy answered, "and just look at him lying there, dead as a nail. Looks like you took his appetite plumb away, Pat."

"Well, you know you gotta come out, Kid, sooner or later. And if you come out shootin', we're gonna drop you right alongside Charlie, there. And that's a fact."

"Looks like you're holding all the cards, Pat. We'll come out empty-handed, if you swear to God you won't shoot us."

"You got my word on it, Billy."

"That's good enough for me," Billy said.

And Billy and his boys gave themselves up. Garrett sent to the Wilcox Ranch for food. It was like a Christmas feast to the prisoners.

Grey took some jerky and dried Velarde fruit from her saddlebag, and a bottle of Durango wine. And at a discreet distance she followed the train into Fort Sumner.

> I wanted just to speak,
> to mutter or cry out;

I wanted just to see
my vagrant enemy—

vagrant as the pale streak
of evening, come about
on the plane of winter,
the long crystal splinter

of despair. Now the
   bleak
dimension of my doubt
comprehends me. I
   wake
and sorrow for my sake.

At Fort Sumner, Billy was allowed by Pat Garrett to say goodbye
to the Maxwell women. María de la Luz Beaubien Maxwell held
his shackled hands and touched a blessing to his forehead. Deluvina, the old Navajo woman, kept her eyes averted and wept, and
she embraced her little boy, her Billito. Grey watched as Paulita
Maxwell kissed Billy; Grey's eyes flashed, taking on the glint of
jealousy. But in her reverie she could see ahead, and she could
afford to be generous. She knew how these women, especially
Paulita, would suffer grief, as she would, as she had so many times
when she dreamed of this place, the Maxwell house, the long
porch, the dark room, the summer scent of orchards. She marveled
at the symmetry of time and place. This very day Billy would be
taken to Las Vegas, then to Santa Fe, then to Mesilla, and then
to Lincoln. And from Lincoln he would escape and he would make
his way back to this house. There would be a curious and somehow

macabre reunion of these very men and women—Señora Maxwell, Deluvina, Paulita, Billy the Kid, and Pat Garrett. And at that reunion Billy would die in the dark room, and there would be a caesura, a perceptible pause in the story, a time of quiet and loss and mourning. She marveled.

The richness of the Plains was a good thing to Grey. The landscape was unending, and there were times, in the early morning or in the sunset, when she felt free of the earth, so great was the space in which she stood. It was as if she had taken place in the sky, among the sun and moon and stars. And when she rode out on Dog, she sometimes lost the sense of distance altogether. There was no such thing as distance; there was space without definition, here peculiarly accessible to the eye. She could see to the horizon, however far away it was, and she knew that she could not reach it, that if she rode to the farthest end of her vision, the skyline would still be that far away. In this landscape the skyline would always recede before her. That was the great mystery and strength of the Plains. What it must have been for her Kiowa ancestors, this land, this great ocean of grain, when they owned a thousand horses and there were a million buffalo on the range! For a people who had been for many thousands of years nomadic hunters, to be on horseback in this landscape must have been the realization of their most ancient and daring dreams. She was glad for them, and for herself in them. She looked with scorn on the fences and roads and townships. They were mean and ugly and unworthy of the wild Plains. But it did not matter. The moment had come and gone, but it had *been*. The great glory had been achieved; that is what mattered. For a moment in the history of the world, the Great Plains of North America shone as the center of highest human experience. Never was there a greater realization of honor, nobility, courage, and moral conduct as there was here, just *here*. That is truly something, Grey thought, almost enough. And she was satisfied, inasmuch as enough and too much come so often simultaneously.

Grey had a hard, uncompromising notion of the Kiowa side of her heritage. The Kiowas were an exclusive people, lordly, tyrannical, domineering. They took advantage of their opportunities; that is how they survived, how they had survived from the time they entered the world through a hollow log. One had to meet them on their own terms or not at all. They could negate you with their stoicism. Not very long ago the Kiowas, and their allies the Comanches, were warriors, horse thieves, and slave traders. They had been invincible for a hundred years, and they had conceived a large idea of themselves. It was Grey's idea, too. There was an arrogance in her, an arrogance of which her Navajo family did not approve. Her father, Walker, had been a proud, hot-tempered man. She imagined that, had he grown old, he would have been a fierce, mad old man like Set-angya, Sitting Bear. Worcester Meat and Milo Mottledmare decidedly did not have the look of warriors, but in their way they were proud men too. And their pride was worth something, Grey knew, even in this long wake of their heyday. Intrinsically they were better men than, say, Dwight Dicks. For in their blood was the blood of great men—Tsentainte, Maman-ti, Set-tainte, Set-angya. Set: bear men, men of *that* power.

The old man Set-angya sat on the ground, his head bent, his legs crossed. Within his reach was the bundle of bones, the bones of his son.

. . .

"**H**ey, Billy, did I ever tell you about Sitting Bear? That was his name, Set-angya. Well, whoa, let me tell you, Billy, he was a Kiowa original. There's a photograph of him in the National Archives, something like yours—quaint, yellow, indistinct. It's a portrait. He looks straight at you, and you just know damned well that you're going to blink before he does. One of his eyes glares; the other is nearly closed, a black slit in his scary face. His hair is long and gray, stringy. And he has a mustache, long, trailing, Mongolian. He wears a robe—buffalo, probably—and a bandolier. He is sixty years old. And on his hollow chest is a medal, embossed with the head of President Buchanan. He was a dreamer, a holy man, a shaman. And he was crazy. He burned with some wonderful madness, like you, Billy.

"He was the chief of the Kaitsenko Society, the Crazy Dog or dog soldier organization of the Kiowa tribe. It was composed of ten men only, the ten most brave. Billy, listen, those guys were camped on the other side of reality. I mean they were *boss* braves. Bravery was their business, you know, their vocation, their profession; they were mean hombres. They were the first and last security of the people. If they should die, everyone should die. Do you see? Each one of them wore a long sash, so long it trailed the ground, and carried a sacred arrow. And in time of battle, each of these Kaitsenko warriors must, by means of his sacred arrow, fix his sash to the ground, and he must stand his ground to the death. Crazy, huh? Neat.

"Well, Set-angya's son was killed on a raid in Texas, and Set-angya went there and gathered up the bones of his son, and from then on he led a hunting horse that bore the bones of his son on its back. And at night he placed the bones in a ceremonial tipi and invited all the people, saying, 'Come, come. My son is at home tonight. Come and visit him. Come and pay your respects.'

"And, Billy, you know what? That crazy old man set up his own death. I mean he directed the scene, for God's sake! Think of it. He was imprisoned at Fort Sill, see? Along with two other chiefs, White Bear and Big Tree, he was placed in the bed of a wagon, to be taken to the railroad, then sent to Fort Richardson to be tried for the raid on the Warren wagon train. Well, as they were going along in the wagon, see, on the grounds of the fort, Set-angya began to sing the song of the Kaitsenko.

"At this, the others became really upset, you know?—because that song was sacred. It could only be sung in the face of death. And when he had sung the song, he said to Set-tainte and Big Tree, 'You see that cottonwood on the side of the road ahead? By the time we reach that tree, I will be dead.' Whoa. And then he pulled a knife, which he had somehow hidden about him, and he attacked the teamster, stabbed him in the leg. Well, the guards, riding close beside the wagon, shot him dead. But he was true to his word.

"Shoot, if you were a Kiowa in those days, Billy, I'll bet you would have been a member of the Crazy Dogs."

"Not me," Billy said at once.

"You could have been, though, huh, Billy?"

"No, ma'am, no."

She was a bit put off.

"Well, why not? You were brave. You were crazy brave at Lincoln and at Stinking Springs and at Fort Sumner."

"I can't sing," Billy said. "Besides, that old man you're talkin'
about, shoot, he was brave in the middle, do you know what I
mean? He was brave on principle, according to an ideal. Excuse
me, ma'am, I don't like to talk this way; it ain't my style, but
you see what I'm sayin'. The truth is, that old man was honest-
to-God brave, and bravery was deep in his mind and in the
minds of his people. Well, not their *minds,* really, but their
hearts. That old man wasn't afraid to die. I don't think I ever
knew a man in my whole life who wasn't afraid to die. You know,
I like to think of that old man goin' after the bones of his son.
Shoot, I wouldn't have done it. You know what? I was scared
to death. I didn't kill men on principle. I killed them because
they damn well meant to kill me. And bravery just wasn't a part
of it. When I ran out to get my rifle and Billy Matthews shot
me, I wasn't brave, I was stupid. Your old man, Sitting Bear,
wouldn't have gone to Texas to fetch a rifle, but he would have
gone, and did go, to claim the bones of his son. Those are two
very different things, aren't they? The one is the act of a boy
who doesn't yet understand that he can die, and the other is the
act of a man who knows all about death but isn't afraid of it. It's
a matter of honor, death. It's your white page, do you see? Or
your shame. Either you're worthy of it or you ain't. To accept it,
to face it with honor and respect and goodwill, to *earn* it, that is
to be brave.

"When Billy Matthews shot me, I had a glimpse of death, sure
enough, *my* death, and I was *afraid.* In the nick of time, Grey, I
knew what it was to be afraid, desperately afraid. You see, I
understood in that nick of time that death was there, right
there—it touched me—and for the first time in my life I couldn't

get around it; it was close, so *close*. And at Sumner, in the last moment of my life, I understood something—the final futility of everything we do. I couldn't help myself. Maybe that is what death is to us, the sudden, absolute awareness that we can't help ourselves. No one and nothing can help us. It is a moment of perfect helplessness. It is irresistible.

"There was the explosion, and the bullet struck me, slammed into me with a force I cannot describe. And there was another explosion which seemed to me even more terrible than the first, though the shot was wild; it did violence only to my brain. And I was falling, and I was dying, and I was dead. It was a strange thing, and it happened in the nick of time, just as I asked who was there, '*¿Quién es?*' There was no bravery in it. That afternoon I had seen a coyote kill a cat."

> But then and there the sun bore down
> and was a focal length away.
> The brain was withered and burned brown,
> then gone to ashes, cold and gray.

He had taken her too far in the fantasy. He had taken her beyond that point at which she wanted the dream to end, at which Billy is poised on this side of the dark door. There is a moon, and the scent of fruit is heavy on the air. He sees the two men on the porch, and he turns and enters into oblivion. "*¿Quién es?*" And the next moment is forever to come.

■ ■ ■

There where I watch you walk
in quiet and in dark
to where your time has come
and you grow old
in ignorance and vain;

there where I hear the shot,
in quiet and in dark,
I think of what you think
and of the cold
that fixes you in thought;

there where you are not, yet,
in quiet and in dark,
I imagine you there
and you appear
and are indefinite.

Too far.

But Grey was a Navajo, too, and she yearned for the home of her
childhood. More and more often now, memories of *dineé bekeyah*,
the Navajo country, returned upon her. She thought of the red
rocks that ran for miles east of Gallup, of the great forested Chuska
range, with its hundred-mile vistas, and of the sheep camps there,
high up in the cold, thin, blue air; she thought of Canyon de
Chelly and of Canyon del Muerto, of the great red and white and
purple walls and of the rock paintings; she thought of the great
monoliths in Monument Valley and of El Capitan and Owl Rock

and of the Three Sisters; and she thought of her mother's hogan at Lukachukai and of the colored earth descending into the long valley to the north, extending to a high-running ridge of sheer pastel walls, succeeding to the sky, forever changing. And her heart ached for it.

She went on with her preparation. She must be patient. The grandmother instructed her and sang to her, and every day Grey became more confident of her learning, of her power, of who she was and of what her purpose was.

Grey, haunted by her reveries, longed to put them aside. But the act of renunciation—how frightening it was to make, even to think of making. She thought of Set and wondered what it was to be a painter. She wished she could transfer her dreams to canvas, to stand apart from them for a moment, to see them as if they were placed on gallery walls, open to public view. Surely that would be the achievement of perspective, objectivity.

In the foreground there is a central human figure in silhouette. It is she. There is a striated shade behind the figure, thin horizontal bands of shade on a white field, an expanse of snow. And beyond that numerous animals: horses, sheep, dogs, deer, mountain lions, porcupines, weasels, buffalo, bear. And each animal is of a different color; there are more colors than she knew existed.

The sky appears as the Atlantic or Pacific or Indian or Arctic Ocean, and it is filled with fish and fowl. The fish are all white, and the birds are all black. The figure in the foreground seems to stand at the very center of the world.

She thought of Set and wondered what it was to be the bear. She thought of him more and more often now, even as the grandmother more and more often spoke his name. The time was coming when she must will him to her.

He was older than she. He had attained a good deal of success in the world; he had traveled widely; he had seen things that very likely she would never see. He had known many women, probably. And he was an artist, which is to say that he had a kind of rare intelligence that very few people have or understand. He could see more clearly, more deeply into creation than others. He intimidated her, because she was still finding her way. But he was losing his, and this she knew better than he. The bear was taking hold of him. Loosing its power upon him, and he did not know what it was. In spite of his considerable knowledge and experience, his fame and fortune, it was she who would bring him to his destiny. She would be his mentor. She would instruct him. She would reveal him to himself. This is what she believed. But she did not believe more than this. She did not know if she could give him medicine strong enough to overcome the power of the bear in him. The unknown was the largest part of the universe.

She did not know where he was. But she knew that he was in pain. He had suffered a great loss. He was dividing himself from the people around him. Like her, he was making an act of renunciation. She felt the weight of her trust. Responsibility gratified her; she had never known herself so consequential.

In the night, in the arbor, she constructed an altar. It was the first altar she had ever made, and it was simple and crude, but it was time for her to do such a thing. From the grandmother's possessions she had collected in a chamois pouch her paraphernalia. This too was simple and crude, but it would do. It consisted of feathers and crystals, pollens and herbs, a buffalo horn, a firestick, and an eagle-bone whistle. Milo had managed to secure for her four peyote buttons. With the peyote she made a tea. Before the altar she laid out the paraphernalia; upon it she placed live coals. There was a small drum, a drumstick, and a gourd rattle.

Jessie and Milo assisted her. She was not yet sure exactly what to do; therefore she did what seemed appropriate. Milo was afraid, but Grey was not. She was very deliberate, and she thought of the grandmother. On the altar the coals shone red and orange, and on them she sprinkled sage and tobacco. She sang songs that she had heard the grandmother sing. She fanned the coals with eagle feathers. Milo recited prayers in Kiowa and English, Kiowa-English. Jessie tended the coals. All three drank the tea and smoked cigarettes made of bark and corn husks. Grey took the drawing of the grandmother and the daubs Set had used to paint her face and held them to the light of the firestick and fanned smoke upon them. These were the only things she had that she and Set had touched together, and so they bore relation to the bear medicine. She laid them on the west side of the altar. At intervals through the night she blew the eagle-bone whistle into a vessel of water. The sound was a strange trill that rose across the silences of the Plains night.

The tea was bitter. In the time just before dawn she saw the head of a beautiful woman, as in a painting. The woman had long, heavy hair like Grey's, and Grey thought it must be the grandmother when she was young. Grey approached the beautiful woman with gladness. Then from the hair and eyes and mouth of the woman, golden eagles emerged and took flight. They beat upward, and they soared and stooped and darted across her vision. They

were majestic and free and beautiful, and she thrilled to watch
them. The air in which they moved was silver and cold and full
of sparkling light.

"Set?"

"Yes, I am Set."

A wind grew up in the arbor at first light.

In San Francisco there were squalls. A storm was gathering off
the Mendocino coast.

Grey knew of course that Billy the Kid was in the vicinity of Fort
Sumner. He was living among the sheep camps, in hiding, at least
by day. At night he stole into the town to gamble, to attend the
bailes, to visit Paulita Maxwell. He told himself and others that
he would make enough money gambling to go to Mexico, where
he would be safe. But in his heart he knew that he would not
leave Fort Sumner willingly. He had many friends, a sweetheart,
a way of life there. He was a young man, barely more than a boy,
and he had never meant to place his life on the line. How had it
happened, he wondered, that he had become famous for being
outside the law? Circumstances, surely. Fate. He was not a mean
man. He was not a "hardened criminal," as they say. He had not
wanted to hurt anyone, much less take anyone's life. He liked to
laugh and to play cards and to be with pretty girls. If only he had
been allowed to go his own way—to laugh and play cards and be
with pretty girls—he would have owned a little ranch and a stage
station at Los Portales, maybe, and he would have been a respectable man of the country; he would have been married, very likely,
and he would have grown old in the way respectable men do, with

children and grandchildren and memories and his rightful share of contentment.

But he was a fugitive from the law, and there was a price on his head. Well, he could make the best of that too. It was, after all, exciting to be so much in the news, so much on the public mind. He had made a considerable reputation for himself. And in that sense he had amounted to something. No one would remember his brother Joe, or his father or stepfather, or even Governor Wallace, or, for that matter, the dying President Garfield, so well as they would remember Billy the Kid, El Chivato. And to a young man whose whole life added up to just more than a score of years, that was a heady satisfaction indeed. There was a vanity in him. He liked it that, when he entered a room, men and women took particular notice of him.

On July 14, 1881, Billy bided his time at the camp of his friend Francisco Lobato. He was bored, restless, and he could not wait for the cover of darkness. It was a long summer day, and the sunset seemed to last forever. The red sun held on the skyline and touched fire to the sky over the Jornada del Muerto and the Manzano and Sangre de Cristo Mountains. It was a brilliant, fiery evening. When night had at last fallen, when the stars were very sharp in the heavens, the two men rode into town. They talked and made jokes, their horses moving easily together through the brushy washes. At a slightly higher elevation, to the northeast, followed a handsome young woman in a white dress. The stars shone upon her copper skin and her blue-black hair, upon the billowing, milky dress, and upon the satiny coat of her big stallion. The cut beads on her dainty moccasins sparkled in the low blue light. There were blood-red ribbons in her hair.

The two men were hungry, and they stopped at the house of Jesus Silva, who would offer them food. Billy the Kid wanted beef, but Jesus had none. He told Billy, however, that Pete Maxwell had butchered a calf that morning, and a side of beef was hanging on the porch of the Maxwell house. Billy would be more than welcome to take some of it for his supper. But first, Billy wanted to get out of his boots and relax. He took his leave of Labato and Silva, and he went to Paulita Maxwell. From early morning there had been a crawling of the skin under his left eye. It was an irritation; he took it to be a sign of weariness.

Just before midnight Billy emerged in the moonlight night, only half dressed, barefoot and naked to the waist, a butcher knife in his hand. The smell of sex was on his hands and face. He was more relaxed than he liked to be, than a hunted man ought to be. He walked briskly to the porch of the Maxwell house.

The girl in the white dress was beyond alarm. Her mouth had hardened, and her eyes bore an expression of cold resignation, or a sadness so old as to be impotent. Her face was sallow in the thinning light. It was itself like a death mask. It was not she; nor was the slight figure of the boy the man she had loved and celebrated and nurtured in the haven of her imagination. The blade of the knife glinted weakly. The boy's upper body, naked, was white as bone, and the boy's eyes were set deep in hard, round shadows. Again, she perceived, he resembled himself in death.

And the next day she was there—after the fact and the commotion and the awful descent of grief upon the Maxwell house— as if she had not moved, and with the same air of resignation she watched as the boy's body was laid in a box and lowered into the fresh summer earth.

Only then did she turn away.

Here are weeds about his mouth;
his teeth are ashes.

For him there is no question
of elsewhere. His place

is just this.reality,
this deep element.

Now that he is dead he bears
upon the vision

merely, without resistance.
Death displaces him

no more than life displaced him;
he was always here.

7

He dances

Dr. Charles Teague Terriman said to Lola Bourne, "Be careful. This man is preoccupied with the thought of being a bear. He wants to be cared for because he has been wounded. But he is trapped in some acute awareness of himself. He is dangerously self-centered. If a hundred women loved him, it would not be enough."

And Lola Bourne said to Dr. Terriman, who was her cousin, "The bear is preoccupied with the conviction that he is a man. Just see, Charles, he rotates his forearms like a man. He stands upright on two legs. He dances. I understand that he is wounded, and I am wary. I would like to care for him, but I am prevented; he stays me with insinuations of things to come. I imagine that I could deal more easily with a hundred bears than with this one."

He hesitated.

"Are you putting me on, Lo? You're putting me on, aren't you?" He cracked half a smile, wanting her to confirm his sense that it was a joke, but she didn't; she was steadfast. He swallowed, peering at her from his fleshy boy's face, through thick green lollipop lenses.

"Help him if you can," she said.

Self-centered? Was that Terriman's term? It had always been to Lola Bourne a term more or less equal to the word *spoiled*. Pampered children were spoiled, self-centered: high school quarterbacks and prom queens. But now it was as if she had grasped the concept *self-centered* for the first time. *Self-centered.* It had the sound of definition; it anchored you; it locked you in. But in his special jargon how had Charles Teague Terriman meant it? What were the professional connotations? She pondered, biting her lower lip. That evening, in a letter she had no intention of mailing, she wrote:

> I know that you are deeply afflicted, that you are sick in your mind, and that you are in great pain. I know that powers of good and evil are at war inside of you. I know that you are angry, that your anger is terrible and blind and destructive. I know that at times you are bent on destroying yourself. I do not know why. The annihilation of the self is far beyond my understanding. I know that I love you with all my heart and that I cannot reach you, help you, save you. My darling, I—

She broke it off, sobbing without tears. And when the spasms stopped she sat at her writing desk in a kind of stupor, still as a stone, late into the night. When at last she got into bed she heard birds singing, and then without relief she fell fast asleep.

8

I am looking for the boy

With dread, Set entered the house on Scott Street and wandered through the rooms. In his mind's eye he could see Lukie lying before the fireplace, blue, angular, contorted in a huge knot, heaving in his breathy sleep, and he sensed the presence of Señora Archuleta in the kitchen, especially, behind the swinging door. But he could not find Bent. He knocked at Bent's bedroom; there was no sound within, and he opened the door and stepped into the dim light that filtered through the drawn drapes. Bent was not there. He drew open the drapes, then the curtains, and the room was flooded with morning sunshine. The bed was made, and Bent's robe lay across the foot. Bent's spectacles lay on the night table. The heels of his slippers were exposed beneath the edge of the bedspread.

Neither was Bent in the study, but his favorite pipe was on the desk, next to an open volume of the writings of Juan Ramón Jiménez. Old, sweet pipe smoke clung to the walls.

Set ventured into his own room, the room he had lived in as a boy. Some of his old drawings were still on the walls, a red pillow still on his rocking chair. He opened the door to the redwood balcony, with its familiar railing and the steps that led down to the path that encircled the garden, within the arc of towering eucalyptus trees. In the center of the garden was a fountain, and upon the fountain stood the statue of a plump, naked boy with thick stone curls and great vacant eyes. A generation ago Set stood many mornings on this little balcony in his pajamas and studied the garden to see what butterflies were there.

Bent was standing, slightly crooked, next to the fountain. He was looking into the eucalyptus trees, and he was wearing the black cardigan, white slacks, and red-soled white bucks. He had forgotten his spectacles again, and he squinted to see.

"Dad!" Set called.

At first, Bent gave no sign that he heard. He continued to peer into the trees, intently.

"Dad, what is it? What are you doing there?" Set's voice carried sharply down into the garden. There was a faint echo.

Then Bent turned and looked up.

"Well, you can see what I am doing, can't you." It was not a question. He looked hard at Set, as if he were trying to recognize him. Set felt a shiver on his spine. "I am looking for the boy."

And then, very slowly, Bent Sandridge faded from sight. He did not disappear at once, but he receded into the bright growth of the garden by degrees, his definition, his substance, becoming steadily softer, dimmer, until it was no longer there. He was gone. Then Set too peered into the trees, looking for the boy. The boy's shadow flitted among the trees; his laughter reverberated on the walls behind Set.

He is capable of violence

Set had lain for six weeks in a hospital bed, and he had become dull and weak with medication. He had suffered a breakdown, he was told, though not in so many words. Everyone spoke to him obliquely, with tact and condescension. He had suffered severe fatigue and depression brought on by stress and strain, they said, extraordinary psychological pressure of one kind or another. It happened all the time, he was assured. Charles Teague Terriman came every other day to talk to him about bears. Set was both amused and resentful. Terriman knew wonderful stories, gleaned from the annals of folklore and witchcraft and medical mythology, but he did not tell them well, and without sensitivity or shame he made crude and intolerable invasions into Set's mind. Set was at first uncooperative, and then he was hostile. On a Thursday morning, two days before he was to be released, Set drove with his right hand a small vase, containing a single rose, into Dr. Terriman's face, just as Terriman was saying, "You see, Locke, the bear is an ancient symbol of the perilous aspect of the unconscious, and—" Two of Terriman's teeth were broken, and his upper lip was lacerated; he required stitches. In deference to Lola Bourne he did not file charges. Set's release was postponed for a week. It was noted on his hospital record that he was capable of violence.

Six weeks before, Set had been found unconscious in his studio. The studio stank of whiskey and vomit and urine, and it was in a shambles. Paints were splattered on the walls and ceiling and the floor. Canvases and papers were strewn about, crumpled and torn. Next to Set was the medicine bundle, open. The little red blanket had been removed, and exposed was the medicine itself, a bag made from the whole skin of a bear cub, including the head and feet. Some of its contents were scattered on the floor: a shriveled grizzly paw with great yellow claws, pouches of tobacco and herbs, small fluorite and quartz crystals, a pipestone carved in the shape of a fish, a hard black twist that Grey would later identify as the penis of a wolf, bits of ancient bone, a yellow scalp. The bag was well preserved, though it was obviously very old. The hair was thick and matted. The claws were small and sharp and well formed. Brass buttons were fixed in the eyes and along the vertical incision on the chest and stomach. There was about it, upon and within it, the odors of bear grease, of mold, of death, of deep, humid earth run through with bitter roots.

Her belief has become absolute

The Washita River ran, bearing sediment and drift and the leaves of trees and the petals of wildflowers. The earth was fresh and fragrant, and the air clean and warm. The Great Plains had become intricate with color. The ruins of the old school at Rainy Mountain, holding against the weather of hundreds of seasons, stood out in the prairie like prehistoric cairns. The tall yellow grass sounded with the drone of bees and the crackle of grasshoppers. Birds drew lines on the sky, and terrapins crept along the creeks. Ghosts convened under the broken walls of Boake's store, where Worcester Meat, when he was a little boy, went with his father to collect "grass money" for the use of Indian land—there were many wagons, a large camp—and Worcester's father, Youngwater, bought hardtack and pickles and buckets and harness and rock candy. Above all, in the withering heat that shimmered in the noon and afternoon, the land was endless. It was the continental reach, beyond maps and geography, beyond the accounts of the voyageurs, almost beyond the distance of dreams. It was the middle and immeasurable meadow of North America. It was the destination and destiny of ancients who, coming with dogs and travois, followed herds of huge, lumbering animals down the long, cold cordillera, following the visions of their shamans, who rattled Arctic bones and cried in the voices of owls and eagles and whose prayers were the lowing of thousand-mile winds. It was the sun's range. Nowhere on earth was there a more perfect equation of freedom and space. Those earliest inhabitants must have beheld the Plains, and each man must have said to himself, "From this time on, I shall belong to this land, for it is truly worthy of my strength, my dreams, my life and death. Here I am. Here, *I am.*" There was an abundance of game and water and grass, and an air full of brilliance to sustain the breathing of warriors and comely women and strong, beautiful children, of grandmothers and grandfathers, of holy people. Here, for those old wanderers, was the center of the world, the sacred ground of sacred grounds.

Grey watched the moon rise, huge and red. She heard the stooping of the wind, splintering in the black limbs of the black clusters of trees on the black islands of the plain. She clasped her hands, laughing. A peace pervaded the dusk, but an excitement was certainly just below, just beyond, in the corners of the night. She could not hold still.

In the morning, with Worcester's help, she butchered a calf in the old way, in the way of the grandmother. She took the raw, steaming liver of the calf in her bloody hands and ate of it slowly, savoring the juices; it would give her strength and clarity of mind. It is what Worcester did too, what Walker had done, and Youngwater too, and his father, and his. It is what Set-tainte and Set-angya had done. It was good, a fitting thing. But now, in her woman's heart, having come to the considerable age of twenty years, she longed to plant seeds in the ground, corn and melons and squash, to tend her mother's flocks, to ride out into the red and blue and purple shadows of Tsegi, "place among the rocks," the place of origin, toward the horizon that was like a rainbow, a horizon in a sand painting or in a watercolor by Beatien Yazz or Quincy Tahoma. She longed to be at home, the home of her childhood. She dreamed of Lukachukai, "place of the reeds bending eastward," of the red cliffs there and of the night sky, so brilliant it had never faded in her memory, which challenged even *diné bizaad,* the Navajo language. The many words and names, all the rich sounds and silences, the shades of meaning, all the images and abstractions, the rhythms and melodies and harmonies, all the aspects of given objects—color, size, feel, shape, taste, age, power, *being*—which in *diné bizaad* are precise beyond the precision of other languages, were reduced to simplicity in the presence of the stars over Lukachukai. She yearned to weave at her mother's loom and to enter into a circle of squaw dancers, to breathe into her lungs the cold air of the canyons and the nutty smoke of the campfires, to take into her nostrils the aromas of coffee at midnight, among cedars and junipers, and of mutton roasting and bread sizzling in an iron skillet, to listen to the beloved songs, ancient, holy, haunting, and the insistent beat of the drums, echoing into the universe, their throbbing like the vibrations of the stars.

"When will he come?" Jessie asked.

"Soon," Grey said.

"Well, *soon.*" Jessie tested the word. She did not want to press, but Grey volunteered nothing, gave nothing away, and Jessie was bursting with curiosity. She waited as long as she could, and then she said, "You said he was sick."

"Yes."

"Well, you know, I was thinking, maybe he *can't* come, he's too sick." Jessie's dress was thin and pale blue, with dark blue and black flowers printed on it. It was a size too small, but it heightened the dark richness of her skin. Sweat glistened on her brow and at the folds below her chin. She slapped at a fly that had alighted between her breasts.

"No, he is better now. He will come."

"Yeah, but it might take some more, you know, *medicine*. Maybe we ought to make smoke again and drink some more of that strong tea, you know? Maybe we ought to sing."

"No," Grey said evenly, with patience real but understated. "It isn't necessary. He's coming."

"When will he come, do you think?"

"Soon now."

Jessie, frustrated, looked out the window, beyond the arbor to the distant, dark band of trees on the river, and sighed. She had come as close to Grey as she could come. They were two women, and there was a bond between them, after all, such a bond as there is between women; in some sense they were sisters. Indeed, they were related by blood. Each could see in the other some trace of the grandmother's physical appearance—or at least a gesture, a tone of voice, an inflection. But Grey was unavailable to Jessie beyond a point. She was not herself curious, as Jessie was, about trivial things, the things that were spoken over the breakfast table, the usual things of the house or the neighborhood, of husbands and wives. She had no taste for gossip. She knew very well how to be frivolous in her imagination, but she cared not to be frivolous in commerce with others.

Like most medicine people, Grey was naïve. She was not at all practical; she was an impractical visionary. When she thought of the things that remarked her essential life, she did not think of numbers or graphs or blueprints or print upon a page. She thought of hawks and horses, the sun rising, and clouds bursting with rain. She thought of deities and mythic heroes, of rodeo riders and warriors brandishing scalps. She thought of Buffalo Bill and Crazy Horse and Calamity Jane. And of course she thought of Billy the Kid—Billy in peril and three dimensions and silver spurs.

But her vision had become redirected and steadily more incisive; it penetrated more and more deeply into certain niches of reality in proportion as she acquired power. What her vision centered upon just now was the man Locke Setman. And the first images that came to her mind's eye were those of his psychic aspect: that is, she saw not only the substance but the shadow as well, not only the physical appearance but also the mental and spiritual conditions; she saw a man in confusion and pain, a man severely wounded in his intelligence, verging upon collapse, a man in danger of losing possession of himself. Often now she took from a drawer in the grandmother's room the drawing of the grandmother. Grey moved her fingers lightly along the edges of the paper, where Set's fingers too had pressed. She could feel his presence then, as a pulse that bore faintly upon her own, a vibration that was peculiarly *his* vitality. It was what she felt, with much greater intensity, when she had handed him the medicine bundle and their hands were upon it for a long moment and it was a bond like blood between them.

Her belief had become absolute. There was no doubt whatsoever in her mind that Set would come, and soon. She knew that as surely as she knew anything. It was something, his coming, that she could bring about—had indeed already brought about—by the sheer strength of her will and her belief. Her will had been expressed in dream and in ceremony. It could not now be brought into question, much less aborted. There was in her, therefore, a deep satisfaction, a contentment like sound sleep. She had only in her wisdom to bide her time. All that must happen *would* happen, and her part in it would be inevitable and indispensable. This she understood with certain humility. Not she but Locke Setman was in the center of her design—she imagined weaving a small, perfect blanket out of old wools, bayeta, cavalry uniforms, trade cloth. It was Set's story that must be told, and no matter how many times the story had been told in the past and would be told in the future, and no matter how crucial was her voice in the present telling, it was he, Set, whose story it was. This was simply, profoundly, so.

To Jessie and to Milo and to Worcester Meat, it seemed that she was waiting. But Grey had no sense of waiting, which was, as she thought of it, a vacuum. She had entered into a quiet stillness, the lull that precedes ceremony, a dimension of peace and restoration. She slept and read and kept to herself, and she gathered her strength for the days to come. She knew that she would need strength—and she knew that Set would need her strength as much as she—and she felt it surging in her blood, taking hold in her bones and marrow. It was not a strength gained by effort. She had drunk tea and eaten meat, but not in days and weeks had she run or ridden her horse hard. Dog grazed on the edge of her awareness, neighing softly, scraping his hooves methodically on the earth. She was wholly invested in a kind of healing languor.

There is a giving over, a reconciliation, a benediction

She knew that soon rain and hail would come driving down with great force upon the plain. The hail would damage the trees and fields and barns and houses, and the rain would run in sheets and cut the traces of numerous lines and furrows in the earth; it would cause the rivers to rise and hold back the currents of the creeks. In the night, lightning would be constant on the whole circle of the sky, and there would be a hard, hot wind. Grey was enlivened by such storms, for they were innately powerful, and their power informed her spirit. In Man-ka-ih she was wholly restored in her spirit.

In the evening, soon after the storm descended, she rode Dog to the east, along the south boundary of the Mottledmare land, along the fence and the red escarpment that lay parallel to the paved road. In the distance she saw the car approaching. And even before it turned and entered the private road she knew that it was he. It had begun to rain steadily, and the skyline before her was obliterated. The car moved slowly, its lights on, and she watched it for a time, and then she turned Dog toward the Mottledmare house. When she passed the cemetery she called above the rain, "Grandmother, he has come!" There remained a long, horizontal thread of brilliant red light on the western rim, and the black sky heaved and shifted above it hugely, slowly. Two hundred yards from the house she drew the horse up and sat huddled, holding her eyes against the rain. The car had rolled to a stop in front of the house, too far away for her to see clearly. Had she seen the two figures emerge, the man would have seemed slighter than she remembered, the woman more comely and graceful than she imagined. Suddenly there was a loneliness in her, like a weight, but it made no matter. There was also a vague, unintelligible excitement, so closely held in check that only she could know of it. What she felt most keenly was relief. Her long preparation for what now must be, so long it seemed she could barely remember when it had begun, was finished. She had the sense that she was keeping calendars. One calendar was now, on this stormy night, being closed. A part of the story had been told; a time had been fulfilled. Now she would begin the keeping of another, even more crucial, calendar.

Then through the curtain of rain she saw the men and women on horseback. They sat sagging, drenched with rainwater, in a tight cluster nearby. She urged Dog slowly among them, approaching very close to some, peering discreetly into their downcast faces. They were imperturbable in their attitude, weary beyond reckoning. They seemed not to see her; even their horses seemed beyond curiosity, fear. Only she and Dog were excited. She had a feeling that she knew these people, these Plains people in their braids and blankets. It seemed to her that she should find the grandmother among them. Dog's ears were pricked and quivering, and for a moment he pranced, his muscles bunching at her knees. She drew near the lean, shadowy figure of a man who kept a small distance apart from the others. Slowly he raised his eyes to hers. She was startled; they seemed to see her and to see through her. She wanted to speak to him at once, but it would have been presumptuous, unseemly. After an appropriate silence she spoke her Indian name, Koi-ehm-toya. And after another he spoke his own, Maman-ti. He brought his right hand from inside the blanket that was draped over his shoulders. The hand was narrow, with long fingers, and it was wholly wrinkled with rain. She wondered why he and the others did not dismount and take shelter. And as if he knew what was in her mind he lowered his wrinkled hand to indicate the ground directly below. She looked down. There were hundreds of tarantulas crawling on the flooded earth. She marveled, and she turned Dog slowly and moved away. When she looked back she could see no one. There was only the black wall of rain.

She felt soaked through with rainwater. There was rainwater in her hair and in her clothing and on her skin; her hat and boots were spongy with rainwater. She slipped the bridle from Dog's head and slapped him away; her hand splashed on his wet, feathery hide. But for the whites of his eyes he had become black with rainwater, and the rainwater ran into his deep crescent prints and shone like shell in the flash of lightning. There was a great crash of thunder, and there came suddenly the next wave of the storm.

She had meant to follow Dog into the barn, but the rain was at full force, and the thunder and lightning were directly upon her. She sat huddled in the arbor. The violence of the weather was extreme, and the din was terrific, but she was strangely unafraid. She was in fact exhilarated. Her heart was beating fast, and she raised her voice in jubilation; and although it was loud and shrill, she could not hear it. She laughed then. The lightning touched her with blue and white light, and the light was throbbing fast, as if shutters were tripping with great speed upon the sheer beam of a powerful spotlight. There in the arbor, in the eye of the storm, Grey might have been a figure, her whole definition stuttering in comic exaggeration, in a Chaplin film.

Locke Setman and Lola Bourne sat with Jessie and Milo Mottledmare in the front room in lamplight. Jessie talked nervously, somewhat louder than was necessary to compensate for the wind and rain that battered the roof and walls. Lola Bourne smiled and tried to chat, but she was clearly out of her element and visibly uncomfortable. Milo grunted now and then and looked down at his hands, his fingers interlaced on his stomach. The journey had left Set very tired, and he slumped in his chair, staring at the floor. Only now and then he tried to acknowledge what was being said by assuming an expression of interest or amusement. Jessie had been taken aback when he entered the room. He had lost considerable weight. His cheeks were hollow and there were conspicuous shadows under his eyes. His skin was sallow and shone with perspiration. Milo, in spite of his pose, was acutely aware of the medicine bundle, which Set had carried in with him and placed on the floor next to his chair. It was for all of them except Set a kind of unacknowledged presence, in fact. It was an extraordinary reaction, as if the bundle were invisible or did not exist. And of this Set could not help but be aware. The presence of the bundle had established a quality of great respect, not to say fear, in the room.

A little later, when the storm was diminished, Grey entered suddenly from the porch and closed the door against the whistling wind. When she turned, her face was drawn and her long hair clung to her head in thick, twisted strings. The others gaped at her, taken aback, startled. She regarded them evenly. For a moment there was only the sound of the rain on the window and the creaking of the door behind her.

"Uh . . . oh, this here is Grey," Milo stammered. "She's the Mayor of Bote, Oklahoma. . . ."

"Grey, dear . . ." Jessie said, and she did not close her mouth.

Grey's expression was benign, nearly blank.

Set, attentive now, caught himself staring at her. The last time he saw her she was altogether contained in a propriety and dignity that astonished him. She was beautiful and composed and graceful beyond words, a vision he had preserved jealously in his memory. Now she was disheveled, weather-beaten, shivering, in some sense pathetic, and yet her eyes were nearly defiant. The disposition of her whole being was proud. She is essentially ambiguous, he thought, essentially unknowable. And he wondered how many people she could be.

Lola Bourne was more than a shade off balance. She looked fleetingly into Grey's eyes and nodded. In some reach of her mind she thought of trying her luck, but in this alien place she had none, and she did not know what to do or say, how to be.

In spite of her appearance, Grey was poised, her shadow slanted on the somber wall. She seemed a wild child, almost ephemeral, with something like shyness in her manner. When she spoke to Set, it was in a voice that conveyed gladness and restraint at once; it was familiar, yet respectful and direct, without conceit. She shook his hand, and then, so naturally that it seemed not a departure, she knelt and laid her hands on the medicine bundle. And she was upright again, all in a second.

"Thank you," she said to Lola Bourne, with simple, unmistakable sincerity.

In that instant Lola Bourne understood beyond the shadow of a doubt that she had no purchase here, that gratitude is all she could have expected or hoped for.

"You are welcome," she replied. The two women held hands without embarrassment, and there was a giving over, a reconciliation, a benediction.

When the rain had stopped, Lola said her goodbyes. She kissed Set sweetly, and a sharp realization of loss passed over her, but it did not take her by surprise. It was easier than she imagined, leaving Set; she no longer knew him. When she drove away she did not look back. She drove fast, with the window open. The air was warm and thick and laden with the clean fragrance of the late rain. She felt suddenly unburdened, one with herself for the first time in a long while. She looked ahead into the darkness and the soft glare of oncoming cars, and she settled back. She breathed deeply and anticipated sleep. Her sleep would be sound, delicious. Nothing could keep her from it.

Past midnight, in the grandmother's room, Grey sat reading by lamplight. Set lay dead to the world in the bed beside her, having been aware in the last moment of consciousness that he was in her keeping. At last the book weighed her hands down, and she dozed off.

She draws lines on the red earth

The old man sat on the ground, his head bent, his legs crossed. Within his reach was the bundle of bones, the bones of his son. There was a sound, and he brought his head up sharply, glaring. The young man was standing a few feet away beside a *pomme blanche,* waiting respectfully for the old man to acknowledge him. Respectfully, too, he was looking not directly at the old man nor at the bones of his son, but to one side, where there was a small stand of willows.

"Haw! How long have you been there?" Clearly the old man was unsettled, perhaps ashamed of being taken by surprise.

"Not long."

"Well, what do you want?"

"I come to pay my respects. I come to visit you and your son. Here's tobacco."

"Haw, *ahó.* You know my son?"

"In a way."

"In a way."

There was a pause in which the old man seemed to ponder this "in a way." He looked down at the bundle of bones, crushing a pinch of the tobacco in his fingers, then up again.

"You are about the same age, I think," he said.

"Yes."

"And do you know me too, in a way?"

"You are Set-angya, Sitting Bear, a warrior and chief as great as his name. Over all the prairies you are famous for your bravery and your deeds. Your mind is true, your words are true, and your heart is true. The eagle knows your name; the buffalo knows your name; the bear knows your name; the white man knows your name. You are Set-angya, chief of the Kaitsenko Society, chief of the Crazy Dogs, chief of the dog soldiers. Yours are the best of warriors; yours are the best of battles; yours are the best of enemies. You are Set-angya, who does not surrender his son to death, who dares to withhold victory from even the greatest of all enemies. Hear me, old man brave to madness, O my warrior!

"You and your son, great chief, you are worthy of each other in your courage and loyalty and love and bigness of spirit. Your son in his bones and you in your flesh and blood are of the same sacred mystery, the same medicine, most powerful.

"Hear me! I am honored to make you this speech, to make you this respectful visit, to stand here in your company, O Sitting Bear, yours and your son's. I have spoken."

"You have spoken well," said the old man softly, gravely, after the appropriate silence. "Now I know *you,* in a way. You are surely a famous orator among your people."

"Well, no, sir."

"My son, I do not admire modesty. I like boasting. I *love* to boast, and I like others to boast, if they have something about themselves to boast of. You have very pretty words about you. Why don't you boast of them?"

"I'm right proud you liked my speech, sir, but, to tell you the truth, it ain't mine. You see, my girlfriend wrote it up, and I learnt it."

"I cannot read, myself."

"I memorized it, and then I declaimed it."

"Why?"

"I wanted you to like me."

"Yes?"

"I wanted to talk to you about death . . . but I am a man of few words."

"Yes, there is something else about you . . . there is a sign, a mark upon you, and there was a mark upon my son, and there is a mark upon me. But I am an old man, and so for me it matters very little. But my son, and you, you are young men, and you are marked men. It is a thing heavy on my heart."

"I have so few words. I wanted you to like me."

"I know you, in a way."

"I am a dead man."

"Yes. Tell me, did you achieve your death in the proper way?"

"I guess so. It happened so fast, and I wasn't expecting it, not at that moment, though I had been looking into the shadows for a long time."

"My son died in the proper way."

"So did you."

"Ah, you have heard about it. So they say. There was not a whimper, no pleading, no shame."

"I had no time for any of that."

"Yes. I think neither did my son. But I had time, and I neither whimpered nor pled. Rather, I sang."

"I can't sing."

At first light she awoke. She would sit for a while longer, arranging her thoughts. She would watch the dawn come about, and then she would go out and lift her arms and pray, and she would see to the sunrise, the lines and streaks of the sun extending up and out and down, striking summer to the earth. Kneeling, then, she would draw lines on the red earth, describing where she and her man must go.

Lines.

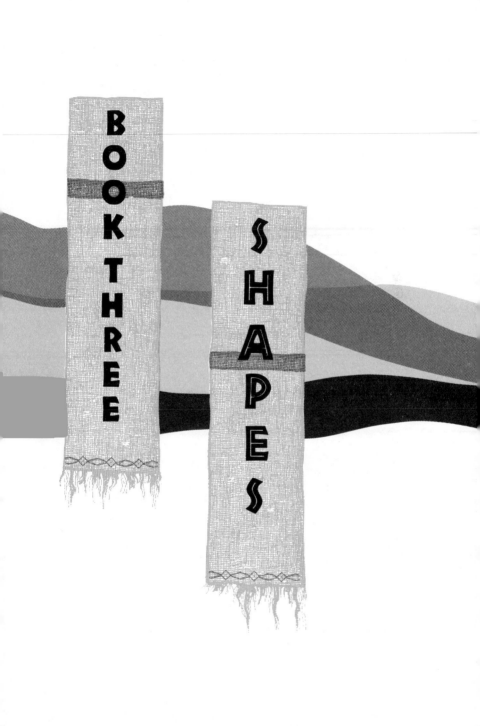

BOOK THREE

SHAPES

A foot
A foot with toes
A foot with toes came
He came with a foot with toes
Aging as he came with a foot with toes

◇◆◇◆◇◆◇

Navajo

■||||||||||||||||||||||||||||||||||||||||||||||||||||| **1** ||||||||||||||||||||||||||||||||||||||||||||||||||||||■

How can we believe in the child?

———————————

But the boy was seen. One by one, hunters returned from the woods with stories in which a bear figured more or less prominently. Sometimes the bear was said to have run upon its hind legs. Sometimes it was said to have approached the hunter gladly, with eager goodwill, as if it had no sense of danger whatsoever. Sometimes it was said to have been defined in a strange light, as if a blue, smoky shadow lay behind it. One hunter, a man with a withered neck, was so deeply enchanted by the bear's behavior that upon its approach he could do nothing but stand with his arms at his sides. The bear came upon him, breathed the scent of camas upon him, and laid its great flat head to the hunter's genitals. In a strange moment in which there was no fear on either side, there was recognition on both sides, the hunter said. The bear cried in a human voice.

Then, too, a Piegan woman whose name was Thab-san, who had been captured by the Kiowas in the Antelope Plains, told the following story:

One night there appeared a boy child in the Piegan camp. No one had ever seen it before. It was not bad looking, and it spoke a language that was pleasant to hear, but none could understand it. The wonderful thing was that the child was perfectly unafraid, as if it were at home among its own people. The child got on well enough, but the next morning it was gone, as suddenly as it had appeared. Everyone was troubled. But then it came to be understood that the child never was, and everyone felt better. "After all," said an old man, "how can we believe in the child? It gave us not one word of sense to hold on to. What we saw, if indeed we saw anything at all, must have been a dog from a neighboring camp, or a bear that wandered down from the high country."

*T*soai, the great stump of the tree, stood against the sky. There was nothing like it in the landscape. The tallest pines were insignificant beside it; many hundreds of them together could not fill its shadow. In time the stump turned to stone, and the wind sang at a high pitch as it ran across the great grooves that were set there long ago by the bear's claws. Eagles came to hover above it, having caught sight of it across the world. No one said so, but each man in his heart acknowledged Tsoai, and the first thing he did upon waking was to cast his eyes upon it, thus to set his belief, to know that it was there and that the world remained whole, as it ought to remain. And always Tsoai was there.

He makes a morning prayer

In the bed of the tan half-ton: the medicine bundle in a green plastic sack; bags and boxes in which were clothing, mementos, utensils, a drawing board, papers and paints; a hundred books, more or less, and the manuscript of "The Strange and True Story of my Life with Billy the Kid"; an ice chest in which were cheeses, apples, boiled eggs, Coca-Cola, and beer; a camp stove; sleeping bags; ceremonial paraphernalia, including four masks and sixteen peyote buttons, an eagle-feather fan, an eagle-bone whistle, and a fluorite crystal with six points and eight triangular sides; a biscuit tin containing Earl Grey and Red Zinger tea bags; four large plastic bottles of water; a saddle, saddle blanket, and bridle; various tools and lengths of rope; a bale of hay and part of another; and two tarpaulins. In the trailer: Dog.

Set had never met anyone remotely like Grey. Her confidence was unassailable, her assumptions sound. The better he knew her, the more enthralled he became. Easily, with simple acceptance and thanks, she held her life. Without question or suspicion she held her life. She held her life not tightly but surely, not jealously but respectfully. Did she know, he wondered, how extraordinary she was? Probably not; there was no sign of it. *Naïve* was a word that came to his mind. She was, he insisted to himself, naïve. She was beautiful and bright and vivacious and enthralling—and naïve.

He did not care to drive, nor was he yet able, and so Grey drove all but a hundred miles of the way, the hundred miles being a concession to his self-respect, a token; it meant not much to either of them, but it was a consideration. The bond that was growing between them was made of small, numberless considerations. Indeed, Grey liked to drive. She sat high; the truck was new and powerful, and the tug and sway of the trailer was a challenge to her hands on the wheel. It was not so fine a thing as riding a good horse—that is, it did not require as much of one's intelligence and skill and coordination and instinct—but it was exciting to be in control of such a powerful and fast machine and to measure precisely its response to her touch. And the novelty was great, for she had never owned a car, and she was not used to driving. Alternately Set slept and looked out on the changing landscape, the sloping of the earth toward the blue ranges. Now and then he glanced at her. She sat relaxed at the wheel, yet alert, wide awake to everything around her. She tapped her fingers to music. Her excitement grew as the landscape changed.

"Tell me again," he said, "where we are going." He knew the answer, but he wanted a better understanding of it.

"Lukachukai," she said. "We're going to Lukachukai."

"It's where your mother lives."

"It's where my mother lives; my sister and my little niece, too."

"There is no man," he said, thoughtfully.

"I told you. My father died some years ago, and my sister's husband—he's in Oregon, I think. My sister threw him away."

After a time:

"What sort of place is Lukachukai?"

"Oh, *hózhón'i!*" she exclaimed. "It is a place of . . . of . . . it is not easy to explain what sort of place it is. You will have to see for yourself. It is a place of great beauty."

"That word in itself," he said. "It isn't descriptive of much, is it? When you say it is a place of beauty, I believe you, but I don't *see* anything. As you say, I shall have to see for myself. Beauty is truth, and truth is beauty. Rooty-toot toot, and rooty-toot tooty."

"Yes," she said, laughing.

"You, I think *you* are beautiful." He hadn't meant to say it, but then it was said. She would assume that he was speaking as an artist, wouldn't she? "Don't you think so?"

"Yes," she answered; then, after a moment's reflection: "Well, I am young and healthy, and healthy young women are more often beautiful than not. Listen, I'm two kinds of American Indian, after all, with no doubt not-too-distant infusions of Mexican and French Canadian and God knows what Scotch-Irish-English blood, and I know something about the world from at least two remarkable and valid points of view, and I am strong and restless and *vital,* and I want my life to be full and exciting and suspenseful and, well, extraordinary. I like to see the sun rise and set, I like to hear birds singing and horses farting, wind and water running, and I like to feel hot and cold, hard and soft. . . . Ah, me, all those good genes, Set. How can I *not* be beautiful?"

"Or romantic, for that matter, except the farting horses."

"Oh, the way I talk. Yeah, I know. I know all the white man's words. But at the drop of a hat I can speak in a correct and genteel fashion. I can be a creature of refinement, Set. My tiny feet are sheathed in dainty slippers, I have a wasp's waist, and my breasts are of alabaster purity."

"I hope not alabaster," he said, "glassy, hard, colorless."

She unbuttoned her shirt and exposed her right breast.

"Just as I thought," he said, "terracotta; let's see, earth colors —burnt umber, raw Sienna, Mars yellow, a bit of white. Swish, swish." He pretended to mix these on a palette.

"You can give them names if you want," she said, braking, trying to see past the tractor and trailer ahead of her.

"Names?"

"My boobs."

"Blueberry and Bunker," he said.

She made a face, shifting down.

"I thought something sweet and old-fashioned," she said. "Abigail and Abiah, maybe."

"Bruce and Evangeline?" he suggested.

"Bruce?"

"I guess not."

"Jeez!"

At Clines Corners they turned north. Set looked out on the arboreal desert with wonder; the air seemed thinner, the light brighter. They had taken leave of one landscape and entered another.

"Tell me more about your mother and sister," Set said.

"Oh, well, you will like them, I think. They are *diné,* real people. But even if you don't like them, it's all right; they are real nonetheless."

"Will they like me?"

"After a while, certainly."

He pondered this.

"You are saying that you don't think they will like me at first." He regretted at once that he had said it; it sounded boyish and petulant.

"They will understand you somehow, that I am meant to keep by you, that you must do what you must do. They will see the necessity and respect it; *then* they will like you very much, I think." She winked at him. "In spite of everything, you are not altogether unlikable."

"Thanks. So it will probably be—uh, uncomfortable—at first, anyway."

"Probably."

"Why in God's name am I doing this?"

"Because you are Set. Don't imagine that you have a choice in the matter, in what is going on, and don't imagine that *I* have one. You are *Set;* you are the bear; you will be the bear, no matter what. You will act accordingly, in the proper way, because there is no other way to act. In the proper way; do you understand?"

"Yes. I am Set."

Near Galisteo and Lamy the land became wonderfully various. There were long reaches of undulant plain, not the plain of the middle of the continent but rolling sand and clay, thick with piñon and mesquite and cedar and juniper, sagebrush and paintbrush, rising to red and white and blue and purple sandstone mesas, round blue mountains in the distance and, in the longer distance, peaks of a fainter blue and snow-capped, and beyond them the blue and silver sky, shimmering.

"I am very curious," he admitted. "Tell me more about them, your family."

She thought for a minute. Dark clouds were building on the Jemez range, to the west. The sun was ranging north. Her window was open, and the rush of dry wind excited her skin.

"Well, my mother's name is Lela. She is a Navajo woman and a traditionalist. She is a member of the Bitter Water clan. She keeps the old ways, for the most part. She speaks the Navajo language as well as any Navajo, I suppose. But she speaks English too, far better than most reservation women of her generation. She's a boss lady; you don't want to tangle with her. She does what Navajo women have done for a long, long time: She cooks, she weaves, she looks after her children—now her grandchild; she even herds sheep. As I say, she keeps the old ways—oh, not exclusively—that's the great thing; she talks on the telephone and drives a Thunderbird. And all of this she does well. She knows exactly how her parents and grandparents lived, and she knows how to live in the same way, knows that it is a good way to live. I know it too, and you will see. Anyway, she lives in the old way much of the time."

"And the rest of the time?"

"She talks on the telephone and drives a Thunderbird."

"She is an anachronism."

"Backwards and forwards."

"Yes, I see."

"And then there is that side of her that is headstrong."

"Meaning what?"

"She makes her own decisions, always has, and she holds to them. She married my father against all the advice of her family. I wish I had been there; it must have been something: the bickering, the resentments, the rows."

"What did they have against your father?"

"Oh, nothing personal. It's just that he wasn't a Navajo, not to mention a clansman. I'm sure my father's family felt the same way. He was headstrong too. But I suppose that arrogance was expected of him; at least he was acting on ample precedent. The Kiowas stole people as well as horses, you know, and it was a good thing, as far as the vitality of the culture was concerned. Look at me; I'm the proof of the pudding, Set. Hybrid vigor. But it was harder on my mom."

"I'm getting to know you. Go on."

"My sister Antonia. She is thirty-one. We are not much alike, she and I. Too much of a difference in our ages, I guess. When I was little she was more like a mother or an aunt to me than a sister. She is more intelligent than I, and much more practical and self-contained. She was not as close to our dad as I was, and not half so spoiled. Antonia takes after that side of our mother that is really, deeply Navajo. She's old-fashioned too; she might have—"

"I like old-fashioned girls."

"She might have cut a figure in our grandmother's generation. And she, too, in another way, is an anachronism. Backwards. But in her this is something very good. It is an originality, a purity, a virtue. She is beautiful—quietly, serenely, natively beautiful. You will see."

"Maybe I will fall in love with her." Set felt better. He was taking a kind of strength from the journey. There was exhilaration just in the going; motion was a principal expression of his life, had he known it, and in it there were properties of healing. It was not that he was going *toward* something, to a destination, to an appointment, though indeed he was and that was all right, but what counted now was the sheer act of going, the blind conviction of purpose and meaning in the simple act of going on.

"Nanibah."

"What is Nanibah?" said Set.

"Nanibah is an eight-year-old Navajo girl. She is my niece, and she is perfect—bright, imaginative, playful, articulate, mischievous, wonderfully mysterious, and irresistible."

"And beautiful, no doubt."

"And *beautiful.*"

On the morning of the second day they drove north from Taos and turned west toward the Rio Grande Gorge. The March light was of a brittle clarity that startled Set. From the peneplain of the Sangre de Cristos he had the certain sense that he could see farther over land than he had ever seen before. And in the foreground of this vast reach of the earth was the gorge. It was etched into the plain so incisively and yet so delicately that it seemed the deepest shadow in the land. It was on the earth and in the earth at once, starkly visible on and in, at once, a thing in nature that seemed almost unnatural, a profound mystery, an old condition of the planet, anomalously vague and definite, like lightning, and the shadow of lightning.

Beyond Tres Piedras they stopped and made tea on their camp-
stove and allowed Dog to frisk and to graze on winter grass by
the side of the road; and all three of them munched on leathery,
tart Velarde apples in the sun.

Thin blue lines of smoke rose above the village of Tierra Amar-
illa, and the air was cold and sparkling and bore the scent of
piñons. An eagle sailed out over the Rio Brazos, hanging for
moments at a time against the great luminous blossom of a cloud;
then it darted and stooped and traced a long curve on the sky until
it was out of sight, and the cloud slowly shifted and roiled. It
became a whale sounding.

"It," she said, sweeping her hand along the horizon, "does you
good."

"I feel good today," Set answered.

"Yes, the air, take it in; it does you good. Place your hands in
the snow; lay them on the warm, sunlit sand. Stand against the
wind. Sing to the earth; it does you good."

"Yes?"

"Yes. It must. The journey must do you good. That is why we
make it. You are gaining strength; you have to be strong. You
will need great strength for what you must do. You *will* be strong,
equal to the thing you must do. Believe me. You have begun to
gain strength."

He thought about this.

"Well, I don't feel strong, stronger, physically stronger, I mean.
But somehow I feel better, better in my head; 'frame of mind,'
they say. My frame of mind is better, maybe."

"It is good to travel," Grey said, "on the ground."

"Yes. I like rolling along, feeling the vibrations, the hold of the tires on the road. I'm not used to it. It's better than flying hundreds of miles an hour and thousands of feet above the earth."

"It's even better riding a horse, or going on your own feet, for that matter."

"I don't know," Set said, smiling. "I doubt it. I like this pretty well, though—you driving, big windows all around, lots to see, a comfortable seat. Yeah, it's like sitting in a rocking chair, looking out at interesting things. Riding high. Yes, by God, I *like* it."

"But after a time it's hard on your ass."

"Your ass dies."

"Wait till you sit a hard horse for a few miles."

He ignored this.

"I feel better," he said.

But later Set told her to stop the truck, and he got out and vomited. It went on for minutes; he could not stop. He broke out then into a cold sweat, and his whole body quaked. On his hands and knees on the shoulder of the road he had never felt worse. He was tearing, drooling vomit, weak and humiliated. He wanted to die.

Grey stood away for a time, and then she came to him and placed a hand on his shoulder.

"Get up," she said. And she said it again sharply, "Get up!"

Set pulled himself together and up. He stood, wavering. He could not look at her. She kept her fingers closed upon his collar.

"Leave me alone!" he shouted, jerking himself violently from her grasp.

She turned from him and took a step away.

"It happens!" she shouted back. "It happens," she said again, placing her voice away, but knowing that he heard. "It will happen again. But you are doing what has to be done; that's all that matters now. The bear invites you, taunts you, reminds you of its power. Just hold on. You are growing stronger."

"Stronger . . ." He made the word strangely in his mouth. It was both a laugh and a whimper. The thing inside him writhed, but he registered what she said.

"I am Set," he said in his clenched teeth, in great pain.

And suddenly he was afraid. Never, not even as a child and an orphan had he felt more completely alone. There on the high plateau of Rio Arriba he would have given anything to hear Bent's voice—and across some unfathomable chasm of time his father's. How could he have become so confused, so disoriented in his mind and soul? How on earth did he come to this? Something had compelled him, but what? Who was he, and where? It was as if he had been uprooted, torn away from his own familiar place. And to what possible purpose he could not imagine. He tried to get it all straight in his mind. He told himself that he was a man like other men, that he earned his living, that he did no harm, that he wanted to give something of himself that was valuable to the world. Dear God, he knew who he was, didn't he? He had said to himself many times, "I am Set." But what did it mean? In his profound loneliness, in his sickness, in his delirium he no longer knew, if ever he had known. And that struck mortal fear in him, and he did not know how to articulate his fear to a living soul, not even to himself. He tried to remember what it was to paint, to put his whole being into his work. He saw paintings in the glare behind his eyes, not paintings that were or had ever been, but the dark, indefinite images of fear that were splashing upon his brain.

Prostrate on the frozen shoulder of a remote road in the high plateau, sick to death, he heard Grey's voice—or was it his own. "Are you Set?"

"No! I . . . I don't know!" he wanted to shout, but he choked on the words. A low, terrible sound came from his throat, like guttural laughter, like a growl. He was grotesquely poised on his feet, his back hunched, and he was helpless. He had heaved himself into a shapeless, quivering thing. He no longer had substance, definition. He had become detestable to himself, like his own bright spittle, the foul taste of the sickness that lay in his mouth. He wanted to cry, but he could only quake and gasp and growl. He had voided his mind and soul. He was empty of all feeling except a consuming, static pain. His eyes were dry and burning, and he could not come to tears. In his throat he repeated her words: "I am growing stronger." Then, "I am Set," and again he emitted the strange, rasping laughter that died away in the cold, glinting wind.

It was a centaur dancing. The man was so concentrated upon the dance that he appeared to take no notice of the half-ton and trailer that pulled up beyond the rails. His head was set. His eyes were downcast, moving laterally with the mare's eyes, on the same axis. His face was rather long and narrow, the flesh hard on the bone. His mouth was wide and straight, with thin lips slightly parted over teeth as white as chalk. His narrow eyes were very black and very bright. His cheekbones were high and prominent. A knife scar ran diagonally across his left cheek, from the top of the ear to the upper lip below the left nostril. At its widest point, where the knife had cut to the skull, it was nearly a quarter of an inch across, and there the scar tissue was taut and glassy; it shone like the scales of a snake. His hair was long and straight and coal-black, knotted at the back of his head, under a dusty black hat. The hat was cocked low on the forehead, and it was a particular thing, a Stetson 10X beaver with a concho band and a pinched crown, a three-and-a-half-inch brim, slightly turned down front and back, slightly rolled at the sides; the blue satin lining had long since been removed, along with the sweatband, which bore the legend WHITEMAN'S BOOTS & SADDLES, CALGARY, ALBERTA. He wore a shearling jacket, Levi's, and Stuart boots made of horse-hide and taped around the vamp between the tongue and the medallion. He was not tall, but he appeared to be tall because he was wiry and compact, like a lightweight or welterweight boxer, with no fat on his body. His hands were long and narrow, with pronounced veins and knuckles, and he held them just above the pommel and centered on the horn, nearly together, the thumbs up but not rigid, the tips of the forefingers slightly curved and articulated like the legs of a crab inward to the center of the man, above an ornate, sand-cast buckle, the hands, sunburned and cal-loused and scarred, held so lightly, tentatively, so much invested in the motion of the dance that they seemed to float on an air of music, an intricate, undulant melody. Lying lightly on the middle fingers might have been reins, which would have been perfectly appropriate to the attitude of the hands, which would have been drawn to no visible tension, which would have been rolled, rippled, played out precisely to the tempo of the dance, which would have strung, as delicately as a spider to its web, the man to the mare. But there were no reins; the mare was unbridled.

The mare, a rangy black animal named Swastika, moved slowly, meticulously, with infinite stealth and cunning. Nothing about her was disturbing, not a step, not an attitude, not even her inexorable advance into the herd. The man, Perfecto Atole, shifted his weight imperceptibly, bringing the barest pressure of a knee to bear upon the mare, and in that instant the object of the dance was realized. Swastika then knew her charge, and the purpose to which she had been bred and foaled, and she crept into the herd and chipped her calf. The calf sprang away, full of agitation and excitement. The mare, her head low, followed, but only a step or two, only enough to place herself, to come upon the center of a strategy. The calf circled wide; the mare sidestepped, prancing, full of grace, only so far as to gain the ground between the calf and the herd. The man sat upright in the saddle, always perpendicular to the spine of the horse. The calf lunged, its nostrils distended extremely, its blowing audible, showing the whites of its eyes, and the mare wheeled, keeping her head low like a snake. Her hooves cracked upon the ground, popping like gunfire. She kept exactly in the calf's way, beautiful and fastidious, imperturbable and discreet. In an ultimate, desperate motion the calf lunged and pivoted, turning sharply around in its skin, and the mare lurched, somehow without desperation, as in slow motion, in some ineffable expression of serenity, barely touching her teeth to the calf's flank, turning it out of the corral, into the holding pen. The man gave no sign of satisfaction—unless it was given

by some barest touch or breath or shift of posture to the mare—
but it was well done. The dance was finished in beauty.

"**C**hiquita, you bring me a hale horse and a broke-down man,"
Perfecto said. "I'll take the horse."

"The horse isn't negotiable," Grey said, "but I wanted you to
see him. He's one in a hundred—a thousand, I guess."

"And the man you brought along. Negotiable?"

"You know what I told you. You know who he is. You can
help him."

"Help."

"Yes. You know what I mean. You know the story. You know
your part in it."

"Yes, all right. I will play my part."

"Thanks."

"But remind me, *chiquita,* what's in it for me?"

"Personal satisfaction, a sense of accomplishment, the certain
knowledge that you have fulfilled your moral responsibility, stuff
like that."

"I'm a cowboy and an Indian," he said. "Talk like that fazes
me, makes me drunk. Tell you what."

"What?"

"Tomorrow. Leave that pretty horse. Take the man out to Stone
Lake. Walk around. Talk to the man about bears. I'll find you
there, do something. Tell you what, I'll help the man along."

"Thanks. I need your help; he does too." She looked down for
a long moment. "What will it cost, your medicine?"

"Arm and a leg, piece of ass."

"No," she said, looking evenly into his eyes now. "We're talking about bears. I mean to be true to this man now. It has to be so, and you know it."

Color came to the scar.

"I remember your body," he said.

"I remember yours," she said.

He looked her up and down, his eyes glittering. She was not the girl whose virginity he had taken away. She was someone else now, a woman he could not have imagined.

"That first time, the boots I gave you that day, the snakeskins, why aren't you wearing them? Be a nice, friendly thing to do. Old times' sake."

"Oh, those boots." She sighed, smiling. "There's something about red shoes or red boots that has to do with the loss of innocence, isn't there? I think so."

"Yellow ribbons and green M and Ms, too," he said. "Those boots, though, *chiquita*. I don't know if you truly appreciate those boots."

"Oh, I appreciated them. How could I not? Red snakeskin Alamos: antelope tops, wing tips and counter foxing on those soft, snakeskin vamps, the scales like mirrors. God, they felt good on my feet."

"And they *look* like a million dollars," Perfecto said. He saw them in his mind's eye; his face and voice were full of admiration.

"And they *looked* like a million dollars," she said. "Black medallions, black beading and piping, three-color flame stitching. They were the most beautiful boots I've ever seen."

The tenses were wrong, but Perfecto Atole was concentrated on a time—a moment, an *instant*—in the past; he teetered on the sublime. He nodded, savoring the image of a lithe, beautiful girl in that most bittersweet moment after she had been deflowered, at the very moment she became a woman, once and for all, after the discreet spotting, the darkening, badgelike stain, her belly and thighs quivering late and reflexively, pulling on the incomparable red boots with tears streaming down her cheeks.

"I cut the tops off," she said.

There was a silence.

"What? You did what?"

"I cut the tops off. Well, I had worn those boots hard, and the soles were shot and the points were scuffed, one of them gouged through almost. I cut the tops off."

"You—"

"I cut the tops off and made shakers out of them, tortoiseshell shakers, stomp-dance shakers, you know?"

"You cut the tops—"

"Off. Clean. Flat off. Clip, snip, zip."

"Shit," Perfecto said.

"Loan you the shakers sometime," Grey said.

"Shit," Perfecto said again, spitting. "Tell you what. I've a mind to put him out of his misery, that man of yours. I got some big loads, you know? He wouldn't feel a thing. Why not? A hunting accident, you know?—you *know* I can bring it off."

"I know," Grey said, sparks in her agate eyes now. "Look, you sonofabitch, you will know how to be. Take my horse if you want. We will be out there early, before sunrise, on this side of the lake. You find us there. We're walking, talking about bears."

Perfecto Atole spat again and laughed.

"Muy bien, chiquita," he said. "I might borrow your pretty horse, and if I like him I will keep him."

"Over my dead body," Grey said.

"¡Madre de Dios!" he exclaimed. *"Two* hunting accidents, and before breakfast!" and he laughed again.

Even when he aggravated her, he appealed. The verbal dueling was a kind of courtship, she remembered, all those hard syllables of seduction. She thought of his hard, pointed weight upon her, his hard mouth and hard hands, his thighs as hard as rock. Had Billy the Kid lived to be thirty, he would certainly have been like this man, she thought, whose teasing and jealousy were formalities. She knew that she could count on him. And Perfecto Atole was the keeper of a bear's paw.

There was a raw wind. The sky in the east was gray and luminous, like smoky quartz, and in the next minute it began to take on the colors of the sun: red and yellow and orange and gold.

The man and the woman, he inappropriately in a camel topcoat and street shoes, she in a long, no less inappropriate, white dress, moccasins, and a Pendleton blanket, red and black, walked on the marshy apron of the lake, in shadows that dissolved at their feet. The wind bore creaking upon the silence of the first light, but the silence held, even as a flock of ducks beat about in the reeds of the lake. Set shivered.

"Bears do not suffer cold, I'm told," he said, his teeth rattling. "The bear takes the warmth from my bod—" He had turned to her and seen that she was looking past him, her expression solemn, her eyes squinting almost. He turned, searching.

A dark figure was approaching from the west. It was at first a nuclear concentration of the darkness beyond, something of the night. Set watched with fascination, speechless. But as the figure approached—slowly, yet more quickly than it seemed—it began to take the shape of a man on horseback, the centaur he had seen the day before. And without knowing why, he felt the goad of fear pressing upon him. He had been unaccountably afraid the day before, but not for himself. He had watched the man on the horse, and never before had he seen such relentless motion of man and beast in total concert. It was even terrifying, the inexorable motion, absolute imposition, unflagging advance of the centaur. He had watched with fear and fascination. He had imagined what havoc must have been in the calf's assaulted brain, what dull, blind panic. Then instinctively he understood that he, Set, was now the object of the centaur's unhurried, irrevocable pursuit. The centaur was coming for *him;* it had no other purpose, no other reason for being. He shot a glance at Grey. Her eyes were fixed upon the figure approaching, her eyes still not wide open but squinting slightly, not quite showing surprise or alarm, but nonetheless a wariness, a sheer concern. In that fraction of a fraction of a second, Set recorded her expression in his mind, against what might come. He understood, with a kind of grudging wonder, that she knew far better than he what was about to be.

Perfecto Atole, in the pitch blackness before first light, had drunk of peyote tea and the juice of a shred of dried venison. His mind was on medicine and provocation and horses. He had taken down the bear's paw, wrapped in chamois, from the cache of his paraphernalia in the wall above his bed. He had taken from Grey's duffel the tortoiseshell shakers. He had gone out into the black cold and touched his hands to the stallion Dog. With his hands he shaped the horse as if it had been a sculpture. With his hard hands he described the horse, the muscles, the bones, the hide and hair. He rubbed his fingers, as if polishing, over Dog's hooves. He touched his mouth to the soft muzzle. "You are something," he said softly, "a whole lot of horse. But, *por favor,* I ride my black mare this morning. She and I are old with each other. If I shift my weight, she shifts hers; if I turn, she turns. And there is something like evil in her. She inspires fear." And he saddled the mare Swastika. He was going to a dance.

A hundred yards away the black figure in the dawn paused and disintegrated. The man dismounted, worked with the saddlebags. He fixed the shakers low on his legs, around the tops of his boots. He drew the bear's paw on his right hand. And then he stepped in the stirrups and the image was integrated again; the centaur resumed its approach. Set stood, watching, waiting. He thought of running, at least moving away, changing his position, shifting his stance. But he was nearly paralyzed; anyway, there was no-where to go. The centaur drew near, the black, lithe body of the horse gliding toward him, utterly calm, graceful, a terrible insinuation in it. And the man loomed at close range in the shearling jacket and black hat, the shakers rattling softly, *Shuh, shuh, shuh,* in time, without menace, the right hand black and huge, held across the man's middle, the eyes invisible under the black hat.

The mare's breath became audible, visible. The centaur moved into the man and woman, cleaving them apart cleanly, as with the blade of a machete. And suddenly the woman was of no matter in the dance. She stood away in the mist, on the frozen mud, watching, catching her breath.

The slow thrust of the mare's head backed Set away. Her head was pointed at his groin. Her head weaved to his awkward retreat. She was in perfect control of her movements; he was careless, off balance, desperate. He tried to feint, dodge, twist away, but she was just there, her head slung low, floating at his belt. She seemed to know better than he how and where he would move. It was not anticipation, not a matter of guesswork, no matter how well informed. It was rather the deepest instinct of the predator. The man on the horse, and by means of the horse, preyed upon the man on the ground. The black mare was his perfect instrument. She related them, struck the keen balance between them, was the center of some ancient design in which there was placed a dance of warriors.

Set ran without purpose. He was weak and disoriented. He had no breath, no strength. He turned away from the centaur at last, for the mare was drawn up, and ran in a straight line for the lake. His eyes and lungs were burning, and there was no feeling in his legs. Then the hoofbeats and the loud, rushing rattle of the shakers came suddenly upon him, *SHUH, SHUH, SHUH!* and he pivoted to his right, to no avail. The mare was at his heels, her breath loud and hard upon his back. She was only inches away. He turned again, nearly falling. When he regained his balance, running, she moved swiftly past, not thundering but gliding with quiet, understated speed. Before he could lunge away, the rider struck him in the throat with the bear's paw, and in that instant Set beheld the man's face, the nearly professional indifference in the glittering eyes, the inflamed scar and the hard set of the mouth. It was a blow that burned and raked blood to the skin, and Set tumbled and rolled on the water's edge. Slowly he brought himself to his hands and knees. The horse and rider stood away. Set glowered. A rage grew up in him so great that there was nothing else. He was beyond sickness and pain, sorrow and confusion and self-pity. In that moment he was mad with hatred, murderous. In his uttermost humiliation something of his will's power was unaccountably restored to him. It was as if he were purged by his own distemper. In the rising morning light, across the mist that floated from the lake, he watched the centaur turn and recede into the distance, memorizing the image, holding on to his anger with all his might, beginning to feel the texture of its use. He made a prayer, a morning prayer.

West of Mexican Water they turned south and drove along Chinle Wash to Round Rock, where they turned toward Greasewood Springs. The plain reached out across endless gradations of color, endless tiers of colored rock and shaded earth as far as the eye could see, smoky pastels, brilliant slashes of red and yellow and purple. In the middle distance were sandy waves of the desert, dotted with piñon and sage and mesquite. In the foreground were blue and green hummocks and red sandstone pillars like obelisks and cairns,

junipers and greasewood. And the sky was vast beyond dreaming
over all, a deep, shimmering blue, in which light played upon
plane after plane to infinity—glancing motes and streaks and facets
of the sun.

"This is Lukachukai," Grey said.

She is beautiful in her whole being

A remarkable change came upon Grey, almost at once. She stood and moved and talked differently. Here, in her mother's home, she assumed an attitude of deep propriety, dignity. With Set she could still tease and joke and whisper words in her old diction, but now she spoke quietly, in a plain and simple way, and her language was made of rhythms and silences that he had not heard before. She put on the bright blouses and long pleated skirts of her mother's people. She combed out her long black hair and fashioned it in the old way, in a queue wrapped with white twine at the back of her head, and she adorned herself with silver and turquoise, old, simple pieces. She wore no makeup, except a pollen on her forehead and cheeks, which after days shone faintly, as from within, an orange-copper glow. Set observed her with wonder. She had been a beautiful girl—he held on to the vision of her in the buckskin dress, with feathers in her braided hair, her face painted—with a free and original and irrepressible spirit. And now, in a wholly different context, she was a beautiful woman, endowed with experience and purpose and grace. She ripened before his eyes. He felt almost boyish in her presence, and indeed, in keeping with the story, he must play out his part as Set-talee, Tsoai-talee, boy bear, rock-tree boy. But Grey had evolved from a girl into a woman, and he had been witness to it. And, fittingly, he began to attend her. One day, while looking at her as she played with Nanibah, it became clear to him that she belonged to him, and he to her. And he felt a happiness beyond anything he had ever known.

That summer they lived in the hogan beyond her mother's house. Little by little Set fitted himself into the rhythm of life at Lukachukai. In the night he went out to see, as for the first time, the innumerable brilliant points of light in the sky. Looking at them he thought he had never seen the night, and he wept and laughed and at last kept the silence of the stars. In the early morning he walked into the dawn's light, slowly at first, stiff with cold, but warming as the flood of light fell from the east, and he saw with wonder and fear and thanksgiving the land become radiant, defined by light and long, color-bearing distances. And when enough of his strength returned he began to run.

The boy ran.

In the days he drew and painted, watching the light change and the colors turn and shift upon the earth, the shadows extend and deepen. His paintings were strong and simple, primary, like those of a child. He listened to the wind and the birds and thunder rolling on the cliffs; in the darkness there was the yip-yip-yipping of coyotes, and at first light the coyotes set up a din that was otherworldly, that was like an electronic music descending from every point on the horizon to the center of creation, to this place, this hogan. And he listened to the voices of Grey and her mother, of Antonia and Nanibah, of old men and women passing by. He listened to the turning of their voices in the element of *diné bizaad*, to the exotic words with their innumerable edges and hollows and inclines—*chizh, dlǫ́ǫ́, tł'izí, tódiłhił*. And he began to understand and use very simple words and constructions in Navajo—*aoo', dooda, daats'i, hágoónee', Set yíníshyé, haash yinílyé?*

At first he did not know how to behave with Lela and Antonia, nor did they with him. But Grey was a good intermediary, and by and large all was well. Nanibah made a great difference, too. She was, like Grey, mischievous and undaunted in her spirit. She took a liking to Set, and she taught him very quickly how to get along with her. He had no experience of children to speak of, and so he walked on eggs. Nanibah adopted him.

One day, when Grey was working at the loom and Antonia had taken Nanibah to Chinle to buy hay and grain, Lela approached close to Set. He was drawing.

"She weaves well," Lela said, under an obligation to speak offhand.

"I think so too," Set said.

"She talks like a Navajo."

"I am glad," Set said.

There was a long pause, which to Set was uncomfortable, to Lela not. He made heavy strokes on the paper with a piece of charcoal.

"She has told us that you are Kiowa."

Set considered. Lela knew from the first that he was Kiowa.

She, having been married to one, knew better than he what it was to be Kiowa. This oblique conversation would have frustrated him at one time; it did not frustrate him now. It was the proper way to proceed.

"I am Kiowa," he said.

"You have strong medicine," Lela said, as a matter of fact.

"Yes."

"Grey knows of this medicine." Again, not a question.

"She gave it to me," he said.

"Yes, so I have heard," Lela said. She was a large woman. She looked him in the eye for a long moment. Wisps of hair turned on the air at her temples. Her hands were at her sides. He could read nothing in her eyes. After a long time she said, "It is a hard thing to be what you must be, *daats'i.*"

"*Daats'i,*" he said. Perhaps.

There was another long pause.

"Do you think you will marry my daughter?" Lela asked. She spoke in a considered way, with measured breath. *Anachronism forwards,* he thought. Her face was shining, especially her forehead and cheeks, and was almost the color of copper. Her face was wonderfully round. She held hands with herself; it was a habit with her. She held them clasped lightly together and low on her abdomen. Her hands were brown and shapely; on three of her fingers were silver rings with bright turquoise stones. She stood with her feet apart. Her stance, and the lines of her body, suggested a fine and firm balance.

Puppies were romping and yelping in the shadow of the house. Butterflies were flitting and floating on the shine of the air. The walls of red rock in the distance appeared to vibrate in the rising heat. The spring had taken hold of the long valley. In looking out across the wide, warming land, Set could conceive of the summer—it was a conception like memory, the remembered summertime of his boyhood at the Peter and Paul Home or at the house on Scott Street; and he marveled to feel his senses awakening —as Lela had conceived of it days and weeks ago, in advance of the final snowfall, when the skies above the Lukachukai Mountains were still curdled and dark. He drew his gaze back upon the closer ground to see Dog standing beyond the hogan, his ears pricked, appearing to search the horizon, standing like some old granitic cairn on the plain, and closer, before the hogan, Grey, at three quarters, sitting, her fine brown fingers picking at the loom.

"I don't know," he said. He looked into her eyes and could see nothing devious there, nothing, unless it was the faintest glint of mischief, a humor so tentative that he dare not count on it. "But it is a thing I have in mind."

"You *want* to marry my daughter, *daats'i?*"

Then he heard himself say, "Yes. Yes, I do. I want to marry your daughter. There is nothing I want more than that."

Then he thought of her asking, You have told her this? And he was ashamed; he searched desperately for some plausible answer: No—not yet. . . . I did not know. . . . I have not been clear in my mind. I am going to tell her now. But it did not come to that. Instead, Lela said, "My daughter is a beautiful woman, like me."

"Yes, she is."

"She is beautiful in her whole being, like me."

"Yes."

"She will bear beautiful children, like me."

"Yes."

Pause.

"But you, if I may speak in a clear way, you are sick. This I have heard. This I have seen. The bear stands against you."

"Yes."

"Yes?"

"Yes. I am sick. I have been sick for a long time, but I hope to be well and strong. I can be well and strong with Grey's help—she knows how to help me. I have become stronger since I have been here, because of Grey."

"*Aoo'*. Yes."

"*Aoo'*, I have been afflicted. The bear stands against me."

"*Aoo'*."

"*Aoo'*. I am the bear."

"*Aoo'*."

In the early mornings, when he inhaled the cold air that ran down from the mountains, and when he touched the earth through the soles of the moccasins Lela and Grey had made for him, he knew how glad he was to be alive. His skin grew darker, and his body began to grow hard, and his hair grew over his ears and shaggy at the nape of his neck. It seemed to him that he could see a little farther into the distance each day and that his legs were hardening and becoming more flexible at the ankles and knees, his stride longer and more regular and persistent. He ran until the sweat streamed on his body, and he tasted the salty exertion at the corners of his mouth, and he ran on until his breathing came in time with his stride and his whole body was fitted into the most delicate and precise rhythm. He entered into the current of the wind, of water running, of shadows extending, of sounds rising up and falling away. His life was in motion; in motion was his life. He ran until running became the best expression of his spirit, until it seemed he could not stop, that if he stopped he would lose his place in the design of creation—and beyond that, until his lungs burned and his breath came hard and fast and loud, and his legs and feet were almost too heavy to lift—and beyond that, deeper into the rhythm, into a state of motion, mindless and inexorable, without end. And when he returned to the hogan Grey bathed him while he stood naked, allowing his body to settle down. Then she gave him water to drink and a kind of gruel, made of crushed corn and goat's milk, piñons and dried fruit, and in the manner of old Najavo men a hundred years ago, he wrapped his loins in white cloth and lay down on a pallet in the shade of a juniper, near the loom, and Grey slowly kneaded the muscles in his shoulders and back and legs. She made a mild abrasive out of sand and oil and massaged his feet, and she sat beside him, singing softly, stirring the air over him with a grass broom, and he sank into deep relaxation. And in the afternoon he drew and painted and dreamed and set his mind upon marriage. He spoke Navajo to Lela as far as he could, and he was not offended when she laughed at him. He played games with Nanibah and put notions of the wide world in her head. He instructed her in painting, and in turn she gave him words, the words of a child, which are at the center of language. And he observed with deep appreciation, wonder, and respect Grey's return to the Navajo world.

In the late afternoon they convened at Lela's table. There was usually lamb or mutton, and dried corn and tinned tomatoes and beans, and dried fruit. There were wonderful breads: fried bread, corn bread, oven bread. Set liked best the dense, sweet oven bread, baked in an *horno* of adobe bricks and mud plaster; it was the bread of the pueblos; Lela had learned to make it when she was a girl attending the fiestas in the ancient towns on the Rio Grande. At dusk Grey prepared a sweat lodge for him, a small conical hogan with an opening on the west. When the stones in the pit were hot and the flames had died down, Grey and Set entered the sweat lodge in breechcloths and sat next to each other. Grey poured water on the stones, and they hissed and let off steam. In the bare light of the embers, before they were extinguished, Set looked at Grey discreetly, saw her smooth skin shining and glistening, as bright beads of water appeared on her forehead, her throat, her shoulders and thighs. The tips of her breasts were nearly as dark as her hair. He watched as she leaned to pour the water, her long side and flank shining, her toes flexing into the sand. Discreetly he watched, the heat of the steam and of his desire coming upon him. And for a time he became dull and heavy, as on the verge of sleep, dreaming of the woman beside him, dreaming longingly of her body, which was so anomalously soft and firm, which was so exciting in its curves and lines and hollows and folds, of the smell of her when she came fresh from sleep, of her casual gestures, of her voice in the day and night when she spoke of this and that with interest or excitement, or with anger or frustration or sorrow, of the breathy cooing of her ecstasy, of her singing softly, of her gentle breathing in the night. And then the drowsiness and the dreaming dissolved, and he felt suddenly refreshed and invigorated and clean and hot, and he began to laugh, and Grey too, and they touched, and their hands slipped over their bodies, describing desire, but yet discreetly, for Lela and perhaps Antonia and Nanibah might be close by. All things in their places. In this little house was peace and purification. Outside the evening air bit them with cold and was sharply delicious. And they walked away from the house and hogan and lay down on a dune, observing the night sky. And later, when the moon was high, they rode horses into the arroyos, among shadows that were like pools of time and eternity.

At the end of April a man came down from the Chuskas, bringing mountain earth. In the center of the hogan he constructed an altar and performed a ceremony through most of the night. Set and Grey sat side by side to the left of the priest. Coals were laid upon the altar, and a firestick was placed in the coals just so, on the east side, so that the pointed end smoldered and shone like a brand. Crystals were placed here and there on the altar's rim. The priest arranged his paraphernalia before him. There were herbs and pollens, a gourd rattle, pots of liquors and teas, peyote pastes, feather fans, a bowl of water, and an eagle-bone whistle. Nanibah slept on a pallet at the wall of the hogan. Lela and Antonia assisted the priest, keeping the coals alive, sprinkling sage and cedar, crushed with tobacco in their fingers, bringing water and coals as needed. Set and Grey glanced at each other occasionally, and sometimes they touched hands, but they were concentrated upon the ceremony. Smoke was fanned upon them, and when it was proper to do so they spoke of their visions. Their visions were very beautiful, and their words were the best that were in their hearts, and their voices were joined in the smoke to other voices, ancient and original. Their voices were soft and everlasting, and in them were laughter and wailing and reverence and awe, and they made stories and songs and prayers. And in the dark early morning, after they had gone out of the hogan to say themselves to the night sky and returned, they stood before the altar, holding each other close. In their honor the priest gave the firestick to the fire, and they knew, though it was not an explicit knowledge, that they were married. In ceremony, in tradition out of time, in a sacred manner, in beauty they were married forever.

He perceives the brilliance of the meadow

Worcester Meat had been ill for sixteen days. At first, Jessie and Milo had insisted that he take to the grandmother's bed, where they could watch over him. They wanted to call a doctor, but Worcester told them no. After thirteen days there was a strange purring in his shrunken chest, he spat up a thick green sputum, and very little of his strength remained. It was then he told Jessie and Milo Mottledmare that he wanted to be thrown away, that he wanted to go home to die by himself; he wanted no one to watch.

When Jessie had said goodbye to him, weeping, Milo and Dwight Dicks removed Worcester Meat to his little house on the other side of Cradle Creek. They laid him on his back in bed and drew a threadbare flannel blanket over him.

"When do you think you will pass away?" Milo asked softly, with respect for the old man's feelings.

"Three days, I think," Worcester said.

"Okay, then, Worcester. We're gonna come back Friday and see. If you're still alive, we won't bother you none, jes' see if you need anything. If you've passed on, we'll see to your remains. We'll bury you right there next to Gran'ma. Here's a water bag and some stuff to eat, crackers and cheese and stuff."

Milo and Dwight shook Worcester Meat's hand, said goodbye, and left him alone.

The next day Worcester sat up in bed and talked and sang to himself. He was perfectly happy to sit there through the day with his thoughts and memories, his dreams and imaginings. When the light began to fade he lay back and fell asleep.

And the next day he awoke and did not know where he was. With difficulty he lifted the water bag to his lips and drank. In the late morning he got out of bed, put on his overalls, and went outside. Very slowly he walked through a small meadow toward the nearer of the two sod houses. There were bluebonnets, yellow violets, and strawberries in patches in the grass. He stopped and stood among the wildflowers. Tears came to his eyes, blurring and magnifying his field of vision. And through his tears he perceived the brilliance of the meadow. The wildflowers were innumerable and more beautiful than anything he had ever seen or imagined. And when he thought his heart could bear no more, a dragonfly rose up, glancing and slipping just above him. In his brimming eyes it divided again and again to effect an iridescent swarm upon the sky. And he took a step, laughing, and another—dance steps. Then he declined slowly to the ground, and he was serene and refreshed in his soul.

They are the shapes of immortality

Through the summer, life flourished at Lukachukai. Horses ran in the valley, and sheep grazed in the hills. Rains came, bringing layers and gradations of green to the land and darkening the long wall of red rocks to the north. For days and weeks on end there were rainbows in the south, over Greasewood and Tsaile and Canyon de Chelly. Water ran fast in the arroyos. In the Lukachukai and Chuska mountains eagles sailed above the black-pointed pines, and deer and bears and cougars came to the high cold streams to drink. Turkeys strutted in the brush, spiders skittered among the rocks, and snakes lay coiled in the sun.

Never had Grey to quest after visions. She dreamed now of Set and of his child within her. In those long summer days her affection for Set became the deep and abiding love of a wife for her husband. All of her joy and passion, her trust and loyalty, were concentrated in him. And as the child grew, so did she in her physical and spiritual beauty. Her own deep vitality was enhanced by the new life in her womb. There was a great radiance in her, and about her an aura of profound peace and contentment. The medicine power she had acquired so assiduously was now refined into a singular presence and a bearing of self-confidence beyond any doubt. She carried herself easily and quietly, with grace and purpose.

As for Set, his love for Grey was a source of endless wonder to him. The greatest thing about it was that it had no definition; it was boundless. He had been moderate in his life, he believed, but in his love he could not be so. He could not account for his years. They were catalogs of loneliness, hurt, acquisition, and accomplishment, but they were not real as compared to this reality.

He awoke, and she was naked in his arms, ascending very slowly from sleep, her eyes closed and her mouth a little open. Softly he said, "Good morning, my darling. This is now my morning prayer: I pray that you are well today. I pray that today you will have all you need to sustain you in your body and in your mind and in your heart. I pray that today you will know peace and joy, that you will have good thoughts of yourself and of me and of our child. I pray that today you will be more deeply in love than you were yesterday or the day before. I pray that today you will give all the good that is in you freely to the world for its own sake, and that you will accept all the good that is given you. I pray that today you will help me to be worthy of you. This is my prayer."

There was part of their life that had not changed. In the night, in the black stillness of the hogan, Set took the medicine bundle in his hands and opened it. The smell of it permeated the whole interior. When he drew on the great paw, there grew up in him a terrible restlessness, wholly urgent, and his heart began to race. He felt the power of the bear pervade his being, and the awful compulsion to release it. Grey, sitting away in the invisible dark, heard the grandmother's voice in her mouth. When Set raised the paw, as if to bring it down like a club, she saw it against the window, huge and phallic on the stars, each great yellow claw like the horn of the moon.

The time came beyond the end of summer. They went to a dance near Oljeto, the place of moonlit waters. They sat late at night with their backs to the fire, waiting. There was nothing to say. A chill wind arose and whipped sparks across the sky. And at last the dancers appeared. They danced in a file, chanting. They wore masks, and their bodies were painted white. They emulated the mountain gods. Their chanting was high-pitched and unintelligible even to themselves. But the dancers were invisible behind the masks, and the gods were visible in them. The gods were real, and they had come from another world. They were the shapes of immortality.

Shapes.

BOOK FOUR

SHADOWS

He comes from the north
he comes to fight
he comes from the north
see him there

I throw dust on me
it changes me
I am a bear
when I go to meet him

◇◆◇◆◇◆◇

Sioux

It is called, therefore, "the land of innumerable long distances"

There were wars and other disasters, and it was determined that the people should leave that place. They journeyed southward into the wide, shimmering country. There the plain was so vast that it could not fittingly bear an ordinary place-name. It was called, therefore, "the land of innumerable long distances."

Those who came after them, whatever people they were, found the round bare patches in the grass of the meadow, the charred wood of the fires, the bones of birds and badgers and deer and dogs—and the tracks of a great bear.

An awful quiet is in his heart

Set walked along the river in the late afternoon. The sun was low now; there was not much daylight left. Patches of the first snow spotted the valley. On a swelling of the ground to the west were cottonwoods, pines, and burr oaks, black and backlighted. Orange shafts of light pierced through them and struck down upon sagebrush and willows and rabbitbrush, and upon the glittering water, and upon his hands and face as he tramped through them. He had been walking for a long time, and he began to feel the cold. The temperature had fallen into the fifties now, and it would reach to freezing in the night. But he did not want to think of the night.

Nor did he want to look up at the monolith, the rock tree. The shadow of Tsoai lay just ahead of him like a dark body of water. When he entered it, it did indeed seem its own element, unlike the earth around it; the air seemed suddenly thinner, darker, colder. It was ominous. He picked up his pace, turning toward his camp, climbing away from the river toward the rock tree, his hands in the pockets of his jacket now, looking down.

He had been there four days, and he had taken nothing but tea. He no longer felt weak or tired, as he had on the second and third days. He was becoming used to the high latitude. He was physically fit now; his strength and endurance were greater than they had been in twenty years. And the clean air of Lukachukai had cleared his mind. He tried to think how it would be later, when it happened, but it was no use. The preparation had been made; that was all. There was nothing left to think of.

When he reached his camp, he made a small fire, taking great care to conceal it, and he heated water. The camp was very simple. Set had brought only water and a tin cup, tea, a bedroll, and the medicine bundle. He made the camp among cottonwoods on the edge of a great clearing on the east side of the rock. He had examined the clearing very carefully on the first day. He had looked for the faintest signs on the ground, and he had probed into the earth with a stick, sifting in his fingers the black and brown dirt, the smallest stones and bits of debris. And he was sure it was the place of which Grey had spoken to him and the grandmother had spoken to her. There was a deep silence. Nothing intruded upon that place; even the wind did not enter there.

Night fell, and he sat down and waited near the fire, his back against a boulder, and began to doze. He closed his eyes and saw Grey sitting at the loom. Her beautiful face bore the look of sadness, but not a sadness like his own. The child was now five months inside of her. Now we live with wonder, Set thought, wonder and thanksgiving and joy. *Oh, I love you!* he cried under his breath, his chest quaking, and he blessed his wife and his child. He took a last look; she placed a hand upon her swollen middle, the gesture so tender and natural. The logs of the hogan shone in late light; the stallion grazed beyond. The purple land reached away. Then there was only a blackness behind his eyes. Hunger had cleared his mind again.

He opened his eyes suddenly to the full moon. It was emerging from the black skyline large and white, and it was soon whole in the east. Set stood then and turned. Tsoai, the rock tree, loomed before and above him in the moonlight. It was changing in the motion of the moon, and it seemed alive. Shapes and shadows shifted upon the great green igneous columns, upon the huge granite planes, across the long black vertical fissures. Set stood in awe of Tsoai. He could not take his eyes from it. He was stricken, spellbound. An awful quiet was in his heart; the thing before him was unimaginable, in some sense beyond knowledge and belief, and he knew that it was sacred. As he looked, the stars of the Big Dipper gradually appeared over it. They became brighter and brighter, riding over the north edge of the rock tree, revolving down the sky. And when he brought his focus back upon the monolith, a strange pitch-black shadow lay upon it, near the base. It was the image of a great bear, rearing against Tsoai. It was the vision he had sought.

In the clearing, he belonged. Everything there was familiar to him. He began to move toward the woods with the others. They were laughing, and they drew away from him. He followed, and they began to shout, taunting him, entreating him to play the game, and Loki began to run. *Set, set!* they shouted. "The bear, the bear!" and ran. And he ran after them. "Yes. I am *set*," Loki called out, flailing his arms and chuffing his breath; he was ferocious. In the trees now, he gained ground. The girls were breathing hard, glancing back and squealing. Suddenly he slowed and began to stagger and reel. Something was wrong, terribly wrong. His limbs had become very heavy, and his head. He was dizzy. His vision blurred. The objects on the ground at his feet were clear and sharply defined in his sight, but in the distance were only vague shapes in a light like fog. At the same time there was a terrible dissonance in his ears, a whole jumble of sound that came like a blow to his head. He was stunned, but in a moment the confusion of sounds subsided, and he heard things he had never heard before, separately, distinctly, with nearly absolute definition. He heard water running over stones, impressing the rooted earth of a bank beyond stands of undergrowth strummed by the low, purling air, splashing upon a drift of pine needles far downstream. He heard leaves colliding overhead, the scamper of a squirrel deep in the density of trees, the wind careening against an outcrop of rocks high on the opposite slope, the feathers of a hawk ruffling in a long stream of the sky. It was as if he could detect each and every vibration of sound in the whole range of his hearing. And the thin air smarted in his nostrils. He could smell a thousand things at once and perceive them individually. He could smell the barks of trees and the rot of roots and the fragrances of grass and wildflowers. He could smell the scat of animals here and there, old and new, across the reach of the hills. He could smell sweet saps and the stench of the deaths of innumerable creatures in the earth. He could smell rain in the distant ranges, fire beyond. He could smell the oils rising to the surface of his skin, and he could smell the breath and sex of his sisters. He caught the sour smell of fear. He looked after his sisters. They too had stopped running. One or two of them had taken steps toward him. He tried to call to them, but he could not; he had no longer a human voice. He saw the change come upon their faces. He could no longer recognize them; they were masks. They turned and ran again. And there came upon him a loneliness like death. He moved on, a shadow receding into shadows.

Shadows.

Epilogue

Koi-ehm-toya's great-great-grandson became a renowned maker of shields. He never saw Tsoai, but he knew Tsoai in himself, its definition in his mind's eye, its awful silence in the current of his blood. On his shields were the most powerful medicines of all, bear claws and eagle wings, human hair and the likenesses of stars. In his old age he dreamed of things that happened before his time. The whole history of the people was played out in the myriad points of light—each one a world and an age—that glided across the plane of his dreaming. And the last of his dreams was that of children moving to a wall of woods. They bobbed and skipped and tumbled away in the distance. He watched them for a time, and then he could no longer see them. They had already entered into the trees, into the darkness.

About the Author

N. Scott Momaday is a novelist, a poet, and a painter. Among the awards he has received for writing are the Pulitzer Prize and the *Premio Letterario Internazionale "Mondello."* He is Regents Professor of English at the University of Arizona, and he lives in Tucson with his wife and daughter.